PLAY THE GAME...OR DIE

The woman whimpered and cried softly.

"I'm not doing it," I said to Darren. "You might as well just let her go."

Darren shook his head. "I'm not gonna let her go. We both know that. But I'm also not going to make you slice her up at gunpoint. Instead, we're going to do this as a game. See the dresser next to the bed? Open the top drawer."

"No."

"Goddamn it Alex, don't get all resistant on me! Open the drawer!"

Avoiding the woman's eyes, I stepped over to the dresser and opened the top drawer.

Inside was a brand new, shiny hatchet.

"It's yours," Darren said. "Take it."

I picked up the hatchet and clenched it in my fist, wanting nothing more than to hurl it at him, to imbed it in his throat.

"Here's the game," he said. "We're going to let her loose in the yard. You have ten minutes to bring me back her head. Nothing else; just her head..."

JEFF STRAND

PRESSURE

LEISURE BOOKS NEW YORK CITY

This book is dedicated to my mother.
(I'd previously dedicated How to Rescue a Dead Princess
to her, but she'll like this one better.)

A LEISURE BOOK®

Jaune 2009

Dorchester Publishing Co., Inc.
200 Madison Avenue
New York, NY 10016

ISBN 10: 0-8439-6253-4
ISBN 13: 978-0-8439-6253-6
E-ISBN: 978-1-4285-0681-7

The name "Leisure Books" and the stylized "L" with design are
trademarks of Dorchester Publishing Co., Inc.

Printed in the United States of America.

10 9 8 7 6 5 4 3 2 1

Visit us on the web at www.dorchesterpub.com.

FOREWORD

Simplicity is hard.

Sometimes the easiest story to tell is the most complicated. Fill multiple plotlines with dozens of characters, and you're guaranteed unending variety. If one plot stalls, switch to a fresh one. You've always got an escape hatch.

But what if you have only a handful of characters, all seen from a single narrator's point of view? What if your story involves one central relationship, which gradually—and ominously—changes and deepens over time?

That's when it gets tough. And if your story plays out over an extended period—not weeks or months, but years or decades—then it's even tougher.

A lot of writers wouldn't tackle that project. Maintaining tight focus in a story that spans a generation is an intimidating prospect. On the other hand, if you can pull it off, you've done something really hard. And really special.

In *Pressure*, Jeff Strand pulls it off.

He gives us a narrator we instantly identify with: the good kid briefly tempted to go just a little bit bad.

And this passing weakness inaugurates a sequence of events that culminates, years later, in passionate hatred and raging violence.

The swift, remorseless unfolding of the story might be almost intolerably intense if it weren't relieved by humor. Fortunately, there's enough of it to keep us from going crazy. The narrator's wry awareness of his own foibles is the lifeline we cling to as we plunge into these dark waters.

But it's a slender lifeline. By the end, there's not much to smile about. *Pressure* takes us to a place we don't want to be, in the company of a hero we wouldn't want to be without.

The title tells you in one word what the book is all about. There's the ticking-bomb pressure of a one-on-one relationship that's increasingly out of control. There's the chronic itchy-palms pressure of waiting, with paranoid certainty, for things to get bad, really bad. And there's the more subtle pressure of social conformity, the pressure to disregard your own scruples and instincts in order to make or keep a friend. This last is the deadliest pressure of all, because without it, the nightmare would never get started.

It would be simplicity itself for our hero to wave off that social pressure and just walk away, saving himself.

But doing what's simple—well, it's hard.

Jeff Strand knows that. After reading *Pressure*, so will you.

Michael Prescott
November 2005

PRESSURE

PROLOGUE

For a while, the bullets were the only things keeping me alive.

It was a sack of one hundred and fourteen of them, each with a date scratched onto the casing. The first date was nearly four months ago, a Thursday. I'd spent that entire morning in the bathtub, tears streaming down my face, the barrel of a revolver in my mouth, garbage bags taped to the wall so the landlord wouldn't have to repaint. I wasn't sure that I really wanted to commit suicide, but yet I couldn't force myself to pry the gun barrel from between my teeth.

Finally I did pull the gun away and removed the bullet. Then I scratched 12/25 onto the casing with a pocketknife, as a reminder that I hadn't killed myself that day.

I was in the bathtub even longer on Friday, but I still didn't shoot myself. This time I wanted to. Desperately. I was biting down so hard on the barrel that when my front tooth cracked I thought for a second that the gun had fired. I'm not sure what ultimately kept me from pulling the trigger—probably cowardice—but in the end I had a second unused bullet and another date.

This became a daily ritual. Sometimes it got really, really bad. There were times, usually late at night, when the only thing keeping me from killing myself was the sight of the bag of bullets, the knowledge that I'd survived each of those days, so why couldn't I survive just one more?

Other times I'd casually put the gun to my head for half a second and then plop down on the couch and watch some TV.

As the sack of bullets grew heavier, it became easier not to want to pull the trigger. My life became less about escape and more about the realization that I couldn't hide away forever. I didn't need to. I'd made it through one hundred and fourteen days.

On the hundred and fifteenth day, I decided that I probably had better things to spend my money on than bullets I wasn't shooting. That freakishly cold evening I dropped the revolver in the sack, tied it tight, and walked six miles to the Winston Bridge. As I tried to ignore the happy father walking on the other side, his daughter perched up on his shoulders, I prepared to fling the sack into the pond below and begin a new era of my life.

Then I thought, no, bad idea. The last thing I needed was for the sack to wash up onshore and some kids to find it. I'd just have to begin this new era of my life without a symbolic act.

I looked at the father again, burst into tears, and walked to the nearest bar, where I got so drunk that I knocked myself unconscious when I fell off the bar stool. I woke up outside with blood in my eyes and the change missing from my pockets.

I'm sure I would have shot myself right then and there, except that the bastards had also taken the sack with my gun and bullets.

I just lay on the ground, shivering, unable to see anything beyond my breath misting in the air, trying to remember if there had ever been happy times.

There had been. In fact, there'd been wonderful times.

But that's not where the story begins.

PART ONE

CHILDREN

CHAPTER ONE

"That's all you've gotta do. Steal the condoms and you're in the club."

I nervously shifted my weight on the propped-up bicycle as we waited across the street (a dirt road that seemed to be comprised of one part dirt, nine parts jagged rocks) from the small drugstore. "I don't know. Can't I just steal a candy bar or something?"

Paul shook his head. "It's gotta be rubbers."

"But what if I get caught? I could go to jail."

Marty chuckled. "Then you can be an honorary member from your cell."

I sighed. At age twelve, I knew the basic function of the product they were asking me to shoplift, but I also knew that we weren't going to be getting any actual use out of it.

"How about this? I'll steal *three* candy bars. That's a lot harder, don't you think?"

"If we wanted candy bars, we could just buy candy bars," Paul explained, scratching the stick-on cobra tattoo on his right arm and then pushing up his thick glasses. "And it's not going to be hard. He's half blind."

"But what are you going to do with them?"

"What do you think?" Marty asked. "Use them."

"You are not."

"Sure we are. They make great water balloons."

"C'mon, guys," I protested. "Let me steal something else. Anything else."

Paul nodded. "Okay, steal a box of Maxi Pads."

"No way."

"Rubbers or Maxi Pads. Your choice."

If I'd still lived in Dayton, Ohio, I wouldn't so much as stolen a soggy straw wrapper for the privilege of hanging out with kids like Paul and Marty. They were both gargantuan nerds who'd somehow convinced themselves that they belonged to the tough-guy crowd. The first time I ever saw Marty, he was sucking on his inhaler after an unsuccessful attempt to rough up a ten-year-old for his lunch money. Paul's mom still cut the crusts off his peanut butter and jelly sandwiches and included a daily note expressing her motherly love, though he always made a big show of crumpling it up and throwing it into the garbage.

But Trimble, Arizona, population 6000, was not an easy place for a newcomer. The children all knew each other, and had known each other their entire lives. The cliques were firmly in place. There was no room for a skinny, introverted, completely nonathletic kid with an ugly purple birthmark covering his chin. I'd sat by myself at lunch for three full weeks, hoping somebody would take pity on me, but the other kids seemed perfectly content to go on pretending that I either didn't exist or carried a communicable disease, perhaps one with an oozing flesh motif.

So when Paul and Marty asked me to go on a bike ride one day after school, I enthusiastically agreed.

"Chicken!" said Paul. "Chick-chick-chick-chicken!" He tucked his hands under his armpits and began making what he apparently thought were chicken noises.

"You sound like a duck," Marty told him.

"I do not."

"Then you sound like a retarded chicken."

"I do not."

"Okay, you sound like a *special* chicken."

"What does that mean?" Paul asked.

"A retarded chicken."

"Kiss my ass."

My fervent hope was that this conversation would continue until it was time for us to go home for dinner, but unfortunately "kiss my ass" turned out to be its natural conclusion. "Do it, Alex," said Paul. "Otherwise you don't get to be in the club."

"I don't even want to be in the club."

"Yeah, right."

Yeah, right. "Are you sure he's half blind?"

"He probably won't even look up," Marty insisted. "We steal stuff from him all the time."

My stomach was churning and I could feel a headache coming on, but I nodded, slung my backpack over my shoulder, and silently walked toward the drugstore. This was stupid. This was so stupid. This was truly, deeply, incredibly, astoundingly, jaw-droppingly stupid.

But I was going to do it.

A bell tinkled as I pushed open the door. Mr. Greystein looked up from his *Christian Living* magazine and frowned. From the way Paul and Marty had been talking, I'd expected some shriveled geezer in his nineties, but Mr. Greystein didn't look any older than fifty.

The drugstore was small and poorly lit; not much more than three aisles and a cooler. Behind Mr. Greystein was a display of cigarettes. "Leave it at the counter," he said.

"What?"

"Your backpack. Leave it at the counter."

I walked over and placed my backpack on the counter. Since the backpack was to be the vessel through which my dastardly crime would be committed, this wasn't a good development.

Mr. Greystein glared at me for a moment longer, and then returned his attention to his magazine. I walked over and pretended to look over the candy selection.

The boxes of condoms were on a rack right next to the front counter. Even if I'd had my backpack, they'd be nearly impossible to swipe. How could I possibly do this? Why was I even willing to try?

My stomach had gone from the churning sensation to outright pain, and the headache was throbbing with full force. I read the nutrition information on a Snickers bar while I tried to decide what to do.

Just leave. Who cared what Marty and Paul thought? Maybe if I bought them each a candy bar, they'd let me join the club anyway; after all . . .

Then I realized something that should have been obvious from the beginning. I didn't need to steal the condoms. I could just buy them. Marty and Paul would never know that they weren't stolen merchandise. I could be a liar instead of a thief.

Of course, not having researched prophylactic purchasing restrictions, I wasn't sure if it was legal for a twelve-year-old to buy them. This wasn't like alcohol or cigarettes, was it?

Quickly, before I lost my nerve, I returned to the register. I grabbed a random box of condoms, set it on the front counter, and then set the Snickers bar next to the box as if that might distract Mr. Greystein from my other purchase.

He regarded me for a long moment.

"How old are you?"

"Twelve."

"Do your parents know you're buying these?"

I shook my head.

"Don't you think you're a little young?"

I shrugged.

"I think you're a *lot* young. I really don't think I should be selling you these. I can't imagine that a boy your age is responsible enough for that kind of thing, can you?"

I shrugged again.

He stared at me for a moment longer, and then his mouth curled up into the beginning of a smile.

"See, I don't think you've fully considered this purchase," he said, tapping the box. "These are lambskin condoms, which aren't as trustworthy as the latex variety. The only reason you would want these is if you or your partner had an allergy to latex. Do you or your partner have an allergy to latex?"

I didn't respond.

"Don't be shy. If you're not comfortable discussing the product, you're certainly not comfortable using it. Do you or your partner have an allergy to latex?"

"No, sir."

"Well, then, this isn't what you want." He shoved the box aside, leaned over the counter, and retrieved another box. "Now, this brand is ribbed for her pleasure. Do you know what ribbed means?"

"No." My ears were ringing so loudly that I could barely hear him.

"It means that it has ridges that help with stimulation. That's definitely something you want. It's only common courtesy. I'm not sure about spermicidal lubricant . . . you seem like you might be too young for that even to be a problem, although I guess by the time you work through the entire box it could be a different story. What do you think?"

"I don't know."

"You can't be an informed consumer with an attitude like that. You wouldn't just grab any old candy bar off the shelf, would you? You'd make sure that if you were in the mood for peanuts, it had peanuts, or if you wanted nougat, that it had nougat, and so on, right?"

"I guess so."

"Of course so. May I ask your name?"

"Alex."

"Tell me, Alex, do you honestly feel that you're ready to buy these condoms? Or should you maybe call the whole idea off? The *whole* idea, if you know what I mean."

I like to call what happened next the trigger event for everything else that was to happen in my life. That's probably not accurate. The trigger could have been agreeing to steal the condoms in the first place, or meeting Paul and Marty, or my parents moving us to Trimble, or, hell, just my being born if you wanted to get technical about it. However, I can say with absolute certainty that in twelve years of a life that included no small number of poor judgment calls, this was far and away the worst decision I'd made up to that point.

I grabbed the box of condoms and ran.

I shoved open the door at full speed and sprinted across the dirt road toward Paul and Marty. "Go!" I screamed. "Get out of here! Go, quick!"

They took off riding without hesitation, knocking over my bicycle in the process. Nearly hyperventilating with panic, I pulled it upright, jumped on, and began frantically pedaling after them.

I didn't dare look behind me because I just *knew* that Mr. Greystein was standing outside of his drugstore, holding a shotgun, not afraid to use it, even on a kid.

I cringed and gritted my teeth, waiting for the sound of the shotgun blast and the unwelcome sensation of my head being blown apart.

It didn't come, but I still didn't turn around. Maybe the only thing preventing my death was his unwillingness to shoot me in the back.

Would he call the police?

Would they be able to find me?

Of course they would. In a town this small, the police would have no problem finding a shoplifter based on Mr. Greystein's physical description . . .

. . . especially when the idiot shoplifter had left his backpack right there on the counter.

I squeezed the hand brakes, leaned over, and threw up onto the dirt.

Just go back there. Return the condoms, apologize, and beg him not to call the police. Tell him you'll pay twice as much as they cost . . . three times, if he wants. You don't have that much right now, but next week when you get your allowance . . .

Marty and Paul, far ahead, turned the corner and vanished from sight.

Still no sound of a shotgun.

I needed to go back.

Instead, I threw up again, and then rode home as fast as I could.

I parked my bicycle behind the house in case Mr. Greystein drove around looking for it. Since he had access to my name and address in multiple places in my backpack, it was unlikely that he'd resort to prowling the town looking for my bicycle, but I wasn't exactly thinking at maximum logical capacity. Then I went to my room, sat on my bed, and stared at my pillow for the next hour until I was called to dinner.

"Did you get your homework done?" my father asked, disinterestedly, taking a bite of broccoli.

"Most of it."

"Why not all of it?"

"Too hard." Not to mention that Mr. Greystein was probably rifling through my backpack at this very moment.

My father made no comment and took another bite.

The phone rang.

My stomach lurched.

My mother got up, pushed back her hair, and went into the kitchen to answer.

I tried to scoop up a forkful of macaroni and cheese, but I couldn't force my hand to work. Even if I could, I didn't see any possibility of swallowing it without puking again.

I waited, desperately listening for some sign to indicate who my mother was talking to. The police wouldn't phone beforehand, would they? *"Hi, Mrs. Fletcher, this is the law. We're on our way to apprehend your son, so if you've got any furniture you don't want riddled with bullet holes, we recommend that you move it into the garage as soon as you can."*

"Mmmm-hmmm," my mom said from the kitchen. Then she laughed.

Thank God. It wasn't about me. Unless the person on the other end had used some light humor to break the ice before informing my mother that her son was a wanted criminal.

My mother talked on the phone for less than a minute and then returned to dinner. I told her that I had a stomachache (the truth) and was excused from the table.

The next morning my stomachache was worse than ever, like I'd spent the night swallowing shards of glass with a chaser of rusty nails. I had to go to school anyway.

I talked to Paul and Marty briefly at lunch. That is, they talked to me, laughing about our close call and welcoming me into the club, while I silently kept a close watch on the lunchroom entrance, waiting for Mr. Greystein to show up, flanked by a pair of armed police officers.

Because I didn't have any of my homework or textbooks, I received two hours of detention, which was a long time to sit after school with nothing to do but worry about whether or not Mr. Greystein had contacted my parents.

When I finally got home, he was seated on the living room sofa.

I immediately burst into tears.

"Go to your room," said my mother, sounding neither angry nor upset. Her voice was barely audible, which was unusual for her. "Your backpack is at the foot of the stairs. Do your homework."

I grabbed my backpack, ran upstairs, sat in my doorway, and tried to listen in on the conversation below.

I could only catch quick pieces. ". . . a good kid . . ." I heard Mr. Greystein say.

". . . no excuse . . ." said my father.

". . . a tough age . . ." said Mr. Greystein.

And finally, perfectly clear from my father: "We'll take care of it."

The front door opened, and then closed.

I sat there, waiting to be called downstairs for my unimaginable punishment.

Five minutes passed. Ten minutes. Twenty.

This was going to be a scary one if it was taking them this long to decide. Usually my mother could blurt out punishments mere seconds after the offending action, or, just as often, before the infraction even occurred. Of course, I'd never done anything nearly this bad before, so there was no precedent for this level of discipline.

One hour.

I wasn't called down to dinner.

I didn't dare go downstairs.
Two hours. Three.
I went to bed. I didn't sleep.

The alarm went off at six thirty and I rolled out of bed, never having undressed. When I looked over, my parents were standing in the doorway. I wanted to cry again, but I forced myself to stay calm. Tears would only make them madder.

My mother sat down on the bed next to me, while my father remained in the doorway. "What did you do with them?" she asked.

"Threw them away."

"Why?"

"Didn't want them."

"Then why did you steal them?"

I shrugged.

"Alex, why did you steal them?"

"To get into a club."

"I see. And you think that was a good reason?"

"No."

"Then why did you do it?"

"I don't know."

"Well, I suggest that you figure that out."

I sniffled. "Am I going to jail?"

"Do you think you should?"

I was silent.

"No, of course you're not going to jail. Mr. Greystein didn't call the police. He wants you to pay for what you stole, and he thinks you should help out in his store, maybe for a few hours on weekends. He thinks you'll learn responsibility."

I nodded, relieved that I wouldn't be spending time in prison with murderers, rapists, and fellow condom filchers. "I'll do it."

"No, you won't. You're going to a new school."

"We're moving?"

"No."

I thought about that. There was only one school for kids my age in Trimble, which could only mean . . .

"*I'm* moving?"

"I'm sorry, Alex."

"You're sending me away?"

"It's not a military school, but it's a school for kids who need the extra discipline. Honestly, your father and I don't know what else to do with you."

The tears started flowing now, and I didn't try to stop them. "But this is the only thing I've done!"

"You know that isn't true."

"It *is* true! I've never done anything like this before! I'll never do it again! I promise! Please!"

"You should have thought about the consequences before you shoplifted."

I shook my head violently. "You can't send me away! It's not fair!"

"It's totally fair," said my mother. "And you need help."

"No, I don't! Can't I prove it? Let me prove it! I'll be perfect, I promise!"

"You had your chance."

"But that was the first time," I said with a whimper.

"And the last time."

I sat alone on my bed, shoulders quivering, tears and snot flowing down my face.

I was a bad kid. A rotten kid. A terrible kid.

I was a thief and a liar.

I deserved to be sent to this school. In fact, I deserved to go to *jail*.

A terrible, rotten, miserable, evil kid.

I looked in the mirror. I stared at myself for a moment, and then began making the most awful faces I could manage. I stuck out my tongue and scrunched up my eyes, contorting my face into ghastly expressions worthy of a kid like me.

A terrible kid.

The worst kid in the world.

It felt good to know I was that terrible. It was refreshing. A relief.

Because otherwise I was a perfectly decent kid whose parents just didn't want him.

Three weeks later, with nothing but clothes and a suitcase with a checkerboard, a magic kit, a small bag of store-bought chocolate chip cookies, and my stuffed walrus Farley, I was in the car on my way to Branford Academy.

CHAPTER TWO

"Here at Branford Academy, you *will* obey the rules," said Mr. Sevin, the headmaster. He was in his sixties, short, mostly bald, and almost absurdly thin, but yet there was nothing even remotely frail about the man. Though my parents and I were the only ones in his office, he spoke as if addressing an entire auditorium full of students.

"You will wake up every morning at five thirty sharp. The concept of a snooze alarm does not exist here. Breakfast is at six fifteen in the common dining hall. Classes begin at seven sharp and continue until lunch at eleven thirty. You will have one hour for lunch, and then three and a half more hours of classes. Mandatory study time is from four sharp until six, followed by dinner. Seven sharp to eight thirty is used for further study time or various group activities, while eight thirty to ten is free time, providing that such a privilege has been earned. Lights out at ten sharp."

He looked at us as if to be sure we understood, and then nodded with satisfaction. "Tardiness to any class will adversely affect your grade. All assignments must be turned in at the time they are due without exception. An A-level paper turned in late will receive an F."

I raised my hand. Mr. Sevin blinked with surprise, as if unaccustomed to such astounding rudeness during his speech. "Yes?"

"What if I'm sick?"

"Students who are legitimately ill stay in the infirmary, and their classroom attendance requirements are determined on a case-by-case basis. While I can assure your parents that we provide excellent medical care, I can assure *you*, Mr. Fletcher, that feigning illness to get out of class is simply not possible. Your days of faking stomach pains to avoid taking a test are over."

"I've never done that."

For a moment, I genuinely believed that Mr. Sevin was going to slap me across the face. "Mr. Fletcher, I realize that your parents are still here, but effective immediately you are to follow the rules of conduct at Branford Academy, and that means you will not interrupt when an adult is speaking. Is that perfectly clear?"

"Yes, sir."

"He just meant that he doesn't fake being sick to get out of going to school," my mother explained.

"I was speaking hypothetically," said Mr. Sevin. "And many new students who are not used to being held to our high standards, or any standards in some instances, *do* attempt to use the infirmary as an escape from their responsibilities. So let me make this clear: it does not work.

"Your dormitory will have four boys to a room. The

rules of conduct will be explained when you arrive there. Infractions will result in a loss of privileges, including but not limited to loss of free time, loss of mail privileges—both sending and receiving—and restriction to the academy grounds on Saturdays. This will apply equally to all four boys in the room. So you are not merely responsible for your own behavior, but for the behavior of your roommates. Are there any questions?"

We had no questions.

Mr. Sevin looked directly at me. "It is not standard policy to admit students after the term has begun, but we had a recent dismissal. I sincerely hope that making this exception will not prove to be a distraction."

He said this as if I should be appreciative that he let me in. I wanted to inquire as to exactly which magical universe he was living in where letting me be a student in this hellhole was doing me a favor, but that didn't seem like a question to which he would respond favorably.

After signing several papers, my parents and I were given directions to the dormitory, Dorm B. I was silent during most of the five-minute walk, trying to force myself not to ask the desperate question that was on my mind. But once we stopped in front of the four-story white brick building, I asked anyway, trying but failing not to sound like I was begging.

"Isn't there *something* I can do so I don't have to stay here?"

There wasn't.

Once inside, there was no real tour to speak of. The guy in charge seemed annoyed that we were distracting him from his newspaper. He gave a cursory wave to where I could pick up my mail (so long as that privilege wasn't revoked), and led us up two flights of stairs to room 308. He unlocked the door and motioned for us to enter.

It wasn't as bad as I'd expected, although at this point my expectation had been barren gray walls, iron bars, and stone mattresses without pillows or blankets. Or perhaps even a personal torture chamber, complete with a hairy gentleman in a black hood. There was a set of bunk beds on each side of the room, and a pair of desks with two chairs each. Though the room was supernaturally tidy, at least based on my personal experience with rooms, a poster of a dalmatian and another of a pug, along with a *Star Wars* movie poster, livened it up.

"The seventh graders aren't back yet," said the guy, who had never introduced himself. "They're at a museum, I think. Probably won't be back for an hour or two. I don't know if you want to go out and get some lunch or something like that."

I almost thought my mother was just going to ask if she could leave me with him, but instead she said, "That sounds fine. Alex, is McDonald's okay?"

I nodded.

I didn't say anything during my Last Meal, and wasn't even able to finish half of my Big Mac. My parents talked to each other about what a great opportunity this was for me, and how it would open up many wonderful doors to my future, and how this summer we'd take a really fun family vacation. I pretended to be excited about this idea, just to let them ease their guilt.

After lunch we went to a mall to buy some last-minute supplies, but since I couldn't think of any last-minute supplies I needed, we wandered around aimlessly for an hour and a half until it was time to go back.

The same guy was there when we returned. My mother cried a little as we said our good-byes, and my father patted me on the shoulder, silently telling me to be brave. The guy led me back upstairs to the room and opened the door without knocking.

"Here you go," he said. I stepped inside and he shut the door behind me without another word.

I stood exactly where I was, unable to move. The three boys looked me over, immediately sizing me up. Two of them were seated on the floor, playing a game of cards, while the other read a hardcover book at his desk.

"Hiya," said one of the boys on the floor. Even sitting on the floor he was obviously quite tall and over-weight, with a chubby face, a blond crew cut, and wire-framed glasses.

"Hi," I managed to blurt out.

"What happened to your chin?"

I self-consciously touched the purple blotch on my chin. "I was born with it this way."

"It's cool-looking."

"Thanks," I said, relaxing a bit.

"What's your name?"

"Alex."

"Alex what?"

"Fletcher."

"I'm Peter McMullen."

The other kid on the floor also had a crew cut,

though he had black hair and an average build. He set down his cards. "And I am . . . Jeremy!" He announced this as if introducing a rock band, and then mimicked loud audience cheers.

"Hi."

"You wanna play?" Peter asked. "It's Crazy Eights."

"Sure."

I sat down on the floor next to them. The boy seated at his desk had a dark complexion and thick black hair that hung almost into his eyes. That was a good sign that at least I wouldn't be forced into a military haircut. The boy looked away from his book and sat there as if waiting for somebody to introduce him. When nobody did, he returned to his reading.

"How come they made you go here?" asked Peter, shuffling the deck.

"I stole something."

"Cool! What'd you steal?"

I considered telling the truth, but then thought better of it. "Some candy."

"That's it?"

"Yeah."

"They sent you here just for stealing some candy?"

"And a bunch of other stuff," I said, scared about what the other boys would think of me if they knew that my parents had just been looking for an excuse to send me away. There had to be something wrong with a kid who was that unwanted.

"Was it good candy?" Peter asked.

"Snickers."

"Yeah, that's pretty good. That's probably what I'd steal." He nodded approvingly as he began to deal the cards.

"Why are you here?" I asked.

"Because I'm dumb."

"He got bad grades at his old school," said Jeremy.

"Yeah. Because I'm dumb."

"I want to know why if grades go A, B, C, D, and F, they don't use E." Jeremy's voice deepened a bit as he made this observation.

"Because F stands for Failed, stupid."

"So what does D stand for?"

"Dumb. Like me." Peter crossed his eyes and let his tongue hang out to make himself look quite dumb.

"I just think that if we go to school to learn things, they shouldn't mess up the alphabet." He set down his cards. "Don't start yet. I'm gonna write that down." Jeremy stood up, hurried over to the desk that the other boy wasn't using, and began to write in a spiral-bound notebook.

"Why's he doing that?" I asked Peter.

"He thinks he's funny." Peter picked up Jeremy's cards and looked at them.

"Is it really bad here?" I asked.

"Sometimes. Not all the time. It can be fun, too, but you have to make sure you get your homework done and keep the room clean and aren't late. For a lot of stuff they punish the whole room, but I'll make sure you know what you're supposed to do."

"Thanks."

"Don't look at my cards," said Jeremy, closing his notebook.

"I wasn't."

"They're in your hand."

"I was just keeping them safe from Darren."

The boy at the desk looked up from his book again.
"Ha ha."

"Hee hee," said Peter.

"Ho ho," added Jeremy.

They all looked at me expectantly. "Har har," I said.

Jeremy sat down and grabbed his cards from Peter.
"So are we playing or what? Who dealt this garbage?
Did you ever notice how everybody on a card has an
upside-down head instead of a butt? They're all a
bunch of butt-heads."

"You've already said that," Peter told him.

"But not to *him*."

"Wouldn't that make them head-butts?" I asked.

Jeremy considered that, and then set down his cards.
"Hold on a second," he said, returning to his desk.

"How come you're here?" I asked him as he opened
the notebook again.

"To babysit Peter."

"No, really."

"Because my parents sent my older brothers here
and it straightened 'em up *real good*, so I got sent here,
too. But I make extra money babysitting Peter."

I glanced over at Darren to ask him the same question, but he'd already returned to his book.

We played cards for about an hour. I was sad,
scared, and missed my parents, but I knew that I'd get
along fine with Peter and Jeremy.

At ten to six the entire residence hall gathered outside, formed a long line, and walked single file to the
dining hall, which was the next building over. After
we took our seats I tried to do a quick count and esti-
mated that there were about four hundred kids in the

room, all between the ages of twelve and sixteen. About ten students pushed carts between the tables, handing a cellophane-wrapped dish and a container of milk to each student.

"That'll be our job every Thursday at dinner," Peter explained.

Dinner was meat loaf, mashed potatoes, creamed carrots, and a roll. All four were indescribably awful. The meat loaf tasted a lot like the mashed potatoes, which tasted a lot like the creamed carrots. The roll didn't taste like anything.

I successfully fought back tears as I thought of my mother's meat loaf, which, to be perfectly honest, was never all that great.

After the meal, Peter and Jeremy took me on a quick tour of the school grounds. There were two residence halls, a library, one classroom building, a small administrative building, and a sports field. Even with my horrible sense of direction, I was pretty sure I could keep from getting lost.

When we got back to the room we talked and played some more cards. Peter told me all about Killer Fang, his cocker spaniel, who at this very moment was guarding his room back at home, defending his valuable possessions against evil intruders. He explained how more than anything in the world, he wished that Branford Academy would institute a policy where he could trade Jeremy in for a dog.

Jeremy made several pointed observations about how people who loved dogs often grew to resemble them, using the pug poster as a visual aid.

Darren kept reading his book.

At ten o'clock, lights out, we went to bed. I was unbearably tired, especially since I hadn't slept the night before, but no matter how hard I tried I couldn't fall asleep.

The next night I did sleep, if only because of my complete mental exhaustion. I slept fitfully for the first week, and twice I woke up crying. Fortunately, this didn't awaken my roommates, unless they were pretending to be asleep in an effort to spare me the humiliation.

But by the third week, I was sleeping more or less soundly each night, and I was getting used to the Branford Academy routine. The teachers were amazingly strict, but the classroom material was less difficult than what I was used to, so it didn't take me long to catch up. I made sure to turn in my homework on time and study thoroughly for every test, and there were no problems.

The dorm rules were straightforward: room spotless at all times, with surprise inspections at least once a week. No noise after ten o'clock, although they were generous enough to allow middle-of-the-night bathroom visits.

I never could get used to the food. Each and every meal was so bad that the chef *had* to be doing it on purpose. Culinary incompetence could explain the first six or seven meals, but more than that had to be culinary malice.

Peter and Jeremy readily accepted me into their group, and the three of us hung out like best friends. Despite living in the same room as him, I didn't talk to Darren much. If he wasn't studying, he was reading, furiously scribbling in his notebook, or staring into space.

I can't honestly say that I'd rather have been at Branford Academy than back at home, but all things considered, the first three weeks weren't such a bad experience.

Twenty-three days after my parents dropped me off, the room's inhabitants were punished on my behalf.

CHAPTER THREE

I hadn't even forgotten my entire history report, just the last page, which had somehow slipped out of the paper clip. Racing back to the residence hall meant I'd be late for class, but that was better than turning in incomplete work. Since I'd never been late before, I probably would have only received a very stern reprimand.

Running on the sidewalks was against the rules, of course, but it wasn't a major infraction. Again, with my flawless behavior record up to this point, it probably wouldn't have earned me more than a warning.

The collision, however, was a definite source of concern.

I ran smack into Mr. Wolfe, my math teacher. The papers he'd been carrying flew everywhere, some of them getting caught in the breeze. Through what I like to think was divine intervention, it was me who was knocked to the ground and not him.

He didn't say a word, and simply began picking up the papers. After standing indecisively for a long, frightening moment, I started to help pick up the papers that had blown onto the grass.

A couple of minutes later I handed him the stack. "Be more careful next time," he said, and then continued on his way.

I walked back to the residence hall to get the last page of my report. Very carefully.

As we returned from dinner that evening, my stomach plunged at the sight of red on our door.

It was a bright red door hanger, like the DO NOT DISTURB signs used in hotels. Officially, it was known as a Summons, but the student body called it the Mark of Blood. You could see the bright red color all the way from the end of the hallway, and that was the point. If your door was "bloody," everybody on your floor knew it. I'd only seen one bloody door since arriving at Branford Academy, and it was serious business. It had been on the second floor, and we'd all gone down to look at it, gawking like tourists.

"Aw, shit," said Jeremy, as we headed down the hall.

"What'd we do?" asked Peter.

I hadn't told any of my roommates about what happened that afternoon. I tried to convince myself that this was a coincidence, and that one of the others had screwed up today. Maybe Peter had spilled scalding hot coffee on a teacher, or Jeremy had projectile vomited on Mr. Sevin's car. Something like that.

Jeremy ran up ahead and pulled the hanger off the doorknob. We hurried over to him, and he held up the Summons so that we could see all four of our names, written in clear block letters. Summons time: Immediately.

At least we wouldn't have to suffer long. Jeremy had told me about some roommates who, several years ago, had received a bloody door on Monday that didn't summon them until Friday. On Thursday, they strung up four separate nooses from their ceiling and simultaneously hanged themselves. Three died; one ended up with a broken neck and was currently living in an insane asylum, paralyzed and constantly screaming in terror because the cruel nurse put a bright red door hanger in his padded cell.

It wasn't a credible story, particularly because I couldn't see any logical reason that a quadriplegic would need a padded cell, and it seemed unlikely that there would be a doorknob on the inside of his cell from which to hang anything, but as my stomach pitched and jerked I could certainly see how a bloody door might drive somebody to madness.

We silently headed back to the stairwell, doomed men on the Walk of the Damned.

We walked to the administrative building. Mr. Sevin's office door was open, and his secretary sent us inside without a wait. We sat down on uncomfortable plastic chairs in front of his desk.

"I understand that there was an incident this afternoon?" Mr. Sevin asked, adjusting his glasses as he glanced at me.

I tried to ignore the dirty looks that Peter, Jeremy, and Darren gave me. "Yes, sir."

"Mr. Fletcher, you do realize that students are expected to have their assignments with them when they report for class, do you not?"

"Yes, sir."

"This is not a difficult concept to grasp. Despite that, under normal circumstances your behavior would only merit a warning. However, due to the . . . ah, unfortunate additional aspect of the situation, I'm afraid I must punish your room collectively."

"But it was an accident," I insisted.

"An accident that will not be repeated," he said. "This weekend's trip to Perkinville is canceled for the four of you. You will remain here, cleaning the school grounds."

Jeremy groaned loudly.

"They didn't do anything," I said.

"Mr. Fletcher, are you questioning Branford policy?"

I shook my head.

"I expect an actual response when I ask a question, not a pantomime."

"No, sir."

"Good. Perhaps in the future you will be sure that you have all necessary materials before you leave the room, and will conduct yourself in a less turbulent fashion."

"Yes, sir."

"Good. The four of you are dismissed."

"This sucks," muttered Jeremy, flopping down on his bed.

"I'm really sorry," I said for the sixth or seventh time since we'd left the administration building. "I didn't mean to get you guys in trouble."

"I've been looking forward to Perkinville all month," said Jeremy. "Why couldn't you remember your stupid assignment?"

"I told you, the page slipped out."

"It's because you're so turbulent," said Peter, grinning. "I hate turbulent people. I think we all need to be a little less turbulent. Jeremy, wipe that turbulent look off your face."

"It's not funny."

"It's kind of funny."

"No, it's not. We were gonna see a movie!"

"Yeah, but it was probably a turbulent movie."

"You don't even know what turbulent means," Jeremy said, and then he rolled over on his side and glared at me. "Just stay away from me for a while."

"How's he supposed to do that?" asked Peter. "You live in the same room, dork."

"Shut up."

"You shut up."

"Leave him alone, Peter," I said. "He's allowed to be mad. I'd sure be mad."

"But he doesn't need to be a whiny jerk about it."

"I'm not being a jerk," said Jeremy. "It's just not fair."

"This whole school isn't fair! That's why we're here. Duh."

"Why don't you guys fight a little louder?" asked Darren. "Let's get ourselves in more trouble. Let's stay on school grounds for the rest of our lives. That'd be fun."

Everybody was silent.

"We don't need to go to Perkinville," said Peter, finally. "Perkinville sucks. We'll have fun here. I promise."

Mr. Wolfe himself administered our punishment. I would have expected him to have something better to do on a Saturday than chaperone our manual labor, but maybe it was something he enjoyed doing.

Branford Academy grounds were kept clean as a rule, so it didn't appear at first glance, or even second or third glance, that there was much for us to do. Our job was to scour the campus lawn for every speck of litter, presumably at the molecular level.

"I don't want to see even the slightest trace of garbage on this grass," Mr. Wolfe explained. "I want you on your hands and knees looking for trash. I should be able to walk through here with a magnifying glass and not find anything but grass, dirt, and insects."

He split us into two groups. Peter was put with Jeremy, and I was put with Darren. Darren and I were instructed to go over the entire front lawn of the classroom building, and informed that there would be an inspection afterward. Since it would not have surprised me a bit to see Mr. Wolfe whip out an industrial-size magnifying glass and Model XL-3000 refuse detector, we took this task seriously.

The objective, of course, was not to create a tidier Branford Academy, but for the other students to see my roommates and I crawling around looking for nonexistent trash. A little humiliation went a long way. Only the seventh graders had gone to Perkinville, so there were plenty of kids around to watch us work while they enjoyed their free time.

Not that any of them would express this enjoyment. From what I understood, laughter, pointing, or a sarcastic comment was a sure way to instantly become part of the group being punished. But I saw the smiles, and the burning sensation in my cheeks and ears wasn't just from the heat.

"I found a dime," announced Darren as we entered our second hour.

"Yee-ha."

Darren sat down. "Let's take a break."

"We'd better not."

"He won't be back for a while."

Mr. Wolfe had just left, presumably to check up on Peter and Jeremy, so Darren was probably right. I crawled over and sat down next to him.

"This is the stupidest thing I've ever had to do," I remarked.

Darren nodded. "Yeah."

"They should at least have us paint a garage or something."

He ignored my comment and just sat there and stared at a pair of bluebirds perched in a lower branch of one of the trees. I looked back to make sure Mr. Wolfe hadn't suddenly materialized behind us, and then watched the birds with him. They weren't doing anything particularly interesting.

"What do you think they'd do if I shot one of those birds?" he asked.

"You don't have a gun."

"If I did have a gun. What do you think they'd do?"

I shrugged. "I don't know."

"They're just birds. Who cares about birds?"

"I'm sure some people do."

"Not me."

"But some people do. Bird-watchers and stuff."

"I'd do it," he said in a soft voice. "I'd kill a bird. I'd kill a fuckin' bird."

He looked at me to gauge my reaction.

"People kill birds all the time," I said. "Chicken, turkey . . ."

"Yeah, but I wouldn't shoot them for food. I used to

shoot at birds with my BB gun. They're hard to hit, did you know that?"

I shook my head.

"They are. 'Course, it wasn't a very good gun. I had to sneak it out of the house. I never did hit one. Or maybe I did and it didn't do anything to them. Have you ever been shot by a BB?"

"No."

"Me either. I was going to shoot myself in the hand to see how it felt, but I didn't know what it would do."

"I knew a kid who got his eye shot with a BB."

"Really? Did you see it happen?"

"No, but he wore an eye patch for a few weeks."

"I would've liked to see that. I wonder what it looked like under the patch?"

"He never showed anybody."

"That's too bad."

I looked over my shoulder again. Still no sign of Mr. Wolfe. "We should get back to work."

"Okay." Darren began to crawl through the grass again, sifting through the individual blades with his right hand. "Yeah, I'd kill a bird."

"What's Darren always writing about?" I asked.

We'd been released from cleanup duty, approximately half an hour before the seventh graders were due to return. Crawling around in the grass hadn't seemed like it would be strenuous work, but after several hours of it we were all totally exhausted. Darren had gone back to Dorm B, while Peter, Jeremy, and I sat underneath a tree, relaxing.

"I dunno," said Peter.

"What do you *think* he's always writing about?"

"I dunno."

I told them about Darren's bird comments. "I've always thought he was kind of creepy," Peter admitted. "I don't like sleeping in the bunk over him. I keep thinking he's going to shove a knife through the mattress or something."

"Maybe we should find out what he writes about," I suggested.

Jeremy began to write with an imaginary pencil. *"Dear Diary, I think tonight I'm going to stick a knife through Peter's mattress and kill him. Love, Darren."*

"Ha ha."

"Hee hee."

"I'm serious," I said. "We should look at his journal."

"It's probably love letters to Ms. Mosher," said Jeremy.

Ms. Mosher, who worked in the library, was a perfectly decent if strict woman, but our objective twelve-year-old opinion was that she was the single ugliest human being on the face of the earth. She looked like a not-so-green version of Yoda. Jeremy's comment ended any trace of a serious conversation, and we broke up into hysterical laughter.

Ten minutes before lights out, Darren left the room to go brush his teeth.

His journal rested on his shelf.

A quick peek couldn't hurt anything, could it? Sure, there was the flagrant invasion of privacy matter, and the chance that he might have forgotten his toothpaste or dental floss and catch me in the act, and the fact that his journal could be somehow rigged to let him know when unauthorized personnel had gained access, or it could even be booby-trapped, but aside from that . . .

It was the wrong thing to do.

I decided to do the right thing. I went to bed.

After the cleanup experience, my relationship with Darren changed. He became a bit more comfortable around me, and I became a bit less comfortable around him. It wasn't just the bird thing; after all, I shared the natural morbid curiosity of any young boy. I'd sun-roasted a few ants in my time, I'd examined the neighbor's cat with fascination after it got run over by a motorcycle, and once I'd even begged my parents to drive more slowly by a grisly traffic accident, though I was secretly relieved when they refused.

But there was something in his tone, something disturbing that I couldn't quite identify. I got the sense that, given a chance, Darren wouldn't just shoot a bird; he'd break its legs and twist its head off. Maybe he'd even press the tip of his tongue against its neck, to get a quick taste.

The remaining weeks of the semester passed, and I made no effort to get a hold of his journal. We spoke more often, usually about schoolwork or TV shows, but we never really crossed the line from roommates to friends. He just made me feel kind of creeped out.

One day I swore I saw him brush a feather off his shirt as he walked into the residence hall, but I searched the entrance for several minutes and couldn't find it.

* * *

"Hi, Mom."

"Hi, sweetie. I can't talk long, we're on our way out, but how are you doing? Are you studying hard?"

"Pretty hard."

"Do you still like it there?"

I'd never actually told her that I *did* like it here. "It's okay."

"That's good. Are you getting along with your roommates?"

"Yeah."

"Have you decided what you want for Christmas?"

"There are some books I want."

"Well, write them in a letter and I'll make sure we get them for you."

"I will."

"I love you, Alex."

"I love you, too."

"Is there anything else?"

"No. I was just calling."

"So, Alex . . . what if we weren't able to pick you up for Christmas?"

I didn't respond.

"Alex . . . ?"

"What?"

"We might not be able to pick you up for Christmas. Would you be really disappointed?"

"I don't know."

"You can tell me if you would be."

I blinked. A tear trickled down my cheek.

"Why can't you?"

"We're going on a trip, but we won't be back before you start school again."

"I could start late."

"That's not a good idea. Don't you have friends who are staying there for the holidays?"

"I don't know."

"They said there are arrangements for students whose parents can't come get them. But we don't have to go on the trip if you don't want us to."

"I want to come home."

"We were going to get you a really big present this year. Maybe we'll even come see you before we leave. That would be nice, wouldn't it?"

"Yeah."

"We'll talk about it later. I love you, Alex."

"I love you, too."

CHAPTER FOUR

"Randolph the red-gunned cowboy, had a very shiny gun, and if you ever saw it, you would drop your pants and run . . ."

Jeremy was singing Christmas carols while he and Peter packed for their two weeks at home. It was painful to watch them, and I had to keep dabbing at my eyes with my index finger when nobody was looking. Darren, who also had to stay at Branford over Christmas break, didn't seem to mind.

"Why aren't your parents coming to get you?" I asked him.

Darren shrugged. "Why should they?"

". . . then one foggy Christmas Eve, the sheriff came to say, 'Randolph with your gun so bright, won't you shoot my wife tonight . . . ?'"

"What are you guys gonna do this whole time?" asked Peter.

"Probably nothing."

While two weeks of homework and tests would not have surprised me, it was actually going to be supervised free time, with some group activities. Nearly forty kids were staying. I wondered how many of their parents just didn't want them around.

Peter's parents arrived first. His dad looked exactly like him, right down to the crew cut, except that he was taller and chubbier. "Tell Killer Fang 'grrrrr' for me," I said, as they walked out the door.

"Actually, Killer Fang's in the car," said his dad, eliciting a whoop of joy from Peter. I went down with them, got my face thoroughly licked by the cocker spaniel, and wished them all a merry Christmas. Jeremy's parents came to get him an hour later, leaving me alone with Darren.

The first day, we spent most of our time hanging out in the library. Two kids we sort of knew from the first floor, Steve and Terrence, sat at a table with us and played Go Fish. Or, more accurately, Steve's variation of the game, where certain cards functioned as automatic weapons or grenades that blew cards out of the other player's hands. The sound effects got us shushed a few times, and from a game design standpoint this rule variation could have used some more play-testing, but it certainly provided us with plenty of entertainment value.

Though lights-out was moved back to 11:00 P.M. in celebration of the holiday spirit, I went to bed at half past ten and was asleep within five minutes.

I woke to the sound of Darren's footsteps. At first I thought he was coming into the room, but the glowing green digits of Jeremy's alarm clock read 12:17. My second thought was that he was simply on his way to the bathroom, but as he opened the door and dim light from the hallway illuminated him, I saw that he was fully dressed and wearing his jacket. He left the room, very slowly closing the door behind him.

I lay there for a while, wondering when he'd return, but fell asleep before he did. When I woke up at 6:30 the next morning, Darren was in his bed.

The next night, just before midnight, he did the same thing. This time I woke up when he returned around three, but pretended to still be asleep. His breathing was heavy as he got undressed and climbed into bed.

Where could he possibly be going that was worth the risk of getting caught?

The next night, December 23, he got up again. I watched him slip on his jacket, pick up his journal, and slowly walk toward the door. I quickly closed my eyes as he glanced over his shoulder at me.

Silence.

"Alex?"

I kept quiet.

"Alex? You awake?"

I could hear his footsteps as he walked toward my bed. I felt his presence as he crouched down beside me.

"Alex," he whispered.

Go away, I silently pleaded.

Maybe he had a knife.

No, that was stupid. He wasn't going to slit my throat.

I could feel beads of sweat beginning to form on my forehead as I tried to sustain the deep, even breathing of somebody who was fast asleep and not desperately praying for his roommate to leave him alone.

Maybe the blade was slowly moving toward my . . .

I opened my eyes.

"I knew you were awake," Darren said.

"No, I wasn't," I said, trying to make my voice sound groggy, like I was still half asleep. "You just woke me up. What do you want?"

"I want to show you something."

"What?"

"You've got to come see."

"What is it?"

"I can't tell you. It's outside."

"We'll get in trouble."

He shook his head. "Nobody will know. They don't care if we go or not, at least not until school starts again. Get dressed."

I pulled the blanket up over my mouth and nose. "I'm not going anywhere," I said in a muffled voice.

Darren grabbed a handful of the blanket and tugged it away. I told him "Knock it off!" as he yanked away the rest of the blanket and threw it onto the floor.

"You'll love this," Darren promised. "It's the coolest thing ever."

"You just wanted to see my underwear."

"Yeah, those yellow stains make me want to sing a happy, happy song."

It was clear that Darren wasn't going to take a whiny "no" for an answer, so I got out of bed and slipped into my jeans and a blue T-shirt. "This better be good," I said, putting on my jacket.

"It is, I swear to God."

We opened the door, made sure nobody was in the hallway, and quietly snuck over to the stairwell. We silently but swiftly moved down the stairs, into the lobby, and out the main entrance. The school grounds were well lit by street lamps, but there was nobody outside.

"See? We didn't get caught," Darren said.

"They can still catch us, easy."

"Nah. Nobody'll be out here this late. It's pretty far, though, so we've gotta hurry."

We broke into a run. It took us less than five minutes to reach the main gate. We easily slipped through the bars and began jogging down the sidewalk along Branford Street.

"How far?" I asked.

"It takes me about forty-five minutes."

"I can't run for forty-five minutes."

"Once we turn off this street we'll just walk."

"What if they check our room?"

"Why would they check our room? Don't be such a baby. Even if we do get caught, this will be worth it, I promise."

Four blocks later, at a railroad crossing, we walked off Branford Street and followed the train tracks. The tracks were poorly lit, and I stepped carefully to avoid the countless broken beer bottles.

It didn't seem like a very safe place for a pair of twelve-year-olds to be walking in the middle of the night. Of course, Darren had made it back alive walking on his own, so it couldn't be *too* dangerous.

"How many times have you been down here?" I asked, stumbling a bit as I nearly stepped on a nail protruding from a piece of wood.

"Eight or nine, counting tonight. I'd come back

every night if I could, but they'll start guarding our building again once school starts back up. Maybe I'll find another way out, who knows?"

A group of kids, probably college age, were standing behind a brick building. A couple of them glared at us, but returned to their conversation and their cigarettes without saying anything.

"Did you ever hear that if you put a penny on the track, you can make a train derail?" Darren asked, picking up his pace.

"I think so."

"It doesn't work. You just get a flat penny."

We walked for another thirty or forty minutes, then left the tracks and came up a small incline about thirty feet behind a small building with a Dumpster in the back. A red lightbulb illuminated the whole area over the dented rear entrance.

Darren knelt down and began carefully brushing the dirt on the incline. "We're here."

"It stinks."

"That's just the Dumpster."

"You brought me out here to see a Dumpster?"

"Shhhh. Not so loud."

I knelt down next to him. "They have Dumpsters back at school that we could look at."

"Make sure there's no glass on the ground," Darren instructed, lifting a scary-looking shard between his fingers and tossing it aside.

He obviously wasn't ready to reveal the purpose of our little field trip, so I brushed at the ground next to him, getting several splinters in my palm. After we were both satisfied that our area was free of glass and hypodermic needles, we lay down on our stomachs.

From this position, we were just able to peek over the incline at the building.

"Isn't this great?" asked Darren. "We can see them but they can't see us."

"So what are we doing?"

"Have you ever been to a strip club?"

"This is a strip club?"

Darren nodded.

"No way!"

"Yes way."

"We're not gonna sneak in there, are we?"

"Nah, there's no way we could do it without getting caught. But we don't need to sneak in. They come out that door every once in a while to empty the garbage or smoke a cigarette."

"The women?" I asked.

"No, not the women. Some sweaty guy who coughs a lot. But sometimes you can see them walking around back there when he opens the door."

"Really?"

"Yep."

"What'd you see?"

"Twice I saw this lady's tits, and the second time she was standing next to this lady who was wearing this thing that almost let you see her whole butt."

"No way!"

"I saw tits, I swear to God."

I looked over at the door. "How often does he come out?"

"I guess whenever he needs to smoke or they fill up the garbage bag. Not very often."

I frowned. "What kind of garbage do they make at a strip club?"

"I don't know. It's probably really gross. Probably used underwear and stuff."

"How long can we stay here?" I asked, glancing at my wrist before realizing that I'd left my watch at the room.

Darren checked his own watch. "At least two hours."

"Cool."

We lay there in silence for several minutes.

"How did you find out about this place?" I asked.

"I forget. I came here a few times during the summer."

I shuddered. Considering how unpleasant the Dumpster aroma was in late December, I couldn't imagine what foul odors lurked in this area during the summer. But, hey, if there were boobs to be seen . . .

I adjusted my position a bit to make myself more comfortable. It might be a long wait, but with the possibility of such a glorious reward, I could be patient.

We talked off and on during the next half hour, mostly speculating about what sights we'd be seeing if we were blessed with X-ray vision. Darren knew countless synonyms for each major component of the female anatomy and wasn't afraid to use them, though I suspected that he'd made up a lot of them himself. While my own vocabulary wasn't as impressive, I made up for it with sheer imagination.

All we needed was X-ray vision, invisibility, and/or the ability to walk through walls, and it would have been the perfect evening.

Then Darren nudged me, roughly, and we both stared, transfixed, as the door handle turned with a loud squeak.

The door opened.

The single most grotesque human being I had ever seen in real life stepped through the doorway. His hairy beer belly protruded from underneath his white T-shirt as if seeking fresh air. He was mostly bald, had an uneven mustache and goatee, and looked to be covered with at least a quart of sweat. Though I knew that I couldn't really smell him from my hiding spot, at least not over the Dumpster odor, the stench in the area did seem to increase by at least 25 percent.

He coughed, twisted his neck around to wipe his nose on his shoulder, and headed for the Dumpster with his small sack of garbage.

This guy got to spend all night looking at naked women. Life wasn't fair.

I realized with horror that I'd been watching the ugly, sweaty, smelly guy and not the open doorway. I quickly gave it my full attention. Red lighting inside, just like outside. No boobs visible.

The guy flung the garbage bag into the Dumpster. For a split second I wondered if he could see us, but I forced that thought out of my mind and focused on the doorway.

Still nothing.

The guy coughed again. "Shit," he muttered. I thought I could see him scratching his ass in my peripheral vision, but it wasn't a sight worth looking away from the doorway.

He headed back toward the building. Only seconds remained before the doorway was shut, perhaps for the remainder of the evening. I furrowed my brow, trying to send brain waves toward the door to entice one of the women to walk into view. There had to be at least *one* of them in there who wanted to see the ugly, sweaty, smelly guy scratch his ass.

He stopped in the doorway, coughed again, repeated the word "shit," and then entered the building, shutting the door behind him.

"Aw, *man*," moaned Darren. "What a rip-off!"

"So what do we do?"

"We wait for the next time."

"How long is that?"

"I dunno." Darren checked his watch. "We may have to head back before then."

Damn.

Damn, damn, damn.

Crap, damn, crap.

What if we waited for another two hours and our only visual treat was watching the guy scratch an alternate cheek?

But what if the door got stuck the next time and they couldn't close it again? Or what if one of the women *came outside?* What if that happened mere seconds after we left?

"There's something else we could do," said Darren.

"What?"

"Knock."

"We'd get in trouble."

"Not if you ran fast enough. Just knock and hurry back here. They won't catch us."

"Why don't you do it?"

"I've already seen inside."

"Right, so it won't matter if you don't get to see it while you're running."

"You're the one who wants to see in there," said

Darren. "Don't worry; I'll make sure you don't get caught."

"How?"

"I just will. I promise. C'mon, go up there and knock."

Since Darren had dragged me along to this place without telling me where we were going, there was a definite flawed logic to the whole "you're the one who wants to see in there" line of thinking. I also had very serious doubts about his ability to make sure I didn't get caught, considering that he would be hiding thirty feet away. I tried to express both of these arguments, but somewhere the line of communication between my mouth and brain was disrupted, and my response was far less articulate than I would have liked: "Uh-uh."

"Fine," said Darren, pushing himself up to a kneeling position. "We'd probably better get going anyway."

"You're right," I agreed, unwilling to back down.

Darren looked over at the building and shook his head sadly. "Biggest tits I ever saw," he said, and then started to walk toward the railroad tracks.

He was bluffing. He was definitely bluffing. There was absolutely no question in my mind that he was bluffing . . . at least for his first two steps. Then I decided that he wasn't bluffing at all and that if I didn't act quickly I'd rob myself of this golden opportunity.

"Okay, okay," I said. Darren looked back over his shoulder at me and smiled. Not the excited smile of a twelve-year-old who might get to see a naked stripper, but the smug smile of somebody who'd convinced his friend to do something against his will. It was, truth be told, a little bit unnerving. But then the smile vanished and his expression turned serious. "All right, I'll watch your back," he said, returning to his spot on the ground. "Just knock a few times, loud, and then run back here."

I nodded, took a deep breath, and walked toward the building. Technically, this wasn't as bad as stealing condoms. There was nothing illegal about knocking on the back door of a strip club and running away, at least as far as I knew. Of course, if I got caught and they called Branford Academy, I'd be screwed in a very big way.

I walked up to the door.

I raised my hand.

I looked back at Darren, who nodded his approval.

I took another deep breath.

I knocked once, twice—

The door opened.

Suddenly I found myself staring directly at a sweat-stained white T-shirt. The ugly guy, one hand out of sight behind him, looked down at me and coughed.

My first and second instincts were to run and to pass out, respectively. I did neither, and instead just stood there in shock.

"Yeah?" the guy asked.

"I . . ." I managed to blurt out, or at least something that sounded like that particular vowel.

"This ain't no place for kids," the guy said. "Whaddya want?"

"I just need to use the phone," I heard myself say, which was a pretty good cover considering that my brain had stopped functioning.

The guy shook his head. "Can't help ya. Go some-place else."

"Yes, sir."

There was movement behind the guy, and I peeked past him. A woman stood there, with long black hair. She was incredibly beautiful, was covered with a thick sheen of perspiration, and was absolutely, completely, gloriously naked. I'd seen plenty of naked women in movies and a couple of times in magazines, but this was my first time seeing one in real life. There were no surprises, anatomically, but the experience was entirely different.

I'm pretty sure I gasped.

The woman made eye contact with me, placed her hands on her hips, and winked.

The guy glanced back at her briefly, then smiled, revealing dark yellow teeth. "Get the fuck outta here, kid," he told me as he shut the door.

I stood there for a long moment.

"Alex!" said Darren in a stage whisper. "Get over here!"

I didn't want to go back to Darren. I wanted to cherish the memory of what I'd just seen. But I also didn't want the ugly guy to open the door again and call the cops.

I ran back past the Dumpster, and Darren and I both ran to the train tracks. "I can't believe you just stood there!" Darren exclaimed.

"Did you see her?" I asked.

"Who?"

"The lady!"

"No, I just saw you and the butt-scratcher. What lady?"

"The naked one."

"She was naked?"

"Oh yeah."

"How naked?"

"All the way."

"Aw, *man*," said Darren. "I should've knocked!"

I grinned and nodded my head. "Yep, you should have. Sucks to be you!"

CHAPTER FIVE

The day before classes resumed, and three days before we found the body of Killer Fang, Peter entered the room in tears.

He'd just returned from Christmas break. Jeremy had arrived several hours ago and was busy constructing a snap-together model World War II ship that his grandmother had given him, which he planned to stomp into thousands of pieces once it was complete.

"What's wrong?" Jeremy asked.

"He's gone," said Peter, in between heaving sobs.

"Who?"

He wiped his nose on his sleeve. "My dog."

"Killer Fang's gone?" I asked. "What happened?"

It took a while, but Peter managed to explain the situation. He'd taken Killer Fang for a quick walk before his parents had to leave, and the cocker spaniel had pulled its leash out of his hands chasing after a squirrel. It ran off, they chased after it, and the dog never returned. They'd looked for it for over two hours, but with absolutely no luck.

After he calmed down, we all went out and helped him look.

No sign of Killer Fang.

His parents had spoken with the local animal shelter and would be contacted if the dog turned up. When we finally quit searching and returned to our room, Peter took out a magic marker and began making LOST DOG signs, working long past lights out.

Though I half expected him to spend the day in the infirmary, Peter got up the next morning and attended all of his classes. A sympathetic teacher agreed to post the signs around town, while the fact that a Branford Academy teacher could be sympathetic came as an amazing shock to the rest of us.

He ate nothing at lunch, but finished half of his dinner. During the meal, I told Jeremy all about the visit that Darren and I paid to the strip club.

"You saw *everything?*" he asked in amazement.

"Yep."

"Upper and lower?"

"Yep."

"And I just got a crappy model ship from my gramma." Jeremy took a sip of milk and sulked for a moment, and then relentlessly quizzed me about the field trip for the rest of dinner.

That night, I awoke to the sound of Darren getting out of bed. He left the room, fully clothed. I lay awake for about fifteen minutes, waiting for him to return, before I fell asleep.

During breakfast the next morning, I quietly asked him where he'd gone.

"Hmmm?"

"Last night. Where'd you go?"

He scratched his lower lip. "To the club."

"How'd you get out?"

"Walked."

"Wasn't there a guard?"

"Maybe."

This didn't make sense. If he'd dragged me out there the last time, why would he be evasive about sneaking out again?

Maybe he'd gone to somebody else's room. Just because I wasn't aware of him having any other friends didn't mean that was really the case.

Why would he hide that?

I didn't push it, but later on I did mention it to Jeremy.

"If he does it again, we need to follow him," he insisted.

"We'll get in trouble."

"Only if we get caught."

"We'll probably get caught."

"Darren didn't get caught."

"We don't even know where he went."

"Right! It could be really great! It might be even better than the strip club! We've gotta follow him!"

"I don't know."

"Yes you do."

"No, I—"

"Yes you do."

Either Darren was quieter, or he didn't leave at all, or I just slept better than usual, but the next night I fell asleep at a quarter after ten and didn't wake up until morning.

The night after that, I awoke to a rather obnoxious finger poking me in the nose. I was not surprised to open my eyes and discover that the finger belonged to Jeremy.

"Stop it," I said.

He poked me twice more. "He just left," he whispered. "Hurry up and get dressed."

I was tired and wanted to protest, but I knew that Jeremy wouldn't relent. I got out of bed and quickly put on my clothes while Peter lay in bed, snoring softly. Jeremy opened our door just a crack and peered out into the hallway. A moment later he opened the door all the way and we left the room.

We hurried over to the stairwell and pushed open the door very carefully. I cringed at the loud squeak. Below, we heard the footsteps of somebody running down the last few stairs, followed by a door opening and closing.

Jeremy made a move to run down after him, but I tugged on the back of his shirt to stop him. "He won't go anywhere if he knows we're following him," I said.

"Yeah, you're right," Jeremy agreed. We cautiously walked down the stairs and paused at the door to the lobby. "How long should we wait?"

"A minute, maybe?"

"We might lose him."

"It's up to you."

Jeremy considered that for a second. "Let's just go. If he catches us, we'll make him take us with him anyway. Two against one."

He pushed open the door and we walked into the lobby.

It was empty. Nobody at the front desk.

We began to walk silently toward the exit, moving casually as if there were absolutely no reason we shouldn't be on our way outdoors for a pleasant evening stroll.

I couldn't be sure, but I thought I heard some giggling coming from the small room behind the front desk. Feminine giggling. If anything, that would certainly explain the ease of Darren's (and hopefully our) escape.

We made it outside without getting busted. There was no sign of Darren.

"We'll just go the way we went before," I suggested. He probably was simply on his way back to the strip club, and was perhaps a bit embarrassed by how much time he was spending in the presence of that most foul of Dumpsters.

When we reached Branford Street, we could see Darren walking several blocks up ahead. Following behind him and hoping that he didn't decide to turn around was probably not the finest shadowing technique ever demonstrated, but we were afraid that anything more sophisticated might cause us to lose him.

Right before he reached the train tracks, he stepped off the sidewalk and ducked into some bushes.

"Is that where you went before?" asked Jeremy.

"Nope."

"I wonder what he's doing?"

"No idea."

"He's probably playing with himself."

I laughed. "He'd at least save that for outside the club."

"Maybe he couldn't wait! We should probably turn back or we might see something really horrible. I'd hate to have to barf all over the place."

"Maybe he stashed some magazines over there."

"Maybe he stashed a *stripper* over there."

We continued walking. "What happens if Peter wakes up and tells somebody that we're gone?" I asked.

"He wouldn't tell on us."

"He wouldn't try and get us in trouble, but he might get worried."

Jeremy shook his head. "Nah, he won't do anything. If he does, we'll just say we were trying to stop Darren. We'd all get in trouble for what Darren did anyway, so we might as well be out here enjoying it, too."

We stopped talking as we approached the thick bushes.

I motioned for Jeremy to stop. We stood there for a moment, listening to the sounds coming from the bushes. They weren't loud, and I couldn't quite tell what they were.

They sounded sort of . . . wet.

Jeremy put a finger to his lips, and together we began to walk toward the bushes as quietly as possible.

The wet sounds continued, vaguely reminding me of my mother peeling the skin off a raw chicken.

Jeremy held up three fingers, counting down.

Two . . . one . . .

"Gotcha!" Jeremy shouted as we simultaneously pushed through the bushes.

Darren cried out and threw up his hands.

A few drops of liquid hit my face.

There was a moment of absolute chaos, as Darren frantically scooted away from us, and Jeremy's face registered pure horror at what he saw, and I was suddenly overwhelmed by a smell that was far worse than the Dumpster outside the strip club.

A pair of garbage bags lay on the ground. On top of them was a furry, headless carcass.

A slit ran most of the way up its belly. Its severed tail rested on the ground. Its head, mouth wide-open in a howl, tongue missing, eye sockets filled with tiny maggots, was propped up between two rocks.

I violently threw up and then crawled out from the bushes, coughing and trying not to choke.

It took me at least thirty seconds to recover enough to focus my attention on anything but my own nausea. Darren stood there, dripping hands at his sides, panting heavily. Jeremy faced him, fists clenched.

"Is that Killer Fang?" Jeremy demanded.

"Let me tell you what happened."

"Is that Killer Fang, yes or no?"

"Yes, but I didn't kill him, I swear to God, I didn't hurt him, I didn't do anything to him."

"You cut his head off!"

Darren glanced around to make sure there was nobody coming. His nose was starting to run and he wiped it with a bloody finger. "I didn't do anything to him while he was alive," Darren said in a whisper.

"Yeah, right."

"He got hit by a car."

"I don't believe you."

"He *did*," Darren insisted. "I wasn't looking for him; I was just going to walk around town. He was lying on the side of the road. He was already dead. I wouldn't kill Peter's dog. I wouldn't do something like that."

"But you would chop him up!" Jeremy accused, taking a step toward Darren and looking ready to beat him senseless. As horrified as I was by what had happened to Killer Fang, I also knew that getting into a fistfight over it would greatly increase the chances of our little field trip being discovered.

"Don't hurt him," I told Jeremy.

"How about I just cut his head and tail off and hide him in some bushes?"

In other circumstances, the "tail" comment would have been highly amusing, but here we didn't even notice the logistical flaw. "When did you find him?" I asked.

"Night before last," Darren said. "That time you saw me go out."

"Why didn't you tell Peter?"

"He would've been too sad."

"You are *such* a liar!" said Jeremy. "You think he'd be too sad to know his dog was hit by a car, but not too sad to know you chopped him up?"

"I wasn't going to tell him anything! This way, he could always think that his dog was still alive. He'd be happier."

"Bullshit!"

"You don't know! You don't know what I was thinking! You're not in my head!"

"Good thing or I'd be in a loony bin! Which is where you're gonna be when people find out what you did!"

Darren looked at the ground. "Do we really have to tell anybody?" he asked in a soft, miserable voice.

"Yeah!" Jeremy sneered. "We're gonna tell *everybody!*"

"Please don't."

"Everybody at school! Everybody you know! The whole world is gonna find out what you did! Especially everybody in the loony bin with you!"

"Please, I'll do anything you want."

"They're going to put you in a straitjacket and you won't be able to move and they'll stick you with giant needles every day and they'll shock you and they'll rip out parts of your *brain* and they'll laugh and laugh and laugh at you!"

"I didn't hurt him. If he was alive, I would've got help and told Peter, I promise."

"I think you killed him."

"I didn't!" Darren wailed.

"I'm gonna tell Peter you killed his dog."

"I *didn't!*"

"And they're gonna jab you with so many needles that you'll look at your arm and it'll be nothing but holes and then they'll strap you down and—"

"Leave him alone," I said.

"Why should I?"

"Because you're not helping anything. We need to get back to school before they know we're gone."

"We can't just leave Killer Fang out here like this," said Jeremy.

"I'll bury him," said Darren. "You guys go back so you don't get in trouble, and I'll bury him."

"You just want to cut him up some more."

Darren shook his head vigorously. "I won't. I'll bury him. You can take my pocketknife."

I'd seen Darren use the blade of his pocketknife to clean his fingernails on a few occasions. It was barely an inch long, and while I wasn't exactly an expert on such matters, it seemed that decapitating a cocker spaniel with such a small blade would be a long, incredibly difficult process. I wondered how many hours he'd spent cutting through the dog's neck, how much effort it had taken to get through the spinal column.

"Okay," I told Darren. "Bury him."

"We have to show Peter what happened," said Jeremy.

"No way. We can't let him see Killer Fang like that. He'd die."

"He would," said Darren. "He'd have a heart attack."

Jeremy held up his fist. "Shut up!"

"We'll let Darren bury him, and we'll go back to the room, and we'll figure out what to do."

"If we let him bury him, then there's no proof."

"There's no proof anyway," said Darren. "I'll just say I found him like that."

"Give me your pocketknife," I said.

"Are you going to tell Peter?"

"I don't know what we're going to do yet."

Darren picked up the dark red pocketknife, snapped the blade back into the handle, and gave it to me.

"See you whenever," I said, and then turned and began to walk back the way we came.

I hoped that Jeremy would follow me, but after I'd gone about twenty feet, I stopped and looked back. He stared at Darren for a moment longer, kicked the ground angrily, and then ran over to catch up with me.

"Sick," Jeremy muttered. "He's totally sick."

"I know."

"He should go to jail. I'll bet you anything he killed the dog."

I shook my head. "He couldn't catch and kill a dog like that with a pocketknife."

"Why not? Sure he could. Maybe Killer Fang was hurt. Maybe he did get hit by a car, but it only broke his legs, and so he couldn't get away when Darren found him. You could kill a dog with a pocketknife, easy."

"Maybe."

"What are we gonna do?"

"I don't know," I admitted. "What do you think Peter would do if we told him?"

"Freak out and kill Darren."

"He won't kill anybody."

"He *should*."

"C'mon, we need to be serious. Nobody is going to kill Darren. We need to figure out what we're going to tell Peter."

"Everything," said Jeremy.

"No. You're right, he'd freak out, and then everybody will find out. You know Darren'll tell about the strip club. And then we'll *all* pay for it, big-time. Mr. Sevin will take away every bit of free time we've got until summer. We might even get kicked out."

Somehow I didn't think my parents would welcome me back into their home with open arms if I got expelled. My next stop would be military school. Probably in a remote location. Somewhere chilly.

"So we're gonna let him get away with it?"

"No, but . . ." I trailed off, unable to think of an alternate solution. We certainly had to let Peter know that his dog was dead, but while I hated the thought of letting Darren go unpunished, was it worth getting in that much trouble ourselves?

I truly believed that Killer Fang had been dead when Darren found him. But maybe next time the dog *wouldn't* already be dead.

Would he stop at dogs?

"What if we . . . I don't know, what if we kept it between us, and we just made sure he never did anything like that again?"

"Kept it between the three of us or the four of us?"

"I'm not sure."

"I'm not gonna babysit him for the rest of my life. I don't care if I *do* get in trouble. He's not gonna get away with this. Peter loved his dog!"

"I'm not saying he has to get away with it, just that we don't have to get anybody else in on it."

"So, what, you want us to give him a spanking or something? He cut our best friend's dog's tongue out! Just for fun!"

Jeremy was right; we couldn't let Darren get away with this. But there had to be a way we could take care of the problem on our own. Maybe just knowing that he'd been caught would keep Darren from doing this kind of thing again, or maybe . . .

"I know what we could do," I said.

"What?"

"We could scare him. You, me, and Peter can figure out a way to scare the hell out of him. We'll scare him so bad that he will never, *ever* do something like this again in his entire life."

CHAPTER SIX

Getting back into the residence hall was ridiculously easy. Parents who paid the tuition with the expectation of a secure environment were getting ripped off, big-time.

On the way back, Jeremy and I worked out a plan. I would have preferred something a little more subtle and a little less cruel, but the end result was one that we could both live with. We also played Rock, Paper, Scissors to determine who had to tell Peter about Killer Fang. Paper covered rock and I won, but after we snuck back into the room I decided that Jeremy's rage about the entire situation meant that he might reveal too much before we were ready, so at the last minute I offered to take on the miserable task.

Peter was still snoring. I shook him gently until he opened his eyes.

"What do you want?" he asked sleepily.

"I have to tell you about Killer Fang."

Peter immediately sat up. "You found him? How is he?"

"He got . . ." My throat closed up and it took me a

few seconds before I could continue. "He got hit by a car."

Peter's lower lip began to tremble. "He's okay, though, right? He's a pretty tough dog. I bet he made it through okay."

"He got killed. Darren found him."

"Darren doesn't know for sure, does he? He could be wrong. Killer Fang's a pretty smart dog. I don't think he'd let himself get hit by a car. He wouldn't do that."

"He got killed," I repeated.

"Oh."

Peter rolled over on his stomach and buried his face in his pillow. His whole body began to quiver. I wasn't sure how to console him, and after standing there for a long, uncomfortable moment, I went to bed.

When we got up the next morning, I was very relieved to see that Darren was there. I'd half expected him not to return to the room, maybe even to run away from Branford Academy altogether. I lingered behind with him as Peter and Jeremy went to take their showers.

"Did you do it?"

"Yeah," said Darren, almost pouting. He held up his hands, which were raw and swollen. "Look what happened 'cause I didn't have anything to dig with."

"Too bad for you." While I hoped that none of his teachers asked Darren to explain what had happened to his hands, I certainly wasn't going to feel sorry for him.

"I should have used the dog's jaw," he said, looking me straight in the eye as if daring me to take offense.

The frightened, pleading Darren of last night was

gone. I couldn't help but take a small bit of pleasure from knowing that soon it would return.

"You were wrong," Peter told me as we returned to the room after lunch to pick up our materials for our next class.

"I was?"

"I talked to Darren. He said he doesn't think it was Killer Fang that got run over. He said it was a little black dog, and that the people who hit it took it right to the vet."

"I guess I was wrong, then."

"I've read a lot about how dogs can find their way home, no matter how far it is. He's pretty fast. It'll probably take him about a week to get back home, so that'll be around Sunday or Monday."

"Well, that's good to hear."

"Yeah. I hope he doesn't get too hungry."

Jeremy and I didn't speak to anybody else about our plan for the rest of the day, or all day Friday. I was growing more and more uncomfortable with the whole idea, but Jeremy was insistent. Darren needed to be punished, and Peter needed to accept the fate of his dog.

"And it'll be fun," Jeremy said.

I strongly disagreed about that aspect, but each time I considered telling Jeremy that he'd have to do this without me, I remembered the headless carcass on the garbage bag. Even though he knew how much Peter missed his dog, how much he loved it, Darren had mutilated its body. He was a sick, scary kid, but when we were done with him, he'd be on his best behavior for the rest of his time at Branford Academy, and hopefully for the rest of his life.

Saturday evening. Jeremy and Peter had already snuck out of the building. Darren was seated at his desk, lost in thought. He held his pen but hadn't written anything for the past twenty minutes.

"Put on your jacket," I told him.

"Why?"

"We're going out."

"Screw you. I'm not going anywhere."

"You are so. You have to apologize to Peter. You're going to take us out to where you buried the dog, and you're going to say you're sorry for lying about it being a different dog."

"Yeah, right."

"I'm serious, Darren. It's mean to let him think he's still alive."

"Then go out there and show him yourself."

"Yeah, and while we're there we'll just show him what you did."

"I don't even know what you're talking about."

I desperately wanted to smash my fist into his lying mouth, but of course I didn't, and not just because I was fairly sure that he could beat the crap out of me if it came down to it. "Don't lie to me."

"I'm not. I have no idea what you're talking about. Leave me alone."

"You have a choice," I said, struggling to make my voice sound as cold and calculating as I possibly could. "You can come with me and help Peter get over this, or we can show him what you did to his dog. We can show him that you ripped his tongue out. Maybe he'll do the same thing to you for lying."

"Ooooh, I'm so scared," said Darren, but his eyes seemed to indicate that the statement wasn't necessarily sarcastic.

"Put on your jacket."

He did.

"Why is he so much in love with dogs, anyway?" asked Darren as we walked along the sidewalk. "They aren't like people. They don't do anything."

"They do a lot of stuff."

"Like what?"

"They catch Frisbees, they fetch sticks, they let you pet them . . ."

"So? What makes that so great?"

"Have you ever had a dog?"

"No way."

"Have you had any pets?"

"Just a goldfish that we flushed."

"So, then, you don't know what it's like."

"I don't need to know what it's like. I can see what it's like. Dogs don't do anything but run around and slobber. Only stupid people like them."

"Well, good, you don't ever have to have one, then." I'd always wanted a dog, but my parents wouldn't allow it. Too much trouble.

We left the sidewalk, and a few minutes later my knees weakened as we entered the moonlit woods. I even felt a little scared, almost as if I were the one with a nasty surprise awaiting me.

What if Darren had another pocketknife?

What if he'd already killed Peter and Jeremy, and their headless bodies were buried next to Killer Fang? Or their chests were slit open, just waiting for Darren to reach inside and—

Stop it. You're being an idiot.

At least I hoped I was.

We ducked through the bushes and stepped into the clearing.

"What the hell . . . ?"

A noose hung from a branch of the largest tree (which wasn't all that large, since this wasn't exactly an immense forest). At least it was *supposed* to be a noose; Jeremy hadn't tied it very well and it was more of a lopsided circle. A wooden crate was positioned directly under the rope.

Movement to the left. I stepped out of the way as Peter came up behind Darren and grabbed his arms, holding them behind his back as Jeremy slapped a strip of duct tape over his mouth. Darren struggled frantically, twisting and kicking, but Peter held him firmly while Jeremy unspooled more of the duct tape, covered his mouth with a second layer, and wrapped it all the way around his head three more times.

Peter wrestled Darren to the ground, and together he and Jeremy taped his hands together behind his back. Darren got in a good kick that nearly knocked Jeremy off balance, but it wasn't long before they'd pulled him back to his feet and dragged him over to the crate.

I was supposed to be helping, but all I could do was watch.

It took nearly a minute of struggle before Peter and Jeremy finally got him on top of the crate. Jeremy pointed to me. "Get over here, Alex!"

I hurried over to the tree, climbed up onto the unsteady crate, and placed the noose around Darren's neck.

"Don't move," Jeremy warned him as I jumped off. "If you fall off this, you'll choke to death. Do you understand?"

Darren shouted something incoherent at him through the duct tape.

Jeremy raised a fist. "Do you understand?"

Darren continued shouting for a few more seconds, but then finally went silent and gave a small nod.

"Good." The three of us stepped away from the makeshift gallows and took a moment to catch our breath.

Peter looked terrible. Even in the poor light I could see that his eyes were red and puffy, and he had the look of somebody who'd spent the past hour being kicked in the head.

"Okay, let's do it so we can get back," I said.

"Darren Rust, you have been accused of the crime of *murder*," said Jeremy in a booming voice. "You hunted down Peter's dog, Killer Fang, and you stabbed him to death with your pocketknife, and you dragged him into the bushes and chopped up his body. How do you plead?"

Darren said something that we couldn't understand.

"Nod for guilty and shake your head for not guilty," said Jeremy.

Darren shook his head.

"We know what you did. We all know. We can look into your very *soul* and see what you did, Darren Rust. And you must be punished."

I'd written the line about looking into Darren's very

soul, and I was amazed by how well Jeremy was able to deliver it.

"You must be punished for your cruel actions, for your taking of an innocent life. You must suffer just as Killer Fang suffered."

Peter glanced over his shoulder. "Did you hear that?"

We all looked back in that direction. We waited for a few moments, hearts racing.

Nothing.

"The words of the Bible say, 'An eye for an eye, and a tooth for a tooth,'" Jeremy told Darren. "To punish you for what you've done, we must chop your head off and shove maggots in your eyes. We must cut open your stomach and make you eat your food again. Maybe we'll even surgically implant a tail so we can rip it off."

That last line hadn't been planned, and certainly wouldn't have been approved by the creative team.

"Peter, as the owner of the victim, do you feel that the punishment of the accused is fair and just?"

Peter nodded. "I do."

"Alex, as the impartial witness, do you feel that the punishment of the accused is fair and just?"

I nodded as well. "I do."

"Then, Darren Rust, you have been fairly sentenced by a jury of your peers, and you must accept the punishment we have decided for you."

The three of us simultaneously took a step forward.

The crotch of Darren's pants darkened.

"The accused has pissed his pants!" Jeremy gleefully announced. "He has wet himself in court! Oh my God!"

I looked over at Peter. He didn't seem amused.

"Did you see that?" Jeremy asked me, laughing. "What a baby!"

"Knock it off," I told him.

"But he pissed his pants!" Jeremy pointed to him. "I can't believe he did that!"

"Shut up, Jeremy."

"Fine, fine, fine." He resumed his booming tone. "If the accused would like to speak any final words before his sentence is carried out . . . well, too bad, because his mouth is taped shut. I guess we should've taped his wee-wee, too."

"Damn it, Jeremy . . ."

"Okay, okay. Darren Rust, upon the count of three the jury of your peers will carry out your punishment. One . . ."

We all took another step forward.

"Two . . ."

Darren looked terrified and frantically began struggling to free his taped hands.

"Three!"

Darren stepped backward to get away from us, and the crate toppled onto its side. I swore I heard a loud *crack* as he dropped. Before I could fully register what had happened, Darren was dangling from the tree, the noose tight around his neck.

"Shit!" Peter screamed.

Darren's legs kicked wildly two feet above the ground as he struggled to get free. Peter and I rushed forward, and I immediately received a violent kick to the chest that knocked me backward several steps, gasping for breath.

"Stop moving!" Peter shouted at Darren, but the accused was too panicked to listen.

Jeremy just stood there, frozen.

I ran back over to the tree, turned the crate right-side up, and pushed it underneath Darren's feet while Peter tried to keep him steady. Once Darren was on solid footing again, I hopped up onto the crate, quickly loosened the noose, and removed it from his neck.

His skin was red and glistening where the rope had dug into it.

Peter and I helped Darren down from the crate. I hurriedly unwrapped the duct tape from around his head, ripping off some hair in the process. Darren sucked in a deep breath, sounding like he was hyperventilating.

"Aw, God . . . look what we did to his neck!" Peter said, his voice frantic.

Jeremy still hadn't moved.

Darren fell to his knees, coughing and choking. I tried to free his wrists, but my hands were trembling too badly to unpeel the edge of the tape.

"Are you okay?" Peter asked. "Can you breathe?"

Darren continued coughing. He might have been sobbing, too, but I couldn't tell.

"We didn't mean it," I insisted. "We were just trying to scare you."

"Get away from me!" Darren managed to shout. "Just leave me alone!"

We all moved away from him. Darren stayed on his knees for an unbearably long time, just staring at the ground and trying to catch his breath.

Finally he spoke: "My neck hurts."

"We're sorry," I said.

"I mean it *really* hurts. It might be broken."

"It can't be broken," Peter said.

"Shut up! You don't know! Get this off my hands!"

It took a couple of minutes, but I finally managed to get the tape off his hands. He held them in front of him, clenching and unclenching his fists; then he touched his neck and gazed at his red fingertip.

"I'll probably have to go to the hospital."

"You might not," said Peter. "It doesn't look that bad."

"Well, it *feels* that bad! You guys made me bleed out my neck! I might die! I hope I *do* die. Then we'll see what happens to you!"

Jeremy suddenly came out of his daze. "So, we're even, right? You killed his dog and we got back at you."

"*I didn't kill his dog!*" Darren shouted, so loud that Peter, Jeremy, and I all instinctively looked back to make sure nobody was around to hear.

"But you cut him up."

"So what? I cut up a dead dog!" Darren ran his palm across the side of his neck and held it up to show us. "Look what you did to me! His dumb dog was already dead when I found it, so all I did was biology. You guys were almost murderers!"

"No, we weren't," I said. "I told you, we were just trying to scare you."

Darren shoved his palm into my face. "That's not what this looks like."

"But it's true. We were going to let you down."

"I don't care. I'm going back to school, and I'm going to tell Mr. Sevin exactly what you fuckers did to me."

He walked off.

We helplessly watched him go.

CHAPTER SEVEN

"He won't tell anyone," said Jeremy, as Darren turned and vanished from sight.

"What do you mean?" I asked. "How can he *not* tell anyone? You think he's just going to wander around with a bloody neck?"

"He can wear a turtleneck! It won't be just us three who get busted if he says anything. He will, too. You think he wants that?"

"He might decide that it's worth it," said Peter.

"Don't be stupid. He's not going to say anything. He's a messed-up dog killer. We might get kicked out of school, but he'll get stuck in a psycho house."

"He didn't kill the dog," I said.

"Then what he did is even *more* messed up! Let him go cry to Sevin. He'll be sorry."

I felt like I was going to vomit. I couldn't get kicked out of Branford Academy. Who knew what my parents would do with me next? It was bad enough what they did when they just didn't want me around; if they were genuinely mad at me, I might end up someplace more miserable than I could imagine.

Or I could end up in juvenile hall.

The police would certainly realize that we'd only been trying to scare Darren, that we weren't really going to rip out his guts, but if he told on us, I was truly, deeply screwed.

"I'm gonna run up ahead and talk to him," I said.

"Don't bother," said Jeremy. "Let the freak go."

"No, I'm gonna see what I can do. He might listen to me."

"Why would he listen to you?"

"I don't know, but he might." We'd bonded over lying outside in the cold waiting to see a naked woman, and a bond like that was not easily broken.

I ran ahead of Jeremy and Peter, praying that I could work this out. I hurried through the trees, and it didn't take long to catch up with Darren. He started to pick up his pace as he heard me approach.

"Darren, wait!" I shouted.

He broke into a run.

"Darren, *please!*"

I'm not sure if it was because I sounded so pathetic or because he figured I could outrun him anyway, but he slowed his pace. "What do you want?"

"What do you think I want? Let's talk about this."

He ran his finger along his neck. "I've got a lot to talk about, but it's sure not going to be with you."

"C'mon, Darren, you know we weren't going to do anything!"

"I don't know that at all."

"Yes you do. And Mr. Sevin will know it, too. And so will the cops. But if we just forget about the whole thing, pretend like nothing happened, then nobody has to get hurt."

Darren lifted his chin to give me a better view of his neck. "Nobody *has* to get hurt?"

"I've already seen your neck, okay? Don't be an asshole about this!"

"*I'm* an asshole?"

Though I was still in a severe state of panic, I was starting to get more than a little angry, too. "Don't act all innocent! You got yourself into this! And if you tell, believe me, I'll make sure they know exactly how sick you really are."

Darren gave me a grin that made me want to break his jaw. "You suck at threats."

"I'm serious."

"Alex, when I tell them what happened you'll be so busy sobbing and blubbering that you won't be able to say a fuckin' word, you chickenshit."

I stared into his eyes, hoping to find some sign that he was concerned, but it seemed to be genuine arrogance. I clenched my fists. "I'm not a chicken."

"What, you can't even say the 'shit' part? You're the biggest loser I've ever met in my entire life!"

He had to be bluffing.

"Fine," I said, shrugging. "Tell them. You'll have fun in the loony bin. Maybe you'll get to cut up a person who *thinks* he's a dog."

"That was kind of funny."

"Yeah. Ha-ha."

"I might not tell anybody. I haven't decided what I'm going to do yet. But you'd better just leave me alone for a while."

"I'm really sorry about this, Darren."

"See? You're a chickenshit."

"But I am sorry."

"Good. Stay away from me."

I let him go. If he was considering keeping this a secret, then all we could do was be as nice to him as possible and stay on his good side.

I walked back and met up with Jeremy and Peter. "So?" Jeremy asked.

"He doesn't know what he's going to do. He might not say anything."

"He'd better not. We can do a lot worse than scrape up his neck."

"Stop it," I said. "Don't say anything mean to him from now on."

"I never said anything mean to him until he did this!"

"Well, let's please not fight with him. Maybe he won't say anything. We'll just all pretend nothing happened."

Jeremy sighed. "Fine. Whatever. But I'd like to see him try to tell on us."

We walked in silence until we were in sight of the campus.

"I don't think he killed Killer Fang," Peter said, his voice hollow. "Killer Fang would've been too fast for somebody like him. He would've ripped Darren's throat out if he tried to hurt him. I think he got hit by a car."

"That's what I think, too," I said.

"My parents should've left him at home." Peter sniffled. "He was a great dog."

"Yeah," Jeremy agreed.

Peter began to cry. Neither Jeremy nor I were particularly well versed in the art of consoling a friend in mourning, so we fell behind to give Peter some dignity as he wept.

When we got back to the room, Darren was under the covers, facing the wall. He had a towel draped over his neck.

"Darren . . . ?" I whispered.

It was obvious from his breathing that his sleep was feigned, but I didn't repeat his name. We all silently undressed and got into bed. As far as I know, nobody slept.

The next day was predictably miserable. I spent most of my time sitting in class, pretending to pay attention while I tried to think of a cover story that would keep us from getting in trouble. But what could we say? The best I could come up with was that we'd been goofing around, playing rodeo, and that one of us had looped the rope around Darren's neck and accidentally yanked too hard. But that was a dumb-ass cover story and would put all the blame on us. No, if the events of last night were discovered, Darren was going to be revealed as the sicko that he was. I'd make sure of that.

Darren wore the same blue turtleneck shirt every day that week (the only one he owned, presumably) and as far as I know none of his teachers questioned the wardrobe choice. He never said a word to us and spent most of his free time furiously writing in his journal.

I noticed that he no longer left it on his shelf. He either kept it in his book bag when he left the room, or he slept with it under his pillow.

I desperately wanted to know what depraved things

he was writing in there, but short of holding him down and taking it by force, I didn't see any way to do so.

That said, after a full week I began to relax. Peter seemed to be more or less over the initial misery of losing his pet, and his cheerful nature started to return. Just a smile here and a laugh there, but it was a promising sign that Darren hadn't destroyed his spirit.

On the other hand, Jeremy no longer cracked bad jokes or interrupted card games to write down witty observations. Several times I caught him just staring at Darren, jaw clenched, filled with so much rage that I thought a few hundred blood vessels in his face might simultaneously burst. Darren was the one with the power, and it was making Jeremy absolutely nuts. And a week of relative peace had done nothing to ease his hatred.

But me, I realized that I could finally eat a meal without being sick to my stomach. That is, sick to my stomach from stress. The food itself remained crappy.

I sat with Peter and Jeremy in the dining hall, eating something for lunch that was either beef, chicken, veal, or some sort of breaded vegetation. It was one of the nastiest things they'd ever served.

"I'd rather eat a dried turd than this," Peter noted. "Jeremy, let me have a dried turd. I know you've got one somewhere."

"Ha-ha."

"Ho-ho."

"Hee-hee," I said, with expert comic timing.

Jeremy finally grinned. "I'd rather lick the butt of a skunk in midspray than eat this."

I nearly choked on my food as I laughed in midswallow.

"I'd rather eat a *hairy* dried turd than this," Peter said.

"That's just gross," said Jeremy. "There's no need for that." He took a bite of his whatever and began to chew very slowly with his eyes closed. "Oooooh, it tastes so much better if you imagine that it's a skunk butt. Oh, yeah, sweet, delicious skunk butt. Skunk butt with parsley . . . that's what I'm eating."

"Mmmmmm . . . dried turd . . ." said Peter, licking his lips.

I was biting the sides of my mouth to keep from laughing and attracting undue attention to our table. Jeremy opened his eyes and took another slow, sensuous bite, but he frowned as Darren sat down in an empty chair next to him.

"What do you want?" Jeremy demanded.

I kicked him under the table. Jeremy kicked me back.

"I just wanted to see how you guys were doing," said Darren.

"We're doing good," I assured him.

"That's cool. And I wanted to say something to Peter."

"Yeah?" Peter asked.

Darren looked Peter directly in the eyes. "Woof-woof." Then he smiled, pushed back his chair, stood up, and casually walked away.

We had no idea what to make of that.

When we returned to our room, the door was bloody.

The four of us sat in Mr. Sevin's office. The stomach pain I hadn't been feeling for the past couple of days had all come rushing back, with reinforcements.

Mr. Sevin sat behind his desk. "I understand there was an incident last week?"

Nobody responded. We all shifted uncomfortably in our seats and tried to avoid eye contact.

"When I ask a question, I do not expect to listen to silence," Mr. Sevin said. "Mr. Fletcher, tell me exactly what happened."

I shrugged. "I'm not sure what you mean."

"Do I look like the kind of man who tolerates liars?"

I shrugged again.

"I expect an answer when I ask you a question," said Mr. Sevin, his voice rising to a frightening level. "You know exactly what I'm talking about, and it is very much in your best interest to cooperate."

"I'm sorry," I said.

"I'm not interested in your apologies, Mr. Fletcher. I'm interested in your explanation."

"Well . . . we accidentally hurt Darren's neck."

"By looping a noose around it?"

"Yeah."

"And you thought that was acceptable behavior?"

"No."

"So you purposely engaged in unacceptable behavior?"

"I guess so."

"Mr. Rust says that you three were trying to get back at him, that the three of you have never gotten along as roommates. Is that an accurate assessment?"

"He killed Peter's dog!" Jeremy blurted out.

Mr. Sevin raised an eyebrow. "I beg your pardon?"

"Peter's dog got away. We found Darren cutting up the body."

Mr. Sevin leaned forward across his desk. "I don't

know anything about a dog. Mr. Rust, would you care to explain?"

"I have no idea what they're talking about," Darren said.

"You liar!" Jeremy turned to Mr. Sevin. "Sir, he's lying!"

"How could I kill his dog?" Darren asked. "Was he hiding it in the room or something?"

"It ran away when his parents dropped him off after Christmas and you know it!"

"These jerks are always accusing me of this kind of stuff," Darren told Mr. Sevin. "I don't know what I ever did to them."

"Why don't we take Mr. Sevin to where you buried the dog?" Jeremy asked.

"Fine. Let's go right now," said Darren, starting to rise up out of his chair.

As Mr. Sevin told him to sit back down, I had a sinking feeling as it became clear why Darren hadn't told on us earlier. He'd been covering his tracks. Moving the corpse.

"He did it," Jeremy insisted. "I swear!"

"Quiet!" said Mr. Sevin, almost at a shout. "Mr. Rust, did you harm a dog?"

Darren shook his head. "Of course not."

Mr. Sevin looked at Peter. "Did he harm your dog?"

"Yes. He cut up his body."

"Did you see this?"

"No."

"Then how do you know it's true?"

"Jeremy and Alex told me."

"I saw it," Jeremy said. "He even cut off its head."

"Mr. Fletcher, did you see this?"

"Yes, sir," I said.

"Why didn't you report it to me immediately?"

"I . . . I don't know. We wanted to handle it ourselves."

"By nearly killing your roommate?"

I was silent.

"I'll take you to where the dog is," said Jeremy.

"Fine, let's go," Darren challenged. "Let's go right now."

"You will *not* speak to each other," said Mr. Sevin. "You will answer *my* questions. I'm sure you all understand how serious this is." He glared at Jeremy. "Write down the location of the dog and we will send somebody to investigate."

"He probably moved it," I said.

"Oh, sure, that's a good excuse," said Darren. "None of you can prove anything because I didn't do anything. I didn't touch your dog." He looked at Mr. Sevin. "They just don't like me. I can't help it if I'm quiet and I like to write instead of playing stupid card games when we're supposed to be studying."

I glanced down at Darren's book bag. His journal was protruding noticeably from the top.

"Mr. Sevin, he's always writing in a journal," I said. "He probably wrote about everything that happened."

"Nothing happened for me to write about, except you guys attacking me!"

"He's got it with him," I said, pointing to his book bag, even though Mr. Sevin wouldn't be able to see it over his desk. "He's always writing in it, and he won't let us see it, and he even started sleeping with it under his pillow. Make him let you read it."

Darren shoved the journal deeper into his book bag, out of sight. "This is private. It's nobody's business but mine."

"Yeah, because it talks about you ripping up a dog!" said Jeremy.

"It does not!"

"Prove it!"

"It's private!"

Mr. Sevin cleared his throat. "Mr. Rust's journal is of nobody's concern but his own. Now I *will* get to the bottom of this. In the meantime, you may all consider yourselves under probation. You will not receive mail, you will not make phone calls, and all free time is to be spent studying. You will not leave your room except to attend classes and for meals. Is that understood?"

We all said that it was.

Mr. Sevin pushed a small pad of paper and a pencil across the desk toward Jeremy. "Write down where the dog is allegedly buried."

As Jeremy wrote it down, Darren bit his lip and looked like he was about to cry. He reached into his book bag and removed the journal.

"Do you promise that you won't tell anyone else what's in here?" Darren asked Mr. Sevin.

"I have no authority to read your personal journal," said Mr. Sevin. "You can put it away."

"I know, but you can read it, if you want. If you don't tell anybody."

Mr. Sevin nodded and took the journal from him.

"Very well. I will retain it in the strictest confidence. Please remain in my office. The rest of you are dismissed."

Jeremy, Peter, and I got up and left his office. "That lying bastard!" said Jeremy as soon as we were out of earshot.

"What do you think's in the journal?" Peter asked.

"I don't know," said Jeremy. "Maybe he's so much of an idiot that he forgot he wrote about Killer Fang."

"Maybe," I said, not believing it for a second. Obviously Darren had written fake entries in his journal, probably woeful musings on his treatment at the hands of his endlessly cruel roommates. He'd let the journal stick out of his book bag so that I'd be sure to notice it. Hell, he'd spent the whole past week making us think he was writing incriminating stuff in there.

How could we prove it was all lies?

How thorough had he been about covering his tracks?

The answers came early that evening: we couldn't, and *very* thorough.

CHAPTER EIGHT

We never found out exactly what Darren wrote in his journal, but apparently it was a heartbreaking chronicle of astounding (yet credible-sounding) abuse. I tried to explain that the journal was faked, but the words sounded ridiculous even as I said them. Mr. Sevin dropped his usual veneer of calm-but-stern authority and screamed at us until he was red in the face (a splotchy sort of red, but red nevertheless) and both Peter and I were in tears. My only solace was that I'd held out slightly longer than Peter before breaking down.

A pair of teachers went out to look for the dog, but found no evidence of any wrongdoing. Had a forensics team been dispatched, I'm sure we would have been fully exonerated, but despite our insistence that the story was true, two teachers were all that we got.

Darren was moved out of our room. We asked where he was going but were told in no uncertain terms that it was none of our business.

We were not kicked out of school, though our parents were called. My dad didn't talk to me at all, while my mom just said in a soft voice that she was very disappointed in me. But she didn't sound disappointed. The lack of emotion of any sort in her voice stung me as if I'd slammed my body against a wall of thumbtacks.

During Jeremy's phone conversation with his parents, he finally broke down into tears. As everybody else had done more than their share of bawling since this whole adventure began, I was glad to have him finally join in the fun.

Our probation was to continue for the rest of the term. No free time. Our door had to remain open until lights-out each evening, with surprise inspections at any moment. Our weekends were spent engaged in manual labor that was exhausting, tedious, humiliating, or (most often) all three.

They did relax the restriction on our incoming mail, which wasn't much of a consolation for me since I never received any. And though I can't prove it, I'm pretty sure that the cafeteria food was made slightly worse on our behalf.

Peter, Jeremy, and I did manage to entertain ourselves by joking about our plight, and we occasionally risked unimaginable punishment by breaking out an unlawful deck of cards like people drinking alcohol during prohibition, but for the most part it was a pretty miserable existence.

Though we were instructed not to interact with him, I'd see Darren each day in the cafeteria and in class. He'd almost always avoid my glance, but every once in a while, when he knew nobody else was watching, he'd smile.

It was the kind of smile that made me think it would be worth getting expelled and going to prison just for the opportunity to nail him to the ground with rusty spikes and punch him in the face over and over until every tooth was shattered.

I hadn't ever thought that I was capable of hate, *real* hate, but there it was.

Ten long weeks after the incident, I sat in Mr. Wolfe's classroom, taking a harder than usual but not unmanageable test. Though it may have created a joyless existence, all of this extra studying did mean that it was pretty hard *not* to ace a test.

"What is this?" Mr. Wolfe demanded, loud enough to make me flinch.

I looked over at him, as did the other boys in the class. Mr. Wolfe hovered over Peter, holding a piece of paper, looking furious.

"That's not mine!" Peter insisted.

"It was on the floor in front of your chair. You're the only one who could've used it."

"But I didn't know it was there!"

"Stand up," said Mr. Wolfe. As Peter did so, Mr. Wolfe grabbed his test paper and crumpled it up. "Come outside with me. The rest of you, eyes on your own paper! I mean it!"

Mr. Wolfe led Peter out of the room and shut the door behind them.

I glanced over at Jeremy. He gave me a confused shrug. When I looked over at Darren, he was staring intently at his test, brow furrowed in concentration, cheek clenched as if trying not to laugh.

For what it was worth, Mr. Wolfe gave Peter a chance to prove his innocence. Peter's answers on the test matched those on the stolen answer key, but of course correct answers were no solid evidence that he'd been cheating. So while Peter sat in an empty classroom by himself, Mr. Wolfe quickly wrote up a new test.

Peter, who was stressed-out, flustered, and terrified, got a C-.

That weekend, we helped him pack his things.

Peter had not officially been kicked out of school, but his parents decided that another approach was needed to straighten their son out. Peter didn't know where he was headed, but he'd been assured by his angry parents that "the vacation was over."

"I didn't cheat," said Peter as he put his clothes into his suitcase.

"Why *would* you cheat? We have to study eighty-five hours a day!" Jeremy took Peter's books off the shelf, slamming each one onto his desk. "Darren did it!"

There was no doubt in my mind that Darren was responsible, but we had no way of proving it, and to even try to bring that idea to anybody's attention probably would've gotten us in still more trouble.

"I'm gonna miss you guys," Peter said. "I probably won't have any friends where I'm going."

"Yeah, you will," I insisted. "You'll have lots of friends."

Peter shook his head. "I bet I won't." He reached for one of the pushpins on the pug poster, then hesitated. "You guys can keep the poster if you want. If you like it."

"Okay," I said. The room wouldn't be the same without the pug poster. "You need to sign it for us."

"Sign it?"

"Yeah. Sign 'Peter was here' on it. That'd be kind of cool."

Peter grinned, found a black magic marker, and scrawled his name on the bottom corner of the poster.

"What you should do is carve your name into the wall with a knife," said Jeremy. "It's not like you can get into any more trouble."

"Nah."

"Then carve your name into Darren's face with a knife."

Peter shook his head. "That wouldn't be right."

"What do you mean, it wouldn't be right?"

"It should be your name. It has more letters."

We all laughed, and then we helped Peter finish packing. His parents picked him up that evening, and I watched through the window as they walked across the front lawn, away from Dorm B and Branford Academy.

Before they were out of sight, Peter's father smacked him so hard across the back of the head that I winced.

Jeremy and I were separated after that. I moved into a room with four other boys who were none too happy to have an extra person in their already cramped living quarters. They weren't outwardly hostile, but they were clearly resentful of this intrusion, and they certainly made no attempts to offer their friendship. Of course, it didn't help that I remained on probation and thus wasn't allowed to be part of their free-time activities. I don't even remember their names.

I talked to Jeremy every day in the cafeteria and learned that he'd ended up with a slightly more sociable group of guys. "Not anywhere near as cool as you and Peter," he assured me with a sad smile.

I did notice that as the days passed, Jeremy seemed more cheerful, more animated. Maybe he just needed a change of scenery.

Me, I wanted our old room back. I wasn't even allowed to put up the pug poster.

The term continued with an excruciating lack of haste. With two weeks left, it was hard to believe that I wasn't thirty-five years old, but no, I was still twelve. Well, thirteen, but my birthday had passed with so little fanfare (a card from an aunt that I almost but couldn't quite remember) that I didn't really even think about officially becoming a teenager.

I sat in the library, studying at a table by myself. I heard somebody sit down at the next table but didn't bother looking up to see who it was until I heard Darren clear his throat.

He wasn't trying to attract my attention. At least, he didn't seem to be. He was scribbling in his journal (that most foul and wretched of journals!), apparently unaware of my presence. I stared at him, hoping that the power of my gaze would cook his brain so that it bubbled and boiled and leaked out of his ears, but it didn't seem to be working.

Finally he looked up. "What are you staring at?" he asked.

"Nothing much."

"You're not supposed to come near me."

"I was here first."

Darren shrugged and rubbed the back of his neck. "You know, my neck still hurts sometimes."

"Like I care."

"It could be permanent damage."

"Like I care."

"You *should* care. If I'd broken my neck you'd be in jail right now."

"I'd rather be in jail and have you dead."

"I'll tell Mr. Sevin you said that."

"Go ahead. Write it in your journal."

Darren sighed. "You know, it's not you that I'm mad at."

"Oh yeah? Peter didn't do anything to you. Why'd you fake that he was cheating?"

"What makes you think I did that?"

"I don't think. I know."

"You don't know anything."

I gave him the finger and returned to my studying. At least I *pretended* that I was studying. In truth, I was terrified that Darren would in fact run to tell Mr. Sevin about my "I'd rather be in jail and have you dead" comment. I wasn't sure what Mr. Sevin could do to me with only two weeks left in the term, but it would be ghastly.

A couple of minutes later, Darren got up. I thought he was leaving, but instead he sat down next to me.

"You're not supposed to come near me, either," I told him.

"Nobody ever said that."

"Well, go away."

"Peter deserved to get kicked out."

"He didn't get kicked out. His parents pulled him out."

"Still, he deserved it. He hardly ever talked to me."

"I never saw you talk to him, either. And you didn't talk to me when I first got here. Peter and Jeremy did, but you didn't."

"I took you to the strip club."

"That was later."

"I haven't been back since . . . since that thing happened. We should go sometime."

I couldn't believe what I was hearing. Was Darren actually suggesting we go out for a social event? Was he trying to become *friends?*

"I can't go anywhere. I'm on probation because you're a liar."

"You could sneak out."

"If I'm going to take the chance of getting in that much trouble, it's sure not going to be to hang around with you."

Darren bit his lip, and for a second I almost thought he was going to cry. My sympathy for him would have been minimal. Instead he smiled. "You're such a jerk."

"Better a jerk than a liar."

"I'm trying to be nice."

"You want to be nice to me? Go tell Mr. Sevin that you made everything up. Tell him that you made up stuff to put in your diary, and that you moved Peter's dog, and that you stole a copy of the test and stuck it where Peter got blamed for it, and that you're a total liar!"

"I didn't do any of that."

"Get away from my table."

"It's not your table."

"I'll tell somebody that you're bugging me."

"Okay," he said. "I'll go." Then he leaned closer to me and spoke in a whisper. "I'm trying to make up. But if you want me to be mean, I can be mean. I can be meaner than anybody you've ever known. I'll fuck up your whole life, Alex."

"You already have."

"I'll do it worse."

God, if only I'd had a tape recorder! Though with my luck, Darren would've gotten a hold of it and cleverly reedited the conversation so that it sounded like I was threatening him.

I just wanted him to go away and let me study in peace. But at the same time, I definitely didn't want him to go away and start brainstorming plans to enact further revenge on me. He'd already proven that he was capable of making good on his threat.

"Okay, fine," I said. "How do you want to make up?"

"Maybe I don't."

"Then go away," I said. I sure wasn't going to beg. "You can't do anything to me."

Aw, crap, I thought, immediately feeling sick to my stomach and wishing I hadn't said that. The last thing I needed to do was taunt him.

"You think I can't?"

"Maybe you can. But maybe you'll get caught this time."

He smiled. "I don't get caught."

"That's what Jack the Ripper said."

"Jack the Ripper never got caught."

"Then that's what . . ." I trailed off, trying to think of a suitable villain who had, in fact, been caught.

"The Joker?" Darren suggested.

"Shut up."

"You should be nice to me."

"I *was* nice to you."

Darren nodded thoughtfully. "Yeah, you were. I

wish you hadn't let Jeremy and Peter do that to me. I wouldn't have come after you. Just them."

I wasn't completely sure what he meant by that. Would he have done something to them even if the whole hangman fiasco hadn't happened? Or was he just not thinking clearly about what he was saying? I decided that I didn't really want clarification and said nothing.

"Did it bother you waiting?" he asked.

"For what?"

"For you to be next."

"What?"

He glanced over his shoulder to be sure that we were still alone. "You know, waiting to be next. Like Peter. I could've done that to you, too, you know."

The way Darren spoke, I got the impression that he'd been *dying* to confess his crime. No, not confess . . . gloat. It probably made him absolutely nuts not to be able to safely say anything, to confirm for certain what we already knew. His frustration at not being able to share his wicked deeds was probably only matched by . . . well, by being the victim of his wicked deeds and not being able to do a thing about it.

"Maybe I'm smarter than Peter," I said, quietly.

"Of course you are. That's what would've made it fun."

Fun. I would've gladly postponed the future loss of my virginity by ten years for the right to grab him by the hair and smash his face into the desk.

"So did it bother you waiting for me to get back at you?" Darren asked.

I couldn't see any reason not to be honest. "Yeah."

"It was probably worse than if I'd just done something right away, wasn't it?"

"Maybe."

"Yeah, it was. Like when you're a little kid and you break something, and your mom catches you right away and you get spanked and grounded. That's bad to a little kid, but it's worse when your mom *doesn't* catch you, and you keep waiting for her to find out who did it. It's probably worse even if you never get caught."

"Then go tell Mr. Sevin what you did."

Darren grinned. "I didn't mean for me."

"Are you here to make up or just to bug me?"

"We could make up."

"Fine. We're made up. Now I have to study."

"Do you want to know how I got the test?"

I perked up at this. Would he really tell me? If he gave away his secret, he might also give away something that could point directly at him as the culprit. Sure, I only had two weeks of probation left, but still, to finally be able to prove my innocence . . . or, more specifically, Darren's guilt . . .

"Yeah, I do."

"Meet me outside of your building at midnight."

I shook my head. "I'll get caught."

"No you won't."

"Yes, I will. I've got four roommates."

"Would they say anything?"

"Of course they would. They don't want to get in trouble for something I did. They don't even like me."

Darren considered that. "That's too bad."

"So tell me now."

"Nope."

"Fine."

"If you really want to know, you'll be outside at midnight. You'll find a way."

"What makes you think that I could possibly care enough about the stupid test to get in that much trouble over it?"

"How about this? Be out there at midnight or I'm coming after you next."

"Screw you."

"I'll get you bad."

"Go to hell."

"I hope I do go to hell. Maybe I'll see Peter's dog there. Or maybe just its head."

I said nothing further. I wasn't going to let him goad me into doing something I'd deeply regret. Without a word, I looked back down at my book and resumed studying. Pretended to study, anyway.

"Alex . . . ?"

I ignored him. I also tried to ignore the sweat trickling down my back.

"I'm talking to you."

I said nothing.

He sat there for a full two minutes (two minutes that seemed like a thousand), staring at me, waiting for me to become so uncomfortable that I'd be forced to acknowledge him.

I didn't give in.

"You are *so* dead," he said, pushing back his seat, standing up, and casually walking away.

CHAPTER NINE

"That's incredible," said Jeremy.

"I know."

"I mean . . . I just . . . I can't even believe it." Jeremy took another bite of his lasagna. "Did they fire the chef or something? This is delicious!"

"Maybe Darren got him," I said. It was the best lasagna I'd ever had. And to be perfectly honest, I didn't even like lasagna all that much, but this was enough to turn me into a fan. I'd had so many awful meals in the Branford Academy dining hall that I'd almost reached the point where I truly believed that food, as an entity in itself, sucked.

We ate dinner in silence for a few minutes, enjoying the bliss of food that wasn't complete crap.

I'd told Jeremy about my conversation with Darren. He was, quite predictably, pissed off. We'd tried to brainstorm plans of action, but there didn't seem to be much we could do. Unlike mine, Jeremy's new room had a window that faced the front of the building, so he assured me that he'd be on watch at midnight. If Darren did in fact show up outside, Jeremy would quickly see to it that he was busted.

But though Darren had gotten cocky enough to come out and admit that he'd been responsible for Peter's removal, we didn't think he'd be dumb enough to just stand outside the building waiting for me, especially because I'd indicated that I wouldn't be coming. And if he *was* out there, he'd probably have some sort of sneaky plan up his sleeve. We weren't quite sure what it could be, but we weren't willing to rule anything out.

For about a tenth of a second we considered going to Mr. Sevin and telling him about the library conversation, but that didn't seem like a good idea. Darren was a much more convincing liar than I was a truth-teller.

Instead, Jeremy and I settled for a vague plan of being incredibly vigilant. If Darren was going to try something, well, we'd make sure we were alert at all times. No journals protruding from book bags were going to get me this time.

Though it seemed unlikely that Darren would confess his crimes a second time, Jeremy and I decided that we needed to carry around tape recorders. Those handheld ones that we could fit in our pockets. Unfortunately, since we were stuck on the school grounds and were unaware of any tape recorders available on campus, there really wasn't much we could do. So we were screwed in that regard, but we did vow to be vigilant.

I lay awake that night, listening as 75 percent of my roommates snored hard enough to make the bedsheets flutter (which was a 25 percent improvement over the usual situation). I wondered if Darren really was out there, waiting for me to meet him at midnight. If he was, what would he do when I didn't show up?

You are so dead . . .

He could've meant that literally.

No. He was a sinister, morbid, rotten kid, but he was just a twelve-year-old. He wouldn't be coming after me with a knife, or a gun, or even a staple remover. Physically, at least, I was perfectly safe.

I wasn't going to live in fear because of him. He wasn't going to have that kind of power over me. No way. He could make all the threats he wanted, but I was not going to let him control my life.

The best he could do is cost me a night of sleep.

And he did it very well.

Darren may or may not have tried to meet me outside. Jeremy, ever vigilant, admitted that he'd fallen asleep and didn't keep watch. But it was a long shot anyway, so I kept the humorously phrased disparaging remarks down to fewer than eight.

I didn't see Darren in the cafeteria at breakfast, which concerned me. I also didn't see him in Mr. Wolfe's class when it started. And I didn't see Jeremy, which concerned me more.

What if Darren had gotten him?

What if he'd *killed* him?

It was a ridiculous thought, I knew, but still . . .

He'd had practice cutting things up. What if he had Jeremy hidden away in some bushes, opening him with his pocketknife, struggling to saw away his head and knowing that with time and patience it would eventually pop free?

Ridiculous.

Absurd.

Maggots in Jeremy's eyes.

Laughable. Ha-ha. Ho-ho. Hee-hee.

His mouth filled with insects instead of a tongue.

Not even worth the brain energy to think about.

Perhaps still alive, unable to scream beneath the duct tape, watching as Darren makes precise incisions, staring curiously at his own blood pooling around the blade . . .

Jeremy hurried into the classroom, out of breath.

"You're late," said Mr. Wolfe, without looking away from the chalkboard.

"I know, I'm sorry, sir. I couldn't find my book."

"Share with somebody else, please."

He scooted his desk next to mine, and we silently read the math lesson while Mr. Wolfe wrote formulas on the board.

Five minutes later, Darren entered the room, bleeding.

His face was bruised, swollen, and bloody, as if he'd been punched several times, hard. There was also blood on his torn shirt, along with grass stains and dirt. He walked with a limp.

Everybody in the class stared at him as he went toward his desk and sniffled pitifully.

"What in the world happened to you?" asked Mr. Wolfe, glancing over his shoulder. He moved over to Darren in two quick steps and crouched down to check out his injuries.

"Nothing," said Darren, sniffling again.

"This is *not* nothing. What happened? Did somebody do this to you?"

Darren shrugged.

"Who?"

Darren pointed at Jeremy.

My first reaction, I'm ashamed to admit, was glee that Jeremy had beaten the shit out of that little monster. That glee was mixed with a sense of disappointment that I hadn't been there to hold Darren down.

But this reaction instantly vanished as I saw Jeremy's face. He hadn't done a thing to Darren. Our common enemy had threatened me, but gone after him instead.

"Is this true?" Mr. Wolfe asked Jeremy.

"No."

"He did it in the bathroom," said Darren, his words somewhat slurred. "That's why I was late."

"I did not!" said Jeremy, almost at a shout. "I didn't do a goddamn thing to you and you know it!"

"Jeremy! Language! Get up!"

"I didn't touch him," Jeremy insisted.

"I said, get up. We're going to visit Mr. Sevin."

"I'm not going anywhere. I didn't touch him."

Mr. Wolfe stared at him with an expression of carefully controlled rage. "I beg your pardon, young man?"

"I—" Jeremy shouted this first word, but then quickly lowered his voice to an appropriate classroom tone. "I didn't touch him, sir."

"He was waiting for me when I came out of the stall," said Darren, wiping his nose on his sleeve.

"You did it to yourself," Jeremy said.

"Oh, yeah, I did it to myself. Real funny. Why are you always lying about me?" Darren's voice cracked, and if I weren't so convinced of the truth behind the matter I would have absolutely believed him.

"I'm not lying," said Jeremy, speaking calmly while shaking in fury.

"Darren, Jeremy, let's go."

"No."

"That was *not* a request."

"I don't care. He's not going to get me the way he did Peter."

"Get up out of that chair this instant!"

Jeremy shook his head defiantly.

"Jeremy, get up," I whispered in a panic.

"*I didn't touch him!*" Jeremy shouted. In any other circumstances, the way Mr. Wolfe flinched would have been absolutely hilarious and fueled several dozen fond mealtime conversations, but now it just made me want to scream for Jeremy to please, *please* do what he was told.

"Stand up."

"No!"

"I said stand up!"

"*No!* I'm not going with you just so you can take his side."

The entire class watched with rapt fascination, collectively unable to believe what they were witnessing.

"Young man, you're making this very bad for yourself."

"You can call the cops. I don't care."

"You *will* care."

"Jeremy, just go!" I said.

Jeremy looked at me, then back at Mr. Wolfe. Then, with a frustrated, furious sigh, he pushed back his chair and stood up.

"I didn't touch him," Jeremy said. "I didn't do a thing to him."

"That's for me to decide," said Mr. Wolfe.

"Mr. Wolfe?" asked Larry Peakin, raising his hand. He was the smallest guy in class, with one green eye and one blue one.

"Yes?"

"I saw Jeremy go into the bathroom after Darren."

"You liar!" Jeremy screamed.

"Quiet!" Mr. Wolfe looked positively enraged. "Jeremy, Darren, Larry . . . the three of you come with me. Now."

"Larry is lying, too!" Jeremy insisted. "I didn't do a single thing to Darren. Look at my hands!" He held up both of his hands, palms facing Mr. Wolfe. "There's not a mark on them!"

"He did it with his book," Darren said.

"I did not!" Jeremy shouted. Then his shoulders fell as the impact of Darren's words sunk in.

"Jeremy, where's your book?" Mr. Wolfe asked.

"I don't know," Jeremy admitted.

"He had it with him when he went in the bathroom," said Larry. "I saw it."

"All right, let's go," said Mr. Wolfe. "Everybody else, read ahead. No talking!"

Mr. Wolfe left the room, followed by Darren and Larry, who seemed happy just to be included. Jeremy looked absolutely miserable as he walked out of the room after them.

I felt absolutely miserable, too, because I had a very good idea of what they'd find. Maybe in a bathroom stall, maybe in the wastebasket, maybe stashed under the radiator, but somewhere between this classroom and the restroom they'd find Jeremy's textbook. His name in the front. Smeared with both his fingerprints and Darren's blood.

I knew that Jeremy was telling the truth. This meant that Darren had stolen his textbook, beaten himself bloody with it, and then convinced (or coerced) Larry to lie for him. Perhaps Larry had stolen the textbook, or even been the one to use it as a tool of violence, but either way it was a preposterous-sounding scenario. Would Mr. Wolfe believe that, or would he believe instead that it was Jeremy who beat Darren senseless?

Things didn't look good for my only remaining friend at school.

Mr. Wolfe returned fifteen minutes later without Darren or Jeremy. Larry followed him and sat down, looking smug.

"What happened?" I asked.

"That's none of your concern," Mr. Wolfe told me. "Everybody open to page two fifty-six. We have a lot to make up."

Neither Jeremy nor Darren was at dinner. I walked over and sat down across from Larry.

"Go away," he said.

"What happened?" I demanded.

"They saw that I was telling the truth."

"You were not."

"Mr. Wolfe found Jeremy's book in the trash can."

"Why would Jeremy be stupid enough to throw his book in the trash? He'd know they'd look there."

Larry shrugged. "Why would he be stupid enough to beat up Darren? Everybody knows he hates him."

"You're going to get caught," I told him. "You're

going to get in so much trouble you won't even be able to believe it. You'll get kicked out of school."

Larry sneered at me. "Yeah, right."

"You'd better believe me. Because I saw you steal Jeremy's book."

The flash of guilt that I hoped to see didn't materialize. Most likely Darren had been the thief. "Uh-huh. You're such a moron. If you don't go away I'll tell that you're threatening me."

"Try it."

Larry immediately called my bluff, raising his hand and looking for the nearest adult. I grabbed my tray and moved to a safer dining area.

I didn't see either Darren or Jeremy the next day. I even went to speak with Mr. Sevin, but was told that it was none of my concern, and that I would do well in life not to hang out with juvenile delinquents in the future.

I made periodic trips to Jeremy's room, risking getting in a hell of a lot of trouble, but his roommates said he hadn't come back.

The next evening, he was packing.

"What did they do?" I asked.

"Mr. Sevin said, 'Under the circumstances, we have no choice but to believe Darren's version of the story.'" It wasn't a very good impression of Mr. Sevin, but I forced a smile nevertheless. "I have to start talking to a counselor and . . . I don't even know what they're going to do. Darren's parents were all freaked out and they said they were going to sue the school and I'm *scared*."

"I can't believe he did that to himself." I'd thought about it a lot. One smack to the face, maybe, but to either beat himself or allow himself to be beaten to that degree just for revenge required some serious mental problems.

"Well, I can! He's a fuckin' lunatic! Why did you get him so angry? It wasn't my fault! You're the one he should've gone after!"

I stepped back, shocked at this outburst. "I didn't do anything."

"You said you did! You said that you made him mad in the library, and that he was going to come after you! Well, he didn't, he came after *me*, and now I have to see a doctor and they're probably gonna give me shots!"

"They won't give you shots."

"Yes they *will!* You don't know what they're going to do! It's all your fault!"

"No, I didn't do—"

"Get out of my room, Alex!"

I just stood there, completely stunned.

"Get out!"

I quietly left the room.

CHAPTER TEN

I lay in bed, eyes closed but not asleep, enjoying the movie in my mind.

Peter, Jeremy, and I kicked the box out from underneath Darren, shattering the wood. As he dropped, we heard the satisfying *crack* of his neck breaking.

He dangled from the noose, slowly turning in circles, the rope getting tighter and tighter around his dead flesh.

His head fell to the ground, followed by his body. We left his body alone, but kicked his head around until it was unrecognizable.

No, rewind . . .

We kicked his still-living, screaming head around until it was unrecognizable. He begged us to stop, but we laughed and laughed. When he tried to bite us, we kicked out all of his teeth.

I opened my eyes.

In my mind, I watched men in immaculate white suits strap Jeremy to a machine. They gave him shots with an oversize needle to keep him calm, and then pulled a lever. His body spasmed, drool gushing from his mouth, blood trickling from his eye sockets.

No, nothing like that would happen to him. You couldn't get in that much trouble for beating up another kid.

Bashing him bloody with a textbook . . .

Jeremy didn't even get the pleasure of the act that he got blamed for.

What did Darren have planned for me?

Nothing.

I was vigilant those last couple of weeks of school. Vigilant to the point of paranoia. But Darren didn't try anything. He returned to classes, face still swollen but healing nicely, but he didn't even make eye contact. He didn't look guilty. He looked . . . satisfied.

The term ended. Because Branford Academy didn't have a summer session, my parents really had no choice except to pick me up, even if they planned to immediately dump me someplace else. My mom hugged me and said that she missed me, and while her words weren't convincing even to a thirteen-year-old, I told myself that on some level, they were true.

We loaded up the car. My dad asked me some superficial questions about life at Branford Academy, and I gave some superficial answers. I really didn't want to talk about it.

As I ran back upstairs for one last check to make sure I hadn't left anything behind, I saw Darren standing by my door.

"You're too late," I said. "You can't do anything to me now."

"I wasn't going to. But you were pretty scared that I was, weren't you?"

"No."

"Don't lie to me." Darren smiled. "I bet you spent every day scared that I was gonna get you."

"If you could get me, you would've done it. You wouldn't have gone after Jeremy."

"I liked you better than Jeremy."

"Well, I hate you."

Darren shrugged. "Doesn't bother me. You coming back to Branford?"

I shook my head. "I don't know where I'm going."

"Did you beg your mom not to make you come back?"

"No."

"I bet you did."

"You bet wrong."

"Yeah, well, maybe I'll see you around. Have a good life."

He chuckled, turned around, and started to walk away.

"Hey, Darren!"

He glanced back. "Yeah?"

"Did you kill Peter's dog?"

"Nope. I found him that way. But I did finally kill one of those fuckin' birds."

He walked away, whistling cheerfully but tunelessly through his swollen lips.

PART TWO

FRIENDS

CHAPTER ELEVEN

There were dead bodies everywhere.

It was the tackiest decorating scheme I'd ever seen. This was my first year of college, and while I fully expected cinder block shelving, pizza box tables, and beer can wallpaper, I really hadn't expected to walk into my dorm room and discover a love shrine to serial killers and their prey.

I tossed my garbage bag of clothing on the unclaimed bed and did a quick survey of the room. Virtually every square inch of my roommate's half of the wall space was covered with graphic photographs and newspaper clippings on the subject. This did *not* seem conducive to an effective study environment.

I'd only spoken to Will, my randomly selected roommate, for a few minutes on the phone before arriving at Shadle University. We'd discussed who would bring the TV, who would bring the stereo, and who would bring the contraband microwave, but the joys of maiming human beings had never entered into the conversation.

Oh well. College was supposed to be all about new experiences, right?

I scratched my chin and looked at one of the photographs more closely. Good Lord, was that a *can opener* protruding from her—?

"Cool, huh?" asked the tall, lanky guy who entered the room. He had blond hair that was cut just above the shoulder and was handsome in sort of a goofball stand-up comedian sort of way. He wore a silver earring shaped like an outhouse, and a T-shirt that depicted a skull about to be hit by a cream pie.

"Uh, yeah. Way cool."

He stuck out his hand. "I'm Will. Either you're Alex or a trespasser that I'll need to shoot."

"Yep, it's Alex."

"Glad to meet you," he said, shaking my hand. "I hope you don't mind that I picked this side of the room, but I got here yesterday and didn't have a whole lot to do."

"No, no, that's okay," I said. I knew that the subject of gory photographs and my objection to having them wallpapering our living space would have to come up sooner or later, but I didn't want to start things off on a bad note.

"So what are you majoring in?" I asked.

"Criminal psychology."

"Big surprise."

"With a minor in cutlery."

I stared at him.

"That was a joke," he explained.

"Ah."

"Actually, I'm not truly a criminal psychology major,

it's just regular psychology, but the criminal mind is my main interest. What about you?"

"Not really into the criminal mind, to be honest."

"No, your major."

"Architecture, I think."

"Hey, cool."

"I haven't officially declared a major, but I figured I'd try a few basic classes and see how I like it."

"Good plan, good plan."

I cleared my throat. "So how long have you been interested in . . . you know, people who passed away?"

Will considered that for a moment. "Since forever, I guess. I know all of them. Jack the Ripper, Jeffrey Dahmer . . . everyone. Here, test me. Name one at random and I'll give you the stats."

"That's all right, I believe you."

"No, you've gotta do it. Pick one. Any one."

"I'm blanking right now."

"You can do it. I have faith in you."

"Fine. Uh, the Boston Strangler."

"Too easy. Albert De Salvo. Thirteen victims, all women, between June 1962 and January 1964. They were all sexually assaulted and then strangled. He usually posed as a—"

"So what non-death-related hobbies do you have?" I asked.

"Computer games. The gory ones, at least. I do like cartoons. Hey, these pictures aren't going to bug you, are they? I can tone it down if you want."

"Nah, that's okay," I said, giving myself a mental kick in the ass as soon as the words escaped from my mouth.

"Cool. Have you been set free yet?"

"Excuse me?"

"Did your parents leave yet?"

"I drove myself here."

"Nice. It took me three hours to get rid of my mom yesterday. I thought I was going to have to fake a demonic possession to make her leave. So you have a car?"

"Yeah. Not a *good* car, but a car."

"Excellent. Have you eaten?"

"Right before I got here."

"Good plan, good plan. Get in that one last meal before you have to face the cafeterias. But don't worry, one of our neighbors is premed, so if you need a stomach transplant he'll be around."

"I heard the food here was pretty good."

"Yeah, the fish sticks I had last night were decent. I just like being cynical."

"Okay. Well. I think I'm gonna head over to the campus bookstore. Did you already get your books for the semester?"

Will shook his head. "I'm gonna hold off, though, in case I have to drop any of my classes after the first day."

Good, I thought. "All right. Nice meeting you. I'll be . . . uh, back."

Okay, so I had a weird, morbid, fairly annoying roommate. I could live with that. I was in *college*, damn it, and I was going to have the time of my life!

I hadn't returned to Branford Academy after that miserable year. Instead, my parents had sent me to Twin Streams Academy, which had no nearby streams and which was pretty much the same as Branford save for the lack of a psychotic little creep like Darren. It sucked but I got through it.

I moved back in with my parents during my high school years. I worked evenings at a movie theater and weekends as a busboy at a restaurant, and while at home made myself as invisible as possible. My mother and father didn't seem to mind having me around when I didn't exist.

Though my grades were decent but not spectacular, I relentlessly pursued college scholarships. And I got them. I ended up with a full ride at Shadle University, an Arizona college that was less than an hour from Branford Academy. One weekend I thought I might make a road trip to my old school and fling a shitload of eggs at whatever campus windows I could find.

But I was here. I was completely on my own. Completely free. Though I was going to work hard and study like an absolute maniac, I was also going to have *fun*. This was my opportunity to reinvent my life, and gosh darn it all to heck, I was going to take advantage of it.

I fell in love for the fourth time, right there in the bookstore line.

I don't mean that I fell in love four times while standing in line, although the length of that particular line would not have made this entirely out of the question. Rather, it was the fourth time in my life that I'd fallen in love.

The first was the day after I turned fifteen. She was sitting on the edge of an indoor fountain in a mall, licking an ice cream cone. Blonde hair, blue eyes, brown lips (from the chocolate). The most beautiful girl I'd ever seen in my life. I vowed that no matter what, I would work up the courage to walk over there and talk to her.

I did not work up the courage to walk over there and talk to her.

I was still fifteen the second time I fell in love. This time it was with Mrs. Vierling, my biology teacher. The spark of love first hit me when Mrs. Vierling consoled Wendy Chandler, who was crying over the dead froggies, and it was a love that sustained throughout the rest of the school year. Since Mrs. Vierling was twenty years my senior, married, and bound by both moral and legal restrictions that prevented her from dating me, it was doomed to be an unrequited love. But I harbored a fantasy that she was secretly into skinny fifteen-year-olds, and that if we'd ever found ourselves trapped in a closet together, she would have ripped off my clothes and taken me roughly.

We did not find ourselves trapped in a closet together.

The third time I fell in love I was seventeen, and so was the object of my affection. Margaret. A redhead. Absolutely gorgeous. We had three classes together, and my time spent gazing at her contributed to me answering more than one question from the teacher with "Huh?"

I confessed my love to my friend Bryan. He shared this news with lots of people. Lots of people shared this news with Margaret. Margaret, whose taste in men did not lean toward those with large purple birthmarks on their chin, was humiliated. She told me to leave her the hell alone (which I guess she meant in a preemptive way, since I'd never even spoken to her). Lots of people witnessed this event. Most of them seemed to enjoy it.

The fourth time literally took my breath away.

Something struck me in the gut so hard that I let out an *ooomph*, pronouncing it exactly that way. Both hands went to my stomach as I struggled not to double over and puke.

Then I stared into the wide, horrified eyes of the girl who'd accidentally bashed her duffel bag into me and was immediately entranced. I was entranced, suffering from physical agony, and embarrassed because the other students in line were staring at me, all at the same time. It was quite a sensation.

"Oh my God! I'm so sorry!" The girl lowered her duffel bag and put her hand on my gut. "Did I hurt you?"

I shook my head. Had she not hurt me so badly, I might have managed a verbal response.

She pushed up her thick glasses. She had long blonde hair that was pulled back, was a couple of inches shorter than me, was thin but not waifish, and was positively adorable. "I'm sorry . . . I wasn't paying any attention to where I was going. I'm such a klutz. Are you sure you're okay?"

I nodded, still struggling to keep my lunch from making a cameo appearance.

She removed her hand from my stomach. "Okay, well, I'm really sorry about that. I'll just go slink off now." She gave me a sheepish smile, the most beautiful smile I'd ever seen in my entire life, and quickly walked away.

I watched her go, regretting that I hadn't thanked her. It took me another fifteen minutes of standing in line to realize that regretting that I hadn't thanked her for bashing my gut was really, really stupid.

Who was she? What was her name? What was in the duffel bag? Why had she been so distracted that she didn't see the long line of students? What was her major? How long had she worn glasses? Where was she born? When did she lose her first tooth? Was she into skinny guys? Did she have any tattoos?

I finally was able to pay for my books. Destitute, I left the campus bookstore and started to head back to my dorm.

"Hey!" somebody called after me. A guy.

I turned around. A dark-haired guy I didn't recognize hurried over to me. "I knew it!" he said with delight. "I'd recognize that birthmark anywhere!"

My hand instinctively went to my chin. Who in the world was . . . ?

"Darren?" I asked.

The guy grinned. "Yep. I *thought* that was you in line. I saw that girl walk right into you. So how've you been?"

I shrugged. My stomachache was returning and I really just wanted to turn and walk away.

"I got here a couple of days ago. They really screw you over with those book prices, don't they? And when we try to sell them back we'll get about a quarter of what we paid. Good racket they've got going here."

"Yeah," I said.

Darren looked at me carefully. I noticed that he'd acquired some serious muscle tone since our Branford

Academy days, which was easily visible through the white Shadle University T-shirt he was wearing. His hair was still shoulder length but stylishly cut, and he'd matured into an extremely handsome guy. Model material, easily. I was still a dork and it wasn't fair.

Darren frowned as he studied me, but then he let out an incredulous laugh. "Holy shit, you're still upset, aren't you?"

I shrugged.

"I can't believe it! Dude, we were just kids! You can't hold a grudge against me for that! C'mon, forget the past. This is the present, Alex!"

I looked him in the eye. "You ruined my friends' lives."

Darren's smile faded. "Okay, okay, I'm not going to pretend that I wasn't a fucked-up little kid. But I didn't ruin anybody's lives. You don't get your life ruined when you're twelve. I was a bully, what can I say?"

Not a bully; a psychopath . . .

"Look, I really need to get back to my room."

Darren shook his head. "No you don't. C'mon, this is no way to act. Let's leave all that crazy shit in the past. You were always a cool guy, Alex."

"And you mutilated Peter's dog."

"I was twelve! There's a statute of limitations, you know. When I was twelve I also farted in a movie theater. It was the nastiest, smelliest, wettest fart you can imagine, and the smell probably soaked into everybody's popcorn and ruined the movie, but I'm sure that by now they've all gotten over it because I was *twelve*."

"Maybe."

"Are you saying that people are still upset over

that fart? Because if they are, I'll apologize to them personally. I'll buy the plane tickets and I'll walk up to their front door and say, 'Hey, I was the kid in the third row center who'd just eaten the burrito, and from the bottom of my heart I apologize for that foul, lingering odor.'"

I couldn't hold back the grin. Darren extended his hand. "C'mon, screw the past."

I hesitated for a second, but then nodded and shook his hand. "All right."

"Cool! So let me buy you lunch."

"I just ate."

"Eat more."

"I've got a lot of stuff to do."

"Okay, so, you're not really screwing the past, are you? You can't do this to me. You can't still think of me as that weirdo. I had issues. So did you. So did everybody. C'mon, we'll hang out, we'll have fun, I'll get you laid."

I chuckled. "Oh, gee, how can I pass that up?"

"You can't. C'mon, let's go."

As we walked to the student parking lot, I took out three beanbags and began to juggle. I'd learned to juggle in high school and when I got nervous, which was often, it helped me relax. Juggling now was not helping me relax. I'd been all psyched for the college experience, and it was already sullied because I didn't have the balls to just tell Darren to go away and find some other freshman to torment.

"Damn, you're good," said Darren. He seemed genuinely impressed.

"Thanks."

"Can you juggle more than three?"

I nodded. "I can juggle five of them without messing up, and I can do up to seven messing up a lot."

"Can you juggle flaming torches or running chain saws?"

"Flaming torches are easy. They're perfectly balanced and easy to throw, so the only trick is to not lose your concentration. Running chain saws, no."

"No way!" said Darren, amazed. "You can really juggle flaming torches? You're not just messing with me?"

"I have some back at my dorm. I mean, ignitable torches, not torches that are on fire right now."

"You hope."

"Yeah."

"So what other hidden talents do you have?" Darren asked. "I bet you know a bunch of magic tricks, right?"

I nodded, increasing the height of my throws. "A couple."

"Do you know how to saw a woman in half?"

"Sure."

"How?"

"It's a very sophisticated animatronic woman that separates in the middle. You have to buy them direct from Disney."

"No, seriously."

"It's a secret."

"So, magic tricks, juggling . . . are you an escape artist, too?"

"Nope, but I can make balloon animals."

"Cool. So are you paying your way through school by doing children's parties?"

"Nah. It's just for fun."

"You have all these marketable skills and you're not

doing anything with them? You know what the problem is; it's that you're such an introvert. You always were. Dude, if I could juggle flaming torches I'd be marching past every sorority on campus, letting the women flock to me."

I caught the three beanbags and shoved them back into my pocket. "Obviously you live in some bizarre alternate universe where women go for guys who can juggle. Being able to do magic tricks is actually a very effective form of female repellent."

"I dunno, it shows that you're good with your hands."

I chuckled. "I just do it for fun. But if you're ever in desperate need of a balloon animal, I'm the guy to call."

"Can you make balloon roadkill?"

"Not without popping it."

We reached his car, which was only slightly less crappy than my own, and drove to a small burger joint called Patties. Our conversation was lighthearted and effortless, and I realized that I was surprisingly comfortable around the guy who'd been responsible for one of the most miserable times in my life.

Maybe he was right. He'd been twelve. Perhaps it was time to get over it.

We sat down at a corner booth and the attractive waitress, who looked to be in her early twenties, was giggly and flirty as she took our orders. Of course, all of the flirting was directed at Darren. She winked at him as she left to get our drinks.

Darren leaned forward and put a shielding hand next to his mouth, speaking confidentially. "I do believe that our waitress has a rather intense desire to fuck me."

I barely stifled a laugh. "I think you may be right."

"Well, I've got a girlfriend back home, and I figure I should be loyal to her for at least a couple of weeks. Our waitress will have to deal. My girlfriend's a waitress, too, actually."

"So waitresses have a thing for you?"

"Waitresses, cashiers, beauticians, accountants, policewomen, political leaders, you name it. It's tough being such a Grade-A stud muffin." Darren shook his head and sighed in mock misery. "So, what about you? Are the women in your hometown going to be doing a lot more masturbating now that you're gone?"

"Oh, definitely," I said. "I'm sure sales of baseball bats have tripled."

Darren grinned. "Seriously, did you have to leave a girlfriend behind?"

"Nah. I didn't date all that much."

"Not all that much, or not at all?"

"Not all that much. There was one girl, Vickie, where we sort of wavered between just friends and more than friends, but nothing really happened."

The waitress returned with our Cokes. Though I couldn't be positive, I was pretty sure that she'd undone an extra button on her blouse. "Can I get you anything else?" she asked, looking straight at Darren.

"I think we're okay for now."

"Well, if you need anything, just wave at me. My name's Stephanie." She left the table, but it looked like she had to pry herself away.

"Oh, yeah," said Darren. "She wants me."

"Do you need me to clear a spot on the table?" I asked. "I can find someplace else to sit."

Darren threw a glance over at Stephanie, who was

taking another customer's order. "I've gotta say, if I were the kind of person who would cheat on his girlfriend this soon, she would be near the top of my list. Did you notice the extra button?"

"I thought I was imagining it."

"So, you don't have a girlfriend, huh?"

"Nope."

"Well, like I said, I'm taken. But I'll bet I could get you together with Ms. Stephanie."

I gasped in pretend excitement. "Really? Do it! Do it! Oh, please do it! I'll be your best friend!"

"I'm serious."

"No, you're not."

Darren nodded. "You want her?"

He looked absolutely serious, which made me a bit uncomfortable. I leaned back in my seat. "What do you mean, you could get us together?"

"I'm not talking a relationship, but I'll bet you anything I could get both of us invited to her place. I'll get her percolating, you can drink the coffee."

I laughed. "That's the stupidest metaphor I've ever heard."

"So, you up for it?"

"I'm thinking no. It wouldn't happen anyway."

Darren shrugged. "Your loss. But, hey, the offer stands."

"Thanks. I'll continue to fail to get women on my own."

"Maybe you should juggle when she comes back with our food."

"Again, I think you're really not tuned in to the dating prospects of magicians."

"Here, let me see one of those beanbags."

I reached into my pocket and took out one. A green balloon came out of my pocket with it and dropped onto the seat.

"Oh, hey, even better. Why don't you make a balloon animal for Stephanie?"

"Nah."

"Why not? You think this place is too classy?"

"I don't feel like it."

"You're such a weenie! Get out a balloon or I swear to God I'll embarrass the living shit out of you. I have no shame, I mean it."

Since I had absolutely no reason to doubt that those words were true, I picked up the balloon and stretched it out a few times.

"Why do you stretch it?" Darren asked.

"Makes it easier to inflate. And it weakens the balloon a little bit so that if it pops it won't send a chunk of rubber flying through your eyeball and into your brain."

"I had no idea balloon animals could be so deadly."

"Oh, they'll kill you like a bullet." I put the end of the balloon in my mouth and inflated it, leaving four inches at the end to serve as the tail. A couple at the table across from us turned to look, and I self-consciously tied a knot in the end. I felt like an idiot, but began to pinch and twist the balloon, locking segments into place, until I'd formed a traditional example of a balloon dog.

"Here, have a pet," I said, handing it over to Darren. The couple at the other table smiled and returned to their meal.

I had a sudden mental image of Killer Fang, decapitated and cut apart, flecks of his blood hitting my face as we caught Darren in the act . . .

"Pretty good," Darren remarked, inspecting the dog and clearly unaware of the irony. He flicked the knot that served as its nose. "Is it housebroken?"

"No, it still leaves air all over the place."

"I think I'll name him Spot." Darren set the dog on the edge of the table. "I'm sorry I forced you to make a balloon animal in a public restaurant. I can give you the names of several top-notch therapists if you want."

"I'll probably survive."

A couple minutes later Stephanie arrived with our burgers and fries. "Oh, how cute!" she exclaimed, looking at the dog, then at Darren. "Did you do that?"

"Nope, it was my friend here."

I expected her to look disappointed, but instead she turned to me and smiled. "What else can you make?"

I shrugged. "A few different animals."

"He's being way too modest," said Darren, as Stephanie put our plates down in front of us. "Alex, you can make a flower, right?"

"Yeah."

"Well then make our lovely waitress here a flower."

"Oh, no, you don't have to do that," said Stephanie.

"Sure he does. It'll only take a minute."

I could feel a burning sensation in my face and was pretty sure that my cheeks were fluorescent red, but I didn't want to drag out the embarrassment by protesting. I took out a few balloons, selected another green one and a red one, and shoved the rest back into my pocket.

"He has to stretch them to avoid killing innocent bystanders," Darren explained as I began the process.

I inflated the red balloon and twisted it into what resembled the bloom of a rose, then inflated the green balloon to serve as the stem. I twisted the two together and handed them to Stephanie.

"Thank you," she said, taking a pretend whiff of the scent. "This is probably the best tip I'll get all day. If you two need anything else, just give me a holler." She left, taking the rose with her.

"I bet you could improve on that tip," said Darren.

"Uh-huh. Right. Eat your burger."

"I'm serious, buddy."

I stuffed a french fry into my mouth. "No, actually the word is 'delusional.'"

"Wanna test that theory?"

"Maybe next life."

"Once again, your loss." Darren picked up his hamburger and took a huge bite, then set it back on the plate and wiped some ketchup off his lips. "But don't worry; I'll wear you down in time. Then we'll have some real fun."

I didn't see Darren during the first week of classes, which was fine because I was busy soaking up the College Experience. The cafeteria food wasn't bad at all, I liked my classes, and even if I didn't make as many instant friends as I would have hoped for, it wasn't like I was sitting in a corner wallowing in misery.

Will was a perfectly decent roommate, primarily because he was gone most of the time. He was annoying when he was around, but it was nothing I couldn't handle, and I quickly got used to the pictures. If I ever found a girlfriend, I'd bring up the subject of perhaps taking them down so as not to disrupt a potentially amorous mood.

Darren called Saturday morning. Early.

Well, it was early to somebody who'd stayed up all night eating cold pizza, drinking an entire vending machine's worth of Mountain Dew, and discussing the deep meaning of *Calvin and Hobbes* with some guys on his floor.

As the phone rang, Will said something incoherent from his top bunk that I translated as "Please answer the phone in a hasty manner so that I am not required to hear that ring any more than necessary, as I consumed a substantial amount of alcohol the previous evening."

"Hello?"

"Alex? It's Darren."

"Oh, hi. How's it going?"

"Are you dressed?"

"Why? Did you want to have phone sex?"

Will raised his head. "Hey, I want to have phone sex. Who is that?"

"It's my mom," I told him. Into the phone I said: "I just got up. Why?"

"Because we're going fishing."

"We are?"

"Yep."

"I don't have a fishing pole."

"That's okay. I'll be there in fifteen minutes."

"I just got up."

"Then I'll be there in twenty."

"Make it half an hour."

"Dude, we're going fishing, not to the opera."

"Fine, twenty minutes."

"Don't wuss out like that," Darren told me. "If you want me to be there in half an hour, say half an hour.

Stand up for your right to take a girlish thirty minutes to get ready."

"Be here in half an hour."

"Will do, sir."

I hung up. "I'm going fishing," I informed Will.

"Why?"

"I don't know. To catch fish."

"You're not cooking them in my microwave."

Exactly thirty minutes later, there was a knock on the door. When I opened it, Darren was outside, in shorts and a red T-shirt. "Ready?" he asked.

"Yep."

"Good, then let's—*Holy freakin' shit look at those pictures!*"

"They're my roommate's," I said, gesturing to Will, who was still in bed. "He's a little off center."

"And proud of it," said Will.

"These are kind of cool," Darren proclaimed, moving in for a closer look. "Whoa, nice work on the blonde. She won't be performing motor functions anytime soon."

"That's Jessica Runyon," Will offered, sitting up. "She was the second victim of the Bay Area Butcher back in 1985."

"Never heard of him, but the man can sure use a knife." Darren turned to Will. "So, you're a homicide major, huh? Made your first kill yet?"

"Nah, that's not until my sophomore year."

"Damn those prerequisite classes. Alex, you ready to go?"

"Way past ready."

CHAPTER TWELVE

Darren drove us through such a complicated series of dirt roads that I started to wonder if he was taking me out to the middle of nowhere to be hunted for sport. Seriously. But finally we arrived at the edge of a large pond, so perfectly round that it almost seemed man-made. The water glistened in the sunlight. I wasn't usually the type of person who'd be impressed by something like water glistening in sunlight, but I had to admit, this was a beautiful pond.

"Nice, huh?" asked Darren, shutting off the engine.

"It's great. Does anyone else know about it?"

"I've seen people around here every once in a while. It's a great place to bring dates. Not that we're dating."

"I'll keep my hands to myself," I promised.

Darren reached across the passenger seat and opened the glove compartment. After searching for a moment, he removed a large hunting knife with a black handle and a leather sheath. The blade looked about eight inches long. "We're carving spears from scratch," he explained.

"You don't have professional spearfishing equipment in the back?" I joked, even though I couldn't help but be a little nervous about that knife. "I'm disappointed. I wanted one of those spear guns like the kind they mount on the side of a ship."

"Do they really mount spear guns on the side of ships?"

"I dunno," I admitted. "It may have been in a movie. Maybe *Moby Dick*."

"*Moby Dick* sucked."

We got out of the van and Darren removed the knife from its sheath. He held up the blade so that it flashed in the sunlight. "Me hunter. Me get stick. You hunter. You get stick, too. It stick-getting festival."

There were plenty of trees to choose from, so I searched until I found a branch about four feet long and the diameter of a quarter. I pulled and twisted it until it was mostly off the trunk; then Darren came over and helped finish the task by sawing it off with the knife.

I jabbed the stick back and forth in the air like an angry native. "Yep, this'll work."

After Darren found and cut off his own branch, we sat on a large rock next to the water. Darren removed his shoes and socks and tossed them out of the way, then let his feet hang down into the water. "Don't worry," he said, "my foot odor shouldn't kill more than a third of them."

"And if it does, we can just scoop them off the surface," I remarked.

"Yeah. You can go ahead and take off your shoes, too, if you want. I'm pretty sure there aren't many leeches."

"Nah, I'm fine."

"You sure?"

"Yeah."

"Suit yourself. The water's pretty nice." He ran his finger along the edge of the blade, then held the knife out to me. "Wanna go first?"

"No, I'll watch and learn from your expert technique."

Darren began to cut away at the end of his stick. He looked up at the sky and smiled happily. "How often do you get outside like this?"

"Not that often," I admitted.

"Did your parents ever take you camping?"

"Nope."

"You probably never even played outside with your friends or anything, did you?"

"Well, yeah, I did that," I said. "I wasn't into sports or stuff like that, but we'd mess around at the park and run around the neighborhood sometimes. But mostly I just watched TV, read books, went to the movies . . . that kind of thing. At least until I got shipped off to boarding school."

Darren blew on the end of his stick and wiped off some extra splinters, then resumed sharpening it. "I never really liked any of those things."

"Seriously?"

"Yeah. They're okay, I guess, but I like to have some control over what's going to happen. When you're watching a movie, someone else controls everything. It's all made up before you even get into the theater. Even if you went back and beat the crap out of the projectionist you couldn't change it. I don't like not having any say in how things turn out."

"But isn't that comforting sometimes?" I asked. "You get to forget about your problems for a couple of hours."

"My problems usually aren't that bad."

"Mine aren't either, I guess. I just . . . I like being entertained. I love to laugh. I've probably seen almost every comedy ever made."

"And it doesn't bug you, watching some actor doing something that you know is stupid and not being able to slap some sense into him?"

"No, that's part of what makes it funny."

"Comedies aren't so bad, I'll admit. But I just about have a stroke when I get dragged to a horror movie. 'Don't go into the attic, you idiot!' 'Turn around and pay attention to the psycho with the ax, you brain-dead fuck!' It's more stress than it's worth."

With a satisfied nod at his makeshift spear, he handed the knife to me. I accepted it and began to cut the end of my own stick.

"Not like that," said Darren after the first stroke. "Never cut toward yourself."

I reversed my cutting direction. I'd fully expected to bumble through the whole procedure, probably ending up with something the size of a pencil, but the hunting knife was seriously sharp and it wasn't long before I had my own perfectly serviceable spear.

"All right," said Darren, pushing himself up to a standing position. "Let's go poke us some fish."

I removed my shoes and socks and pulled up my pant legs. We waded into the water, stirring up dark clouds as our feet sunk into the slimy muck. "You'd tell me if this pond was a haven for broken glass, right?" I asked.

"You'll be okay," Darren assured me. "Just don't step on a crab."

"Ah, yes. The ponds of Arizona—the perfect breeding ground for crustaceans."

"See? You at least know enough about the great outdoors to be sarcastic."

Darren stopped once the water was knee-high, and I followed his lead. We stood about ten feet apart, holding our spears with the points facing the water.

"Now what?" I asked.

"We wait for the water to clear."

"All right. Let the thrillfest begin."

We stood there without speaking for a moment, as if silence would cause the muck to settle faster.

"So, do we just sort of stand here until a fish swims by?"

"Yeah."

"Do you even know if there are fish in this pond?"

"There are. I've seen them jump."

I was quiet for a long moment.

"We don't stand a chance in hell of catching a fish, do we?"

"I wouldn't think so. Not standing knee-deep in a mucky pond with a couple of sticks."

"And why exactly are we doing this?"

"When you woke up this morning, did you think you'd wind up going spearfishing?"

"No."

"Then that's reason enough."

I thought about that, and then broke into laughter.

"What else would you have done today?" Darren asked. "You would have watched a movie or two, wandered around campus, looked at some of your roommate's freaky pictures, pretended to study, and gone to bed. By Monday, the whole day would be gone from your memory. But instead you're here with me, and I guarantee you that ten years from now you're going to remember the time you stood in a pond with a stupid fake spear looking like an absolute ass."

Now my laughter was getting out of control, and I had to jam the spear into the pond floor to keep from topping over as my body shook.

"You're disrupting the water!" Darren exclaimed. "The fish are gonna escape!"

For reasons that I couldn't even fathom, that made me laugh harder. I wiped a tear from my eye and lifted the spear out of the water. "Look! I caught some slime!"

"Hurrah! We'll eat well tonight, my friend!" Darren shoved his own spear into the ground and scooped up some black sludge. "I've caught some, too! The gods are smiling upon us this day!"

With a flick of his wrist, Darren sent the sludge flying at me. It wasn't a direct facial hit as was no doubt intended, but it splattered all over my shoulder.

"Sorry," said Darren. "Muscle spasm."

"That's okay," I assured him, bending down. "I have no intention whatsoever of retaliating. I'm just going to reach down into the water for reasons that have nothing whatsoever to do with revenge and get myself a nice, gooey handful of pond glop."

"Glad to hear it."

"Okay, here we go. I've now retrieved a huge handful of slime in an action that in no way is related to anything having any connection to vengeance." I flung the muck at Darren, who dodged just in time. "Damn."

Instantly we both threw our spears aside and crouched down, scooping up as much pond glop as possible. And then the missiles flew. It wasn't long before Darren had several blobs stuck to his chest, arms, and legs, and I found myself almost completely coated.

"All right, all right," I said, spitting out a particularly flavorful mouthful. "Truce."

"No truce. But I'll help you get cleaned up."

Darren rushed at me, arms outstretched. I tried to grab some muck off my shirt to throw for a vicious close-range hit, but didn't make it in time. I let out a loud grunt as Darren tackled me and we both splashed into the water. I prepared to wrestle myself to freedom, but Darren backed off, allowing me time to sit up.

"Do you surrender?" Darren asked.

"You got my wallet all wet."

"You're a college student. There was nothing in it anyway. Do you surrender?"

"How about . . . no!"

"Fine. I hope you're hungry for pond scum!"

My fearsome opponent charged, and I nailed him point-blank in the face with a previously hidden handful of muck. Darren cursed, threw his hands up against his face, and stumbled backward.

"Are you okay?" I asked, genuinely concerned, although I also scooped up some more ammunition in case he was faking it.

Darren nodded through his hands.

"Did I get you in the eye?"

"Your clump had a rock."

"Oh, jeez, I'm sorry! I didn't mean to!"

Darren lowered his hands, revealing a small red mark. "It's okay. No big deal." Then he gave me a wicked grin. "Except that you're seconds away from gaining about fifty pounds in pure pond crap."

The battle raged again.

I lost. Big-time.

By dunking ourselves underneath the water a few times, we managed to get mostly cleaned up. I had some mud deep in my ear that I couldn't quite manage to get out and which I explained to Darren would probably later cause me severe hearing problems and ultimately death. Darren told me to quit being such a pansy and to accept my imminent fatality like a man.

We wandered around the area for a while to give the sun a chance to dry our clothes. As demented as it sounded, I felt a lot more relaxed around Darren now that we'd pummeled each other half to death with muck.

We listened to music, talked, and laughed the entire way home. It had been a great day.

I couldn't believe it. Darren and I were friends. Actual friends. I wondered what Peter and Jeremy would think about that.

They'd understand. People change.

Two weeks after classes started, I saw her again.

Darren and I were at the library, doing homework. Or, to be more accurate, I was doing research for an English paper while Darren sat at our table scoping out hot college chicks.

"Check her out," Darren said, pointing to a brunette

with gargantuan breasts. "If she ever toppled over she'd bounce right back up. She can suffocate me with those things anytime."

"What about your girlfriend?" I asked, amused.

Darren checked his watch. "My loyalty period is just about to expire."

"You're such a sleaze."

"But I'm a lovable sleaze, and that's all that's important. Ooh! Ooh! There's your space cadet!"

Darren pointed over my shoulder. I turned around and saw the girl who'd accidentally walloped me in the bookstore. She was carrying a ridiculously tall stack of books and having a bit of trouble managing it.

"She *is* cute, though," Darren noted.

"Very."

I looked back at Darren. He was grinning.

"What?" I asked.

"You've never agreed with me before. You usually just tolerate my obnoxious misogynistic behavior."

"Yeah, well, you were right, she *is* cute."

"So's the girl with the mammoth tits."

"Don't say that."

"What? Tits?"

"No. Mammoth tits. I'm not turned on by woolly breasts."

Darren grinned even more broadly. "I can't believe it. You're trying to change the subject. You've got the hots for the spacey chick, haven't you?"

"Nah."

"You can't lie to me. She's got you *mes-mer-ized*. So don't sit here yapping with me, dipshit, go talk to her."

"She's probably busy."

"That's the weakest possible excuse you could come

up with. If you let her go, I promise you, she'll smack into some other guy and he'll be doing her doggy-style before the day is over."

"Sleaze."

"Go talk to her. I've got a private room, so you two can use my place for your thrusting and moaning."

"No."

"Go talk to her."

"I don't have anything to say."

"Offer to help her with the stack of books."

I glanced over my shoulder. "She's gone, anyway."

"She went around that corner," said Darren, point-ing. "Go talk to her or I swear, I'll scream at you to take your hand off my dick. I'll do it. You know I'll do it."

I closed my book, pushed back my chair, and stood up. My heart was pounding as I headed in the direc-tion that Darren had pointed, but it was pounding in a good way.

As I turned the corner, I saw her, still struggling with the stack of books. I hurried over, walked behind her for a few steps, and then walked up beside her.

"Hi," I said.

She glanced over at me. "Oh my gosh! How are you? You're not still hurt, are you?"

"No, no, I'm fine."

"Oh, good. I felt like such a geek."

"Can I help you with that?" I asked, gesturing to her stack of books.

"That would be awesome. There don't seem to be any empty tables in this place."

I took the top half of her stack, about ten books. The top book was something about Egyptian mummies.

"Oh, that's much better," she said. "Thanks. They

should give you shopping carts. 'Course, I'd just bash into people with that, too. Could you do me a huge favor and push up my glasses?"

I quickly adjusted the stack of books and used my free hand to push up her thick glasses.

"Thanks so much."

"No problem."

"Oh, thank goodness, there's an empty table up there."

As we made a beeline toward the table, another student sat down at it. The girl sighed in frustration.

"There's another one," I said, doing a half sprint toward it and nearly dropping the stack of books. Fortunately, I made it to the table without the unbearable humiliation of dropping them and she breathed a sigh of relief as she set down her own stack.

"Now I just have to camp out here for the rest of the semester and I'll be fine," she said, sitting down.

I stood there helplessly. Should I leave? Should I ask if I could join her? Should I make an informed yet witty comment about Egyptian mummies?

"Are you busy? Did you want to sit down?" she asked, sparing me from any decision making. I loved her for it.

"Sure," I said, sitting down across from her.

"Did we introduce ourselves after I hit you in the stomach?" she asked.

"No."

"I didn't think so. I'm Melanie."

"Alex."

"Nice to meet you."

"Nice to meet *you*."

We just looked at each other in awkward silence for a long moment, until Melanie burst into giggles. "Wow, we're the best conversationalists *ever!*"

"We're brilliant!"

"Astounding!"

My mind went blank as I tried to think of another adjective, and Melanie burst into giggles again.

"What's your major?" she asked. "Please don't tell me communications."

"Architecture."

"Like it?"

"It's okay so far. I only have one class on it so I can't tell yet."

"I'm history. I don't know what I'm gonna do with it yet, but I always liked history." She pushed up her glasses again. "I really should get contacts one of these days."

"Why haven't you?"

"I'm not sure I want to touch my eyeball. I don't think you're supposed to do that. And I'd always be worried that I'd blink and the contact would slide up onto the top of my eye and come off and get lost back there. Yecch."

"The glasses look good on you."

"You think so? I'm going for the nerd look. I got bored with the whole beauty pageant queen, super-model, Greek goddess thing."

"It works for you."

"Thanks."

We continued talking. We talked about high school, movies we loved, movies that sucked, our favorite authors, our favorite music, how the first two weeks of college were going, foods we liked, foods that made us queasy, our roommates, our hobbies, and our childhood. Once we got started, the conversation was effortless, even when I told her about my parents. Oddly enough, we didn't share many of the same tastes, but talking to her made me want to experience Italian cinema and listen to Dar Williams music and eat a slaw dog. I didn't even like cole slaw, but a slaw dog sounded wonderful.

We talked so long that we didn't even realize that there were now plenty of open tables. It wasn't until a librarian told us that they were closing up that we realized we'd been sitting there for several hours.

"Oh my gosh, I didn't get *anything* done!" Melanie exclaimed. "I mean, I got a lot done, I loved talking to you, but I didn't finish any of my research!" She smiled. "Darn you for being so interesting."

"Did you want to go get something to eat?" I asked.

"Oh, I'd love to, but I have to turn in the first draft of this paper tomorrow and I'm going to be pulling an all-nighter. I don't write fast. I'll just have a vending machine dinner."

"Okay."

"Are you busy this weekend?"

"Not at all."

"Wanna go to the movies?"

"Yeah," I said, because screaming *"hell yeah!"* at the top of my lungs would have made me seem needy.

"You can pick it, but I get veto power."

"It's a deal."

"Wanna help me get these to the checkout counter?"

"Sure thing."

After she'd checked out her books, I walked her

back to her dorm, which was disappointingly close to the library. One of her friends was walking in at the same time and offered to share the load, so Melanie gave me a hug and reminded me to call her.

I walked away from the dorm, feeling like I was glowing. In a good way, not the radioactive 1950s monster-movie way.

Wow.

I knew what I should do. I should pick her up something good for dinner and drop it off so she wouldn't have to eat candy bars from the vending machine. Maybe I'd get a rose to go with it.

Nah, I didn't want to come off like a stalker. I had to play it cool, like Darren would. Just give her a call tomorrow night as planned.

I headed back to my dorm, but I didn't really feel like going inside. It was too nice of an evening. I strolled around campus until nearly midnight, feeling good about everything in my life.

I felt less good when the alarm woke me up at 6:15 A.M., but I forced myself to get out of bed, attended all of my classes that day, and even paid attention in most of them. After all, getting kicked out of school would adversely impact my ability to keep seeing Melanie. And if we were to get married and have kids, I'd need a good job, so it was important to study hard and get excellent grades and make sure that I . . .

Yes, I was eighteen years old and envisioning an elaborate future with a girl I'd really only gotten to know the day before. Call me a romantic.

I gave Melanie a call after dinner. Because she had to study for a test, we only talked for two hours instead of the desired sixteen, but it was a wonderful conversation, hampered only by Will's frequent "gagging" gestures. We weren't even saying any lovey-dovey stuff.

When we finally hung up, even the mutilated bodies on our wall seemed to be radiating love and happiness. Ed Gein, the inspiration for *Psycho* and *The Texas Chainsaw Massacre*, looked like Cupid.

The phone rang.

"If she's calling you back already, I'm going to puke," Will informed me.

"Keep it on your side of the room." I picked up the phone. "Hello?"

"Dude, I've been trying to call you for the past hour!" said Darren. "You've gotta come over here."

"Why?"

"Because you do. It'll be worth it, I promise."

"I've got homework."

"Screw homework. I've got life lessons here, Alex. This is education that you'll remember forever. Get over here."

"All right, all right. God, you're pushy."

"Get over here quick."

"I will."

"No lollygagging."

"I won't."

"I'll kick your ass if you lollygag."

"Maybe you should chill."

"Maybe you should get over here before it's too late."

I hung up the phone. "I'll be back," I told Will as I headed out the door. Darren's dorm was on the other side of campus and I jogged most of the way. I walked

up the stairs to the third floor and knocked on his
door.

Darren answered and quickly ushered me inside.
The first thing to catch my attention was the nearly
naked woman on the bed.

CHAPTER THIRTEEN

She looked a couple of years older than us, and was dressed only in black panties and a tube top. Under other circumstances she was probably an incredibly attractive woman, but her brown hair was messed up and her makeup was smeared. She smiled and gave me a clumsy wave as Darren shut the door behind us.

"Alex, meet Trisha," Darren said.

"Hi," I said, politely but warily.

Trisha nodded. I couldn't quite tell if she was looking at me or at something behind me.

"So what's up?" I asked Darren.

"She's pretty hot, huh?"

I shrugged. "Yeah."

"You want her?"

"What?"

"She's yours if you want her. You're not gonna get many chances at a body like that. She's horny as all shit."

I looked back at her. "Darren, she's drunk off her ass."

"So? Dude, I'm offering you an end to your virginity. C'mon, I told her all about you. She said she'd do both of us."

"You can't be serious."

"I'm completely serious. But we don't have to share her. You can have her all to yourself. Now *that* is friendship."

"Is she a student here?"

Darren shook his head. "Nah, just some waitress I met."

"You and those waitresses." I forced a chuckle. "I've gotta get going."

"This is exquisite pussy you're passing up. You can't just walk out on this. At least get her shirt off and check out what I'm offering."

"I've got a girlfriend." I was pretty sure that Melanie didn't quite count as an official girlfriend yet, but it did seem like a good excuse to get me out of here.

"The spacey chick?"

"Yeah."

"You fuck her?"

"None of your business."

"Because if you didn't fuck her, there's no commitment yet and you can do whatever you want. And if you did fuck her, then she's a slut who puts out on the first date, and you shouldn't have any commitment there, either. C'mon, nobody will know. I won't say a word."

"I'm not doing it."

"Why not? Give me one reason."

"She could have diseases."

"That's what rubbers are for."

"It could break."

"So you let her use her mouth."

I took a deep breath and tried to speak in such a way as to allow no room for argument. "I'm not doing anything with her, and that's final. I appreciate you thinking of me, but my first time is not going to be with a drunk lady that I met thirty seconds ago. I'm not going to mess things up with Melanie before they even start."

Darren shrugged and let out a deep sigh. "All right. I was just doing you a favor."

"Thanks."

Darren looked at Trisha, then back at me and lowered his voice. "You could hit her."

"Say what?"

"She's more than just drunk. She wouldn't feel it."

I gaped at him.

Darren slapped me on the back, hard. "Aw, I'm just playing with you, buddy. You go back and get some sleep. Tell the spacey chick I said hi."

"I will."

He opened the door for me. "Yeah, I'm gonna make me some sweet, sweet love. Give me a call if you change your mind. We'll be here all night."

"Okay."

I stepped out into the hallway and he closed the door. I walked toward the stairwell, desperately craving a shower.

Darren called late the next morning.

"I am *so* sorry," he said. "That was totally uncool. I'd had way too much to drink and I just got out of hand. It'll never happen again, I promise."

"All right," I said, not convinced.

"I didn't even sleep with her. I sent the skank home. You were right, who knows what kind of filthy diseases she could've been carrying? She could've melted the condom right off me."

"Yeah."

"Aw, c'mon, you're still pissed off. Don't be pissed. Let me make it up to you."

"Nah, it's fine."

"Things are working out with that library girl, huh?"

"Melanie, yeah."

"Good to hear. You gonna be around?"

"For a bit."

"Cool. I'm on my way."

When Darren showed up at my dorm room, he was holding a piece of red licorice. "Peace offering," he said, handing it to me.

"Thanks."

"I apologize again for last night. I will never mix Jack Daniel's and Snapple ever again. I'm glad you turned me down . . . if both of us stud muffins had gone at her, she would've been paralyzed from the lips down."

"You just wanted me to observe your penis."

"Yeah, well, there was that, too." He sat down at Will's desk. "So when are you getting together with Melanie again?"

"Friday for a movie. Maybe before that for lunch or something. I don't know."

"You bringing her back here?"

"Not with you in the room."

"No, seriously, are you bringing her back here?"

"I haven't planned that far. I doubt it."

"If you do, do you want her to see all this crap?" Darren gestured to Will's decorations.

"Not really."

"So get rid of it."

"I was going to ask Will about that later."

"Why haven't you asked him already?"

"I just haven't gotten around to it."

"You're not going to get any action if you've got all this serial killer stuff up on your walls," said Darren, standing up. "That is, unless Melanie's a necrophile, and necrophiles are hard to come by in a college setting. Let's make this stuff go bye-bye."

"I said I was going to ask him about it."

"Why ask him? It's your room, too, right?"

"Half of it."

Darren reached over and plucked a color photograph of a decapitated head off the wall. "See, why does he need this? It's not like he severed the head himself." He crumpled up the picture in his fist and tossed it onto the floor.

"Hey, whoa!"

"Whoa what? What's he going to do to you? Beat you up? You can take him." Darren yanked a newspaper article off the wall and crumpled it up as well.

"Seriously, don't do that," I said, picking the photo off the floor and straightening it out the best I could. "It's not my stuff."

"But you have to look at it."

"Yeah, well, I'll take care of it tonight."

"Let's take care of it now." Darren ripped a second newspaper article off the wall.

"Damn it, knock it off!" I said. "I have to live with him!"

"That's exactly why you shouldn't let him push you around."

"He's not pushing me around! I never asked him to take them down! I said I'll ask him tonight. Quit wrecking his stuff."

"Wow," said Darren. "I've never seen you pissed."

"Yes you have, you just don't remember. Now quit it. I mean it."

"You need to control your life. Let Will know that you're in charge of this room. Let that morbid little freak know that it's *your* room, and you're just being nice enough to let him hang out here. C'mon, let's rip all this shit down and show him that there's not a thing he can do about it."

"He can sure go tell the resident advisor."

"Yeah, and . . . ?"

"And get me in trouble."

Darren rolled his eyes. "He's not gonna tattle on you. If he does, you say you asked him over and over to take these pictures down because they made you sick and he refused. Say you were in fear for your life. Worst-case scenario, you get switched to a new roommate. You'd be better off."

"The pictures don't even bug me."

"Bullshit. Okay, look, I'll make you a deal. Tear one down. Just one. You'll feel better, I promise."

"I'll feel better when you let this drop."

"I'll let it drop when you tear one down."

"Fine." I glanced around the wall and located a picture of a woman's body lying on a mortuary slab. I removed the pushpins and took down the picture. "Are you happy?"

"Crumple it up."

"No."

"Just that one. Crumple it up."

"He's been collecting this stuff for years."

"And you have the power to take it away from him. This stuff isn't enriching his life, Alex. Somebody who would subject his roommate to this crap without asking permission deserves to lose it. Crumple it up. When he gets back and asks what happened to it, look him right in eye and say that you did it. There's not a thing he can do."

I set the picture on Will's desk. "I think you're still drunk."

"C'mon, one picture. Wreck one picture. Or an article. Wreck an article. I'm sure he's got copies. Wreck one of them and I swear I won't say another—"

I slashed at the wall like a cat, ripping down several of the articles. *"There! Now will you leave me the hell alone?"*

"I certainly will."

"Crap." Pieces of the articles were still stuck under the pins, so I removed all of the pins and scraps. "Will's gonna throw a fit."

"So what if he does?"

I gathered up all of the articles and photos and set them on my own desk. I wasn't sure what Darren's problem was all of a sudden, but I didn't need a friend who acted like this. I had Melanie. I could handle my roommate disputes perfectly well on my own, thank you very much.

I refused to admit that ripping down those articles *had* felt pretty good.

And I refused to admit that instead of dreading it, I was actually kind of looking forward to seeing Will's reaction when he got back.

He returned about forty-five minutes later, while Darren and I were watching television. He walked into the room, got himself a soda from the refrigerator, then frowned.

"What happened there?" he asked, pointing to the blank spot on the wall.

"Oh, jeez, I'm sorry," I said. "We were messing around and they sort of got—"

"We tore them down," Darren explained.

"Oh." Will snorted a laugh. "What were you guys doing, having a wrestling match?"

"No," said Darren. "We just felt like tearing them down."

Will looked at him as if unsure whether or not he was kidding. "You didn't throw them away, did you?"

"We burned them."

"They're on my desk," I said.

Darren looked at me expectantly. "Ask him."

Will frowned. "Ask me what?"

"Oh, uh, do you think you could tone it down a bit? The pictures, I mean. Melanie might come over this weekend and I don't want her to get creeped out."

"Yeah, sure, it's not a problem." Will picked up the decapitated head photo from my desk and glared at me. "Did you do this on purpose?"

"No," I insisted. "We were just roughhousing. I'll pay for it."

Darren punched me in the arm, so hard that I winced.

"If you two have become gay lovers, that's fine with

me," said Will. "You can do all the S&M you want,
just keep it on your own side of the room."

I tried to think of a joke to add to that, but nothing
immediately came to mind. Darren stood up, making
no attempt to hide his frustration.

"I'm outta here. If you want people to push you
around your whole life, that's fine. I hope you're happy.
Maybe you'll luck out and Melanie *will* be a necrophile.
See ya." He left the room, not slamming the door
behind him but certainly shutting it harder than was
necessary.

Will gave me a confused look. "What the hell was
that all about?"

I shrugged. "No idea."

"Why were you hoping that Melanie is a necrophile?"

"I wasn't. It's . . . it's hard to explain. I'm not sure
what his problem is today."

"Well, if the pictures and stuff bothered you, you
should've said something. I asked you about it before."

"I know, I know. Actually, though, I'm going out
with Melanie on Friday and if we decide to come back
and watch TV or something it might be nice if you
could maybe, I dunno, get rid of some of the sicker
ones."

"Sure. It's your room, too." Will didn't sound like
he believed it. "Don't harbor stuff like this, Alex, it's
not healthy."

"I wasn't harboring anything, I was just . . . uh,
thanks for taking it down."

"No problem."

* * *

I lay in bed, almost asleep, wondering what to do about Darren. I still thought of him as my best friend, but he was getting way out of control. Threatening to accuse me of touching his dick in a crowded library to get me to talk to Melanie was something I could live with, but demanding that I rip up Will's property for no good reason was going too far. The incident with Trisha I'd blame on alcohol, even though Darren hadn't seemed drunk and I hadn't smelled any booze on his breath.

I wondered if that creepy kid from Branford Academy was still there. Not the one who mutilated dead dogs, but the one who took great delight in knowing how much power he had over me. I could still see the sadistic glee in his eye when we spoke that last day before school let out.

"Don't lie to me. I bet you spent every day scared that I was gonna get you."

I fell asleep. I dreamed of mummies bursting from their sarcophagi and tearing long, bloody strips of flesh from my bones.

CHAPTER FOURTEEN

My date with Melanie was a disaster from beginning to end, and one of the best times of my life.

First of all, somebody stole all of my laundry out of the dryer. This was an ongoing prank at our dorm. If you weren't watching your clothes, the unknown culprits would swipe them and return them in an amusing fashion. Our next-door neighbor found his clothes on a female mannequin that had been placed in the kitchenette. The guy down the hall found various pairs of his underwear clogging each of the toilets. Nobody knew who was responsible, or how you could even get a mannequin into the building without anybody noticing, but we'd already had two mandatory meetings about the situation and it was supposed to stop *immediately*.

I knew that I deserved whatever creative fate befell my clothing, simply for being dumb enough to leave the dryer unattended, but my favorite blue shirt had been in there and now I had nothing nice to wear. Will, ever helpful, offered to let me wear his black Charles Manson shirt, but I declined.

Then I accidentally dropped my electric shaver, breaking it against the bathroom floor. So I had to shave with a regular blade, which meant that I acquired several lovely nicks and attractive pieces of toilet paper stuck to them to stop the bleeding.

Not to mention that I was having a bad hair day. Admittedly, I was not the kind of person who ever had *good* hair days, but this one was particularly abysmal. Cowlicks I'd never formerly possessed sprung up like weeds and no amount of hair gook would keep them in place. Will helpfully suggested that I shave my head and offered to track down a machete to speed up the process, but I declined.

The walk to Melanie's dorm passed without incident.

Melanie looked gorgeous. We weren't going anywhere fancy (I hadn't yet gotten a part-time job and my money was running low) but she was wearing a red blouse that looked new and was wearing just a hint of makeup. Her roommate Sally gave me a good-natured interrogation, and then we were off.

My car wouldn't start. Though it was a crappy car and had been crappy when I bought it, this was the first time it had ever failed to start. I lifted the front hood and spent a few minutes pretending that I knew what I was looking at, all the while making jokes that were much funnier than my usual standard of nervous jokes.

When it became clear that my car wasn't going to start without professional assistance or supernatural intervention, we returned to Melanie's room to get permission to borrow Sally's car. The interrogation this time was substantially less good-natured, but we

were allowed to borrow the car after promising that if
we were in an accident, we would bleed on the pave-
ment and not the upholstery.

Then Sally's car wouldn't start. After a few frustrated
tries, I realized that this was because, like a dumb-ass, I
was using the key to my own car and not Sally's. Fortunately, instead of taking the more reasonable approach of shaking her head sadly, getting out of the
automobile, and leaving the dumb-ass to live a life of
well-deserved solitude, Melanie had a gentle laugh
over it and we finally got on the road.

When we got to the movie theater and bought our
tickets, I realized that I'd misread the starting time
and that the romantic comedy Melanie wanted to see
had been on for half an hour. She didn't seem bothered by this, and we decided to see *Threads of the
Noose*, which neither of us had ever heard of.

I bought us each a small drink and a large tub of
popcorn to share. I allowed Melanie to take on the responsibility of butter application, and she drenched it
with more butter (technically, butter-flavored product) than I had ever personally witnessed coming into
contact with popcorn. I was pretty sure that an alarm
went off at a nearby hospital, preparing them to dis-
patch an artery surgeon at a moment's notice. But
even though I generally liked dry popcorn with just a
hint of salt, sharing this semisolid glop with Melanie
sounded delicious.

Threads of the Noose sucked. I mean, really, really, really, really, really sucked. It was boring and depressing
and badly acted and incoherent and featured not one,
not two, but three graphic shots of the actors throw-

ing up, which is not what I pay to see when I go to a movie, especially when I'm eating from a tub of semi-solid popcorn glop. But we were the only two people in the theater, which allowed us to loudly and glee-fully share our disdain for the movie and have a won-derful time.

When we got back to Sally's car, I couldn't get Melanie's door unlocked because, again, I was using my own keys. I acknowledged that I was a dumb-ass, while stating that in my own defense, at least I wasn't the kind of dumb-ass who would make a movie like *Threads of the Noose*.

We went to dinner at a small, inexpensive seafood place that turned out to be inexpensive for a reason. But though we left most of our food untouched (I was full from the butter-flavored product anyway) we stayed there until closing time, just talking and laugh-ing and thoroughly enjoying each other's company.

"I really had a good time," said Melanie as we drove back to campus. I was still basking in the personal vic-tory of using the right key this time.

"Me, too. I had a great time."

"We should watch more crappy movies together."

"Absolutely."

We were silent the rest of the drive home, but it was a nice, comfortable silence. We didn't have to say anything.

I walked her back to her dorm. We looked at each other for a moment, she let out a soft giggle, and then I put my arms around her and kissed her.

The rest of the evening had been an enjoyable dis-aster, but this first kiss was perfect.

When we finally parted, Melanie pushed up her glasses and smiled in an almost giddy manner. "Do you want to do something tomorrow?" she asked.

"Yeah."

"Good."

She kissed me again, quickly this time, and then went inside the building. I stood there for a moment, just collecting my thoughts, then decided that I didn't want anybody to think I was the kind of creep who stood around outside girls' dormitories after dark, so I went home and walked in on Will having sex with a Goth chick in a position that didn't look comfortable for either of them or good for his desk.

He paid me ten bucks to sleep out in the lounge, and I cheerfully accepted. The couch was uncomfortable and too short, but I got the best night's sleep I'd had in a long time.

I woke up all hot and sweaty, feeling like there was an incredible weight on my chest. There was. The jackasses who'd stolen my laundry had left the pile on top of me while I slept.

"If you could kill one person, who would it be?" asked Darren, nibbling on a piece of pizza.

"I dunno. I wouldn't kill anybody."

Darren shook his head. "Cop-out answer. You have to give me a name. Somebody at this school."

"I'd kill my English teacher for giving me a B-minus on that paper. That was a good paper."

"Who else?"

"That's it."

"C'mon, that can't be it. Let that inner hostility out."

"Let's just drop it."

"Dude, it's just a conversation starter. I'm not saying, 'Let's go out and kill some people,' I'm just asking who you would kill if you could."

"Yeah, then tomorrow morning their heads will end up in my bed."

"Nah, I'm a strangler, not a decapitator."

We were sitting out on the lawn in front of Booker Hall. I'd just been sitting out there studying, but Darren had noticed me on his way back from the cafeteria and joined me.

"So who would you kill?" I asked, picking off a mushroom before taking my next bite.

"I'd probably take the teacher route like you did. I hate that they think they can rule me, telling me to do homework and take tests and all that shit."

"Yeah, those damn teachers ruin college for everyone."

"They sure do."

"So why'd you go to college anyway, if you don't like people telling you what to do?"

"What are my other options? Military would be a million times worse, or I could get some lousy job and have a boss order me around all the time. College seemed to have the most freedom."

"You could always be a panhandler."

"Nah. I don't do well without my creature comforts. Like this pizza." He took a great big bite.

"You didn't even ask how my date with Melanie went."

"How'd your date go? You fuck her?"

"No."

"Couldn't get it up, huh? I've got a little crane you could borrow next time."

"I've got a piece of pizza I could smear in your face."

Darren held up his own piece of pizza in a defensive pose. "You know I'm just kidding. How'd it go?"

"It was great!" I told him about the entire evening from beginning to end, not even censoring the part with the car keys. Darren listened to the whole tale, laughing in the right places and seeming genuinely happy for me. One thing I'd always liked about him . . . even if he had a tendency to ignore protests on matters of sleeping with drunk women named Trisha and ripping down photographs, he did always listen rather than just wait for his turn to speak.

When I told him about the kiss, he slapped me on the shoulder to congratulate me for a job well done. "Well, I'm thrilled," he said. "I'm so thrilled that I won't make my usual crude comment."

"Oh, go ahead. I wouldn't want to cause you psychological distress."

"Okay. When're you gonna fuck her?"

I punched him on the arm.

"Sissy punch," Darren noted.

I hit him harder.

"That one hurt. Don't do that again." He chuckled. "Yeah, I can see it now. You two will be spending all your free time together, and there'll be no room for Darren Rust. I'll just stand outside your window, making puppy dog noises for attention."

"And if you're really good, we'll let you come inside and stay in a cage."

We both laughed, but it occurred to me that it *was* kind of odd that such an outgoing guy didn't seem to have any other friends. At least none that he spoke about, although it wasn't like we spent every free moment together.

"We could always take her fishing," Darren said.

"Or we could fish out of the library toilets and have just as much success."

"Yeah. You know, my parents have a cabin and some property, about a twelve-hour drive from here. I was going to go up there for Thanksgiving break. We could all go together."

"You have parents?"

"Of course I have parents."

"You've never said anything about them. I figured you were a test-tube baby, or else you spontaneously generated from the muck underneath a city or something."

Darren grinned. "I wish. Wanna know why I never talk about my home life? Because it's so boring that you would slash your wrists with a tin can lid before I'd gotten five minutes into it. You cannot *imagine* how boring my parents are. My dad goes to work at an office Monday through Friday—I don't even know what he does there—and my mom vacuums the house and watches daytime television. They're like zombies without the cool flesh-eating. Do you have a tin can lid handy?"

"In my other pants."

"They don't even use the cabin. They inherited it but have never been there. Walking into my house is like walking into this energy-sucking pit where all creativity and inspiration just goes *whoosh*. They're like nonentities. I have no idea how I turned into such an interesting guy. Man, they suck."

"Sounds like it."

"So what about the cabin idea?"

"Believe it or not, Melanie has a family that would miss her if she didn't come home for Thanksgiving."

"Imagine that!"

"Yeah, it's freaky."

"Well, if you ever want to go up there, let me know. It's too far for just a weekend trip, but Thanksgiving, Christmas, spring break—any of those are cool."

"Is it a nice cabin or an outhouse with a bed?"

"Real nice cabin."

"Sounds good. I'll let you know."

Darren made it a point to ask at least once a day if Melanie and I had finally fornicated. Five weeks and a day after our first date, my answer changed.

Having a girlfriend was a new experience for me and one that I cherished. We saw each other every day, though we didn't get to spend as much time together as I wanted. Melanie was a straight-A student, but as she frequently said, "I have to struggle for every grade." I knew that she could get equivalent grades in half the study time, and wasn't convinced that the fourteenth draft of a term paper could be notably superior to the eleventh, but her obsessive attention to detail was just one of the many, many things I loved about her.

After our first study session together, we were forced to admit that perhaps we were not the best study partners (something vague about kissing being preferable to quizzing each other) and I respected her need to devote much of her free time to schoolwork.

I got a part-time job bussing tables at a much better restaurant than the one I'd bussed tables at during high school. This gobbled up some of my spare time, but I still had time to hang out with Darren. He'd begun to date regularly, and he, Melanie, and I had gone out on a few double dates, each time with a different girl. He and Melanie seemed to get along fine. Darren could be remarkably charming when he put his mind to it.

Melanie and I had a few heavy petting sessions. She was technically a virgin ("but only technically") and after working out an "if the room's a-rockin', don't come a-knockin'" arrangement with Will, who was still seeing the Goth chick, Melanie and I spent some quality time on my top bunk. I remained a virgin by definition, but a happy one.

Then Will went home for a weekend, and Melanie decided that she was caught up enough in her studies to take the weekend off. I traded shifts at the restaurant and spent all day Saturday and Sunday in my room with her. We dragged the mattress onto the floor, watched bad movies, ate worse pizza, and cuddled.

We fell asleep in each other's arms.

When we woke up, I told her that I loved her.

She kissed me in response, and for a second I thought she was doing it to avoid an answer, but then she whispered: "I love you, too, Alex."

We kissed some more, and then made sweet, gentle love.

Then we made sweet, gentle love again.

Then we had some more pizza.

Then we made love once more, though it wasn't quite as sweet and definitely not as gentle. But it was fun. Lots of fun.

"Oh my God, you're holding out on me!" said Darren. "You fucked her, didn't you?"

"Like I'd tell you."

"Did she come?"

"Like I'd tell you."

"Is she loud?"

"Like I'd tell you."

"Was she a wild animal? Did she hurt you? Do you want me to check you for claw marks?"

"I'm not telling you a damn thing," I said, putting on my best smug expression. "You'll just have to use your imagination. Your vivid, wet, dripping imagination."

"That's just gross."

"And yet I feel no regret for saying it."

"I hope you were careful."

"Of course."

"Because you know, when a man and a woman love each other a lot, they take off their clothes and try to make a baby."

"Shut up, dork."

"Well, I'm happy for you," said Darren. "I'd shake your hand to congratulate you, but I have a pretty good idea about where it's been."

"Sleaze."

"Don't call *me* a sleaze! You're the one who's out there engaging in rampant sexual activity. Oh, by the way, you won't find this in any book, but the first time you have sex your testicles swell up to watermelon-size and you have to hide yourself from society for a few weeks. It's a ritual that people don't like to talk about. It takes about two days for the swelling to begin . . . when did you do her again?"

"I can't believe I'm hanging out with you instead of her."

"I know. Why is that?"

"She's studying."

"Ah. So are you going to keep seeing her, or are you going to dump her like a scoundrel and move on to the next conquest?"

"I told her I loved her."

Darren raised an eyebrow. "Really?"

"Yeah."

"Did she say 'I love you' back?"

"She sure did."

"Wow. That's great." His expression turned serious. "To celebrate, I'm going to quit making any and all crude comments about you two. I'm serious. If you two are in love, I couldn't be happier."

"Thanks."

"I meant after this conversation, of course. How did her pussy taste?"

"You are *such* a prick."

"Kidding. I'm just kidding. Congratulations, man. You deserve it. And I mean that."

"Thanks."

Two days later, Darren and I walked into my room. Will was seated at his desk, reading a new book about serial killers.

"Hi, Psycho-Boy," said Darren, plopping down on the floor in front of the television.

"Hi," Will replied, not looking up from his book. "How was class?" he asked me.

"Not too bad. How was yours?"

"Eh."

"Yeah." I glanced at the wall, frowned, and then stepped over to look more closely. I felt a sudden burst of rage beyond anything I'd ever experienced. *"You sick motherfucker!"*

CHAPTER FIFTEEN

"What the hell . . . ?" asked Will, flinching and nearly falling back in his chair.

I tore the picture off the wall. It was a black-and-white picture of Melanie (a photocopy of the same one I kept on my desk) that had been doctored to look like she was a severed head. The only color was the red blood gushing out of her mouth.

"You think that's funny?" I demanded, waving the picture in his face. "You think that's fucking funny?"

"I didn't do that! I didn't even see it there!"

"Bullshit!"

Darren stood up and hurried over. "Hey, hey, calm down, there's no reason to . . . oh, Christ."

I glanced back at the wall. The severed head picture wasn't the only one of Melanie. Her face had been taped to a shot of a woman strapped to a gurney, several knives protruding from her chest. Another picture had her hanging from a meat hook, while yet another showed Melanie dismembered, her body parts stacked in a pile, bloody head on top.

I tore them down.

"Is that your sense of humor?" Darren asked. "Or were you really planning to do that?"

"I didn't—" Will protested, right before I took a swing at him.

He blocked it easily. "You sick fuck!" I screamed, not caring if the entire goddamn dorm could hear. "You sick motherfucker!"

"It wasn't me! Chill the hell out!"

I threw another punch. Will grabbed my hand and tried to hold on to it, but I pulled free. Darren came up behind him, dragged Will out of his chair, and pulled him to his feet.

"You touch Melanie, we'll fuckin' kill you," Darren said, wrenching Will's arms behind his back.

"Get your hands off me!" Will shouted, struggling violently.

I looked at the picture of Melanie on the floor and punched Will in the face as hard as I could. His head rocketed back against Darren's face, and as it slumped forward, I could see blood spurting from Darren's nose.

"Oh, jeez, I'm—"

"It's fine! Hit the fucker!"

I punched Will again, so blinded by fury that the punch didn't even hurt my hand. Actually, it felt good. Invigorating.

The door flew open. "Knock it off!" I heard Michael, our resident advisor, shout.

I raised my fist to deliver another punch, but hesitated. "You do that again and I'll kill you!" I screamed at Will.

"Enough!" Michael shouted, pulling me away. "Let him go!" he told Darren.

Darren shoved Will to the floor. He hit the ground hard, groaning in pain. I tried to pull free of Michael, to kick that son of a bitch in the stomach while he was down, but Michael was a big guy and his grip was too tight.

"Enough, I said!" Michael repeated. "Everybody calm down! I'll call the police if I have to, so let's get through this."

For a moment nobody spoke. We just stood there, catching our breath.

"What happened?" Michael asked.

Darren picked up one of the pictures and handed it to Michael. Michael sucked in a deep breath. "Jesus, Will, that's not funny."

"I didn't do it," said Will from the floor.

"If he touches her, I'll fucking kill him," I said.

"Okay, now Alex, you really need to just calm down," Michael told me. "He wasn't threatening your girlfriend; he just has a warped sense of humor." He looked back at the doorway and the crowd that had gathered outside. "All of you, get back to your rooms, I'm handling this."

Will lifted his head and wiped his bloody mouth off on his sleeve. "I didn't do it. It was probably your friend."

"Yeah, right," said Darren. "I'm *so* into the idea of covering the walls with shredded corpses."

Now my hand was really starting to hurt, and with the initial rage fading, I wished I hadn't attacked Will like that. It had obviously been a joke. A joke that wasn't the least bit amusing, but still, a joke *intended* to be harmless.

"It wasn't me," Will insisted, looking at me.

My stomach lurched as I suddenly realized that I believed him.

"I don't want to have to make a big issue out of this," said Michael. "Alex, you're going to be my roommate tonight. Will, I'm going to get you to the nurse. You, too," he said, nodding at Darren.

Darren wiped some blood off his nose and looked at his hand. "I'm okay," he said with a smile. "It was worth it to watch that freak get what he deserved."

"Fuck you," said Will.

"Okay, go back to your own dorm," Michael told Darren. "Until we get this sorted out, I'm going to ask you to stay away."

Darren shrugged. "Not a problem. Alex, I'll give you a call." He walked out of the room, letting blood drip onto his shirt.

"I'm sorry, Will," I said, feeling queasy.

"Go to hell."

"Enough! Alex, do you need ice for your hand?"

"No, I'm okay."

Michael helped Will to his feet. "We'll be back. Don't go anywhere."

"I won't."

Michael led Will out of the room. The crowd of spectators hadn't dissipated, so I shut the door.

I sat down at Will's desk, gathered up the pictures, and tore them to pieces, ignoring the pain in my hand as I did so. I wanted to burn them, dunk them in the kerosene I used for my flaming torches, but that had been confiscated weeks ago.

No way in hell had Will made those pictures.

I picked up the phone and dialed Melanie's number.

"Hello?" she asked on the third ring.

"Hey."

"Hi! How's it going?"

"All right."

"Are you okay? You sound weird."

"No, no, I'm fine. I just wanted to call."

"I'm glad you did."

"I need you to do me a favor."

"Sure. Anything."

"Just . . . just make sure you keep your door locked tonight, okay?"

There was a long silence on the other end.

"You there?" I asked.

"Yeah. Is there something wrong, Alex?"

"No, there's nothing wrong. It was a funny dream I had, that's all. Sorry if I scared you. Look, I should go, I fell asleep at my desk and woke up in the middle of a nightmare, no big deal."

"We can talk as long as you want."

"No, you need to get some sleep; you've got an early class."

"I could come over."

"No, really, I'm fine. Just got kind of spooked."

"I love you."

"I love you, too."

I wrote Michael a note promising him that everything was fine and that I'd be back in the morning and slipped it under his door. Then I left the building, walked to Melanie's dorm, and found a good vantage point where I could sit outside and keep watch throughout the night.

* * *

As the first students started to emerge from their dorms and head off to class, I walked to Darren's room and knocked on his door.

"Hey, Alex," he said, grinning as he answered. His nose was red and swollen. "That was one hell of a punch you threw. I think you probably hurt me as bad as you did him."

"Can I come inside?"

"Jeez, aren't we Mr. Formal? Yeah, c'mon in."

I walked inside his room. Darren shut the door behind me, then went across the room and plopped down on his bed. "Did you even sleep?"

I shook my head.

"Why not? Hand hurt too much?"

"My hand's fine. Did you do the pictures?"

"Dude! I adore Melanie! You're all glowy and stuff when you're around her. I'd never do something like that. Why would you even think that?"

"Because Will said he didn't do it and I believe him."

"You believe that freak?"

"Yeah, I do."

"I'm hurt. I'm really hurt. Do you really think that putting up death pictures of your girlfriend is something I'd do?"

"You faked a journal to get my friends kicked out of school."

Darren let out an incredulous laugh. "I was twelve! Holy shit, I thought we were long over that!"

"I thought we were, too."

"How could I have even done it? I don't have a key."

"You've heard me complaining to Will lots of times that he leaves the door unlocked."

"So, what, you think I made up some pictures of Melanie, snuck into your room, stuck 'em on your wall, and waited for you to blame Will?"

"Yeah."

"Why would I do that?"

"That's what I'm here to find out."

Darren gave a slight nod. "Did you notice that you haven't backed down?"

"Huh?"

"You haven't backed down. I said I didn't do it, and you didn't apologize and pretend everything was okay."

"So?"

"So that's good. How did it feel to punch him?"

"That's not what this is about."

"That's *exactly* what this is about. How did it feel?"

"It felt good."

Darren grinned. "That's how it was supposed to feel."

"It felt good when I did it, because I was more pissed off than I've been in my entire life. Then I realized that he wasn't the one who deserved it, and it felt absolutely sickening."

"That's understandable. But you can get over that. Focus on how good it felt to finally let that son of a bitch know what you thought about him."

"That's *not* what I thought about him. I made a mistake."

Darren was silent for a long moment. "Do you want a Coke or something? I've got some in the fridge."

"No."

"Yeah, I made the pictures. But don't flip out on me . . . hear me out, okay?"

I nodded as I clenched my fists.

"I swear to you, it wasn't because I have any bad feelings about Melanie. None at all. I just wanted you to let out some frustration. It felt good, right?"

I didn't respond.

"Yeah, it felt good," said Darren, standing up. "If we'd thought to lock the door, I could've held him while you beat him into a bloody smear."

"He didn't do anything."

"Maybe not. But it still would've felt good."

"You stay away from Melanie."

"You're not listening, Alex. This isn't about Melanie. This is about you. This is about feelings that you have that you need to let out. I watch you. I know what you're like."

"What am I like?"

"You're like me."

I shook my head. "I have no idea what you're talking about, but I don't want to see you ever again."

Darren chuckled uncomfortably. "Are you breaking up with me? Shouldn't we have a trial separation first?"

"It's not funny."

"No, it's not. I'm sorry." He crouched down, reached underneath his mattress, and withdrew a dark red pocketknife. It looked just like the one he'd had as a kid. The one he'd used to cut up Killer Fang. He snapped out the blade, rested it on his mattress, and stepped away. "Pick it up," he told me.

"Why?"

"I want you to cut me."

"You want me to *what?*"

"Cut me." He bent his left arm in front of his chest. "Not deep or anything, not so that I need stitches, but a few cuts to draw blood."

"There's something really wrong with you," I said, turning toward the door.

"*No!* Hear me out! Please!"

I turned back to face him.

"Take the knife and slash my arm a few times. I promise I won't retaliate. I just want you to know how it feels."

Suddenly I understood. "You want to tell the cops that I cut you, right? Show them my fingerprints on the knife? Nice try, asshole."

"No, no, but that's good. Calling me an asshole is good. How about this? Tell me what to cut. Nothing deep, nothing to get me sent to the hospital, and I won't mark up my face, but anything else is fair game. Tell me where to cut myself and I'll do it."

"So, what, you're a sadomasochist now? Get some help, Darren!"

Darren violently shook his head. "No, you've got it all wrong. I don't *want* to cut myself. But I want you to see how it feels to *make* me do it."

"I'm outta here."

Darren quickly grabbed the knife and lifted his shirt. "Tell me to do it."

"No way in hell."

"Damn it!" Darren flung the knife at the mattress. I flinched as it bounced up, thinking that it might fly across the room at me, but it struck the wall beside the bed and dropped to the ground.

"I just wanted to help you," Darren said, his voice weak.

"Get help for yourself first," I told him. I left the room. He didn't follow me.

* * *

Michael had always been a fairly easygoing guy, but now he was absolutely furious.

"You had me worried sick! Do you realize that Will is talking about pressing charges? I've got him calmed down, but you need to take this seriously."

"I am."

"Then act like it!"

"Okay," I said, and then I told him everything.

By the time school officials got there, Darren was gone. He'd left most of his stuff behind, but he'd taken the knife.

Technically, he'd committed no crime, and so while I would've preferred an all-out police manhunt, he was merely considered a missing person.

His parents had no idea where he was.

Two days later, his car was found in a grocery store parking lot, but there were no clues as to where he'd gone.

Upon my recommendation, the police checked the cabin owned by his parents, but nobody had been there since they'd last used it during the summer.

I offered Will the most heartfelt apology I could manage. He told me to go fuck myself. But he didn't press charges against me, asking only that he get the room to himself. I moved in with Anthony, a personality-free elementary education major who was more than a little annoyed to be losing his single room.

Melanie was completely creeped out by the whole thing. She made me describe the pictures for her, which I did, very reluctantly.

The week following the incident was pretty bad, but then things settled down and returned more or less to normal. Instead of staying at campus over Thanksgiving break, I went home with Melanie and met her fantastic parents. They loved me as much as I loved them. In fact, they were so gracious that I turned Melanie down when she offered to sneak into the guest bedroom with me the second night . . . no sense risking an awkward, unpleasant situation by getting caught. I was not quite as strong-willed when she slipped into the shower with me the next morning, but the spray of water covered the noise.

After Thanksgiving, I got promoted to head busboy. The cooks and servers still gave me shit, but the dishwashers and other busboys were under my command.

I continued getting good grades on my tests and papers.

Melanie and I said "I love you" a ridiculous number of times a day. In a rare demonstration of personality, Anthony kept count in a notebook.

And just before Christmas, as I was walking along the sidewalk after dark, listening to loud music to relieve some of the stress of studying for final exams, a black van pulled up alongside me.

I turned down the volume and kept walking, picking up my pace.

The driver side door opened and somebody got out.

As he broke into a sprint, I did the same, but he tackled me from behind and knocked me to the ground. A gloved hand punched me in the face. Something jabbed into my side. I stopped struggling as everything went blurry, and then dark.

CHAPTER SIXTEEN

When I woke up, my hands were tightly bound together with duct tape and covered by yellow mittens. My bare feet were bound together as well, and another strip of tape was over my mouth. I was in the back of the van, lying on a comforter that didn't live up to its name. I went into an immediate panic attack, unable to breathe through my nose fast enough to get the oxygen I needed, terrified that I was going to suffocate.

Darren glanced back at me from the driver seat. "Hey, easy back there! Calm down! It's going to be okay. I'll get that tape off your mouth as soon as there's a good place to pull over."

I screamed at him through the duct tape.

"Don't freak out on me, dude," Darren said, returning his attention to the road ahead but adjusting the rearview mirror so that he could watch me. "You know I'm not going to hurt you if I don't have to."

I didn't know that at all. I rolled onto my side and frantically tried to pull my hands apart, but of course the duct tape didn't give. I tried to pull my feet apart and had the same lack of success.

"If you want to tire yourself out, that's fine with me," said Darren. "We've got another eight hours left. When we get to a rest area, I'll give you another shot if you'd like to sleep some more."

I didn't want to sleep some more. I wanted to find out what he was planning to do with me. And I wanted to know if he'd done anything with Melanie.

"Do you want to listen to some music?" he asked. "The stations here are crap, but I've got some CDs. How about something mellow? You like Neil Diamond? I've got his greatest hits right here." Darren put the CD in the player and turned up the volume. "If you want me to change it, just nod your head, okay?"

I rolled onto my back again and continued to struggle. I scraped the mittens against my mouth, trying to get the duct tape off.

"Exit in four miles," Darren said. "I'll pull off there and then we can make you more comfortable."

I stopped struggling. This wasn't going to work. If I was going to escape, I'd have to surprise him, and to do that, I needed to conserve my energy.

God, what if he'd done something to Melanie?

I lay silently, listening to "Sweet Caroline." We were definitely on a freeway, but I couldn't see outside of the van to pinpoint our location beyond that. All I knew was that it was dark outside.

As the song ended, the van slowed down and took the exit. A couple of minutes later the vehicle came to a stop. Darren turned off the engine and looked back at me.

"How are you feeling?"

I knew he couldn't see me giving him the finger

through my mitten-covered hand, but I did it anyway. Darren leaned over and reached for something that was blocked by the passenger seat. I heard him open the glove compartment. When he looked back at me, he had a gun.

"I don't want to shoot you, Alex. I really, really don't. But let me make this clear. If you try anything, I won't shoot you in the head; I'll shoot you in the arms, legs, and stomach and let you bleed to death. It's not a fun way to go. Do you understand me?"

I nodded.

"Let me add to that. If you try anything, I'll also hunt down Melanie and do the same thing to her. Got it?"

I nodded again. I was still absolutely terrified, but at least now I had the relief of knowing that Melanie was safe. For the moment.

"Good." Keeping the gun pointed at me, Darren got out of the driver seat and moved into the rear of the van. He pressed the gun tightly against my stomach. "It takes a long time to die from gut-shot wounds," he informed me. "Don't make me prove it. No bities." With his other hand, he ripped the duct tape from my mouth.

There were a million questions I wanted to ask and a million profanities I wanted to scream, but I remained silent except for my panicked breathing.

"Don't hyperventilate on me," said Darren. "Just breathe in . . . breathe out . . . breathe in . . . breathe out . . . envision a happy little meadow . . ."

"Where's Melanie?" I asked.

"I don't know. I didn't touch her. This is about *you*,

Alex. You and me. I know you're scared and I know you're angry, but it's all going to work out, I promise."

"Where are you taking me?"

"My parents' cabin. Duh."

"The police will find us there."

"I hope not. I'd rather have you as a partner than a hostage. Anyway, we won't be there long. Do you have to go to the bathroom?"

"No."

"I brought a little jar if you decide that you do. I've got some drinks and snacks in the cooler. Beer, too." He grinned. "Wouldn't it be funny to get arrested for underage drinking?"

I didn't return his grin. "Are you going to undo my hands and feet?"

Darren looked genuinely apologetic. "I can't, dude. It's not that I don't trust you, but I'm going to be driving and I can't keep the gun on you the whole time. You've got plenty of room back here so you can change positions whenever you want. You'll be okay. Do you want another shot? It'll make the ride go quicker."

I shook my head. No way in hell did I want to sleep through a possible escape opportunity.

"Do you want a beer?"

"No."

"Mountain Dew?"

"No."

"Chips? Beef jerky?"

"Nothing."

"Okay, suit yourself. We'll stop at the next rest area if you change your mind."

"Darren?"

"Yeah?"

"I changed my mind."

"About the beer?"

"No."

"Then about what?"

"About the knife. I'd like to cut you now."

Darren let out a high-pitched laugh that hurt my ears. "See, *that's* why I like you so much," he said, moving back into the driver seat. "We're gonna have some great times."

We didn't speak during most of the ride. I had nothing to say. I accepted a few gulps of Mountain Dew and two strips of beef jerky at the next rest area, but regretted it when the need to urinate became too much to bear. Fortunately, I was able to manage the process of peeing into a jar well enough despite the mittens and Darren's assistance was not required.

After three hours that felt like thirty, I started to wish that I'd accepted the shot.

I wondered if anybody was looking for me. Anthony would assume that I was with Melanie. Melanie would assume that I was in my room asleep. I had no exams scheduled until late this afternoon, so I could easily go that long without being missed.

I smiled involuntarily at the irony that, given the choice, many students would rather be trapped in a van with a psycho than face their final exams. Perhaps Darren would let one of them trade places with me.

Six hundred eighty-three hours later (in mental time), Darren pulled off onto a dirt road. "We're almost there," he told me.

An extremely bumpy twenty minutes later, Darren stopped and shut off the van. "Gotta check on a couple of things," he said. "Back in a sec."

He got out of the van, taking the keys with him. I lay there for a moment, and then frantically began to struggle with the duct tape. Sure, there was virtually no chance that I'd be able to free myself in time to deliver a surprise kick to the face, but maybe the gods were smiling upon me and the tape would rip.

The gods were not, in fact, smiling upon me. I at least hoped they weren't laughing at me.

The rear doors to the van slid open. Darren stood outside, pointing the gun at me. "Scoot over here," he said.

I obliged. The comforter bunched up beneath me as I tried to slide toward the rear door, but I managed well enough.

Darren reached into his jeans pocket and took out the familiar knife. He snapped out the blade. "I'm going to cut your feet free," he said. "Again, please don't make me shoot you."

"I won't."

He lowered the gun a bit, aiming it at my groin. "Make sure you don't."

"I said I won't."

Darren sawed away at the duct tape. He'd used a lot of it, and it took a couple of minutes, but finally my feet were free. Darren stepped back from the van.

"Get out and walk around a little bit to stretch," he said. "But don't try to run away. You know what will happen if you do."

"Enough with the threats," I said, with a lot more courage than I actually felt. "I understand that you have a gun, and I understand that you'll shoot me if I do anything wrong, so quit harping on it."

"You know, if you were like this all the time, we wouldn't be here right now. Go on, get out and stretch."

I got out of the van and nearly lost my balance, but managed to remain upright and slowly walked around, grimacing at the tingling in my legs.

We were in front of a small, one-story cabin. It was unpainted but didn't look at all rickety. There was no grass, but there was cactus everywhere.

Most notable was the fence. I couldn't tell how far back it went, but the left and right sides were each about five hundred feet from the cabin. Behind me, I could see that the fence was topped with razor wire.

I watched as Darren went to the front gate and slammed it shut, trapping us inside the prison. He locked a thick, black padlock and pocketed the key.

"What do your parents *do* here?" I asked.

"This is my recent addition," Darren said, gesturing to the fence. "Good thing we don't have any neighbors or they might get suspicious, huh?"

"You put this all up by yourself?"

"Of course not. I hired some people. There's no law against being a paranoid whacko who wants to keep the New World Order out."

"So why are we here?"

"Because I have a surprise in store for you, my friend. Here, give me your hands."

I held out my hands and Darren cut off the duct tape. I shook off the mittens and massaged my aching wrists.

"We're going inside now," he said. "I know you said to quit bringing up the gun thing, but if you freak out,

I have to shoot you. Don't freak out." He tossed me a small key. "Go open the door."

I walked over to the front door of the cabin. There were two windows but both were covered with dark red curtains on the inside. I inserted the key into the lock, turned the doorknob, and slowly pushed open the door.

The cabin seemed . . . well, like a normal cabin. I stepped inside. The floorboards didn't even creak.

Darren came in after me, turning on the light. "Not too shabby, huh?"

"What am I supposed to see here?"

"Nothing here. It's in the first bedroom. To your right. Door closest to you. Use the same key."

I unlocked the door and pushed it open. A woman lay on a small bed, gagged, her hands and feet tied to the bedposts. For a second I thought it was Trisha, but an instant later I realized that though there was a resemblance, this woman was several years older. Her face was tearstained, her wrists and ankles were raw and bloody, and she was wearing only a bra and panties.

My stomach dropped as if on the longest, tallest, scariest roller-coaster ride ever built.

I looked back at Darren. "I'm not going to hurt her," I told him.

Darren smiled sadly. "Yeah, I know. It'd make things a lot easier if you would. I've got a straight razor. You can't believe how tempted I was to use it, but I wanted to keep her fresh for you."

I shook my head. The gesture wasn't meant for Darren but for myself, to deny that something like this could be happening. The horror I was feeling was too intense to be real. If I closed my eyes, maybe it would all go away.

But I didn't close my eyes. It wasn't going to go away. I needed to keep myself focused to save this woman's life.

"I'm not doing it. You'll just have to shoot me."

"I don't believe that. I think if I shot you in the leg you'd do it. I think that if I put my gun in your mouth you'd do it. Don't you think it would be fun? Her skin parting. She'd scream and scream but we'd be the only ones to hear and appreciate it. She's a crack whore; nobody will miss her."

The woman whimpered and cried softly.

"I'm not doing it," I said. "You might as well just let her go."

Darren shook his head. "I'm not gonna let her go. We both know that. But I'm also not going to make you slice her up at gunpoint. Instead, we're going to do this as a game. See the dresser next to the bed? Open the top drawer."

"No."

"Goddamn it, Alex, don't get all resistant on me! Open the drawer!"

Avoiding the woman's eyes, I stepped over to the dresser and opened the top drawer.

Inside was a brand-new, shiny hatchet.

"It's yours," Darren said. "Take it."

I picked up the hatchet and clenched it in my fist, wanting nothing more than to hurl it at him, to embed it in his throat.

"Here's the game," he said. "We're going to let her loose in the yard. You have ten minutes to bring me back her head. Nothing else; just her head. If you don't do it, I'll find you, shoot you, and leave you to bleed to death while I laugh in your face. Then I'll cut her into pieces so thin they'll be invisible to the human eye. How does that sound?"

"I'm not doing it."

"Then how about we add another little twist to the rules? Follow me."

Darren backed out of the bedroom, keeping the gun pointed at me. I wondered if there was any possibility of flinging the hatchet at him before he squeezed off a shot. Pretty damn unlikely. But if he really did aim for my arm or leg, and I managed to get him in the face . . .

It wasn't going to happen. He'd shoot me before the hatchet even left my hand.

I walked back into the main part of the cabin. Darren used the gun to gesture to the other door. "Open it," he said. "Same key."

I did so. It led to another bedroom. And another person tied to a bed. A little girl, probably not more than six.

"Oh my God . . ." I whispered.

"Her mommy and daddy are probably frantic," said Darren. "She's been missing for two weeks now. Don't worry; I haven't done anything to her. But here's the deal: you have ten minutes to bring me the woman's head. After ten minutes, I start hurting this little girl. I start hurting her bad. She has tiny little arms and I bet they come off real easy. I will hurt her until you finish the game, or until I decide that it's game over. Now, is there any confusion whatsoever about how this is going to work, Alex?"

I shook my head, feeling as if I might pass out at any second. Or throw up. Or both.

"Close the door."

I closed the door, trying but failing to avoid looking at the little girl's frightened, pleading expression.

"Remember, Alex, I'm doing this for you. This is what you want. You just need a little nudge, that's all."

"You're completely sick in the head."

"But I embrace it. Think of it like escargot. Escargot is delicious once you try it, but first you have to get over the whole idea of eating snails."

"You're comparing murdering a woman to eating some fucking *snails?*"

"Maybe not a great metaphor, but yeah, I am. You'll see. Go sit on the couch."

"Darren, you don't have to do this."

"I know! That's the whole point! I don't *have* to do this, I *want* to do this! And you'll realize that you want to do it, too. I promise. Sit down."

I sat down on the couch, which was a good idea because my knees were about to give way beneath me anyway.

"Don't get up," Darren said. "I'll be back."

He went into the woman's bedroom. Ten seconds later he poked his head out. "Good boy," he said. "Keep doing that."

He disappeared again. I stayed where I was. Getting shot was not going to help my situation. I had to stretch this out as long as I could, figure out a way to get out of this. I was a smart guy . . . there *had* to be a solution.

The question was, could I come up with one in ten minutes?

A moment later, Darren poked his head out a second time. "You shifted," he said.

"No, I didn't."

"I know. Just messing with you."

As Darren left again, I glanced around the cabin, looking for anything that might be helpful. Nothing looked remotely beneficial to my plight. If only there was some way to get him to put down the gun, just for a second.

The woman stepped out of the bedroom. It clearly hurt her to walk, and her lips were trembling with fear, but she kept her head up, defiantly.

Darren followed her. "Sorry that she won't be much of a challenge to catch," he said. "I think I tied her too tight."

"I'll do it," I told him. "I'll cut her."

Darren looked at me and raised an eyebrow. "Really?"

"We can cut her together. That's what you want, isn't it?"

"Yeah. I'd love that. And we'll be doing a lot of it. But right now I think you're just trying to screw with me, so we're sticking with the game." He jabbed the barrel of the gun into the woman's back, hard. "Keep going."

He walked her over to the front door. "Tell him your name," Darren told her. "Prey is more fun when it isn't anonymous."

"Andrea," she said, voice cracking.

"Andrea who?"

"Andrea Keener."

"I'm sure Alex is pleased to meet you, Andrea Keener. Now, I'm going to give you a very short head start. Your first instinct is going to be to go for the van, but it's all locked up and you'll just be wasting your time. Open the door."

Andrea opened the front door.

"On your mark . . . get set . . . *go!*"

He shoved Andrea out the door. Then he pointed the gun at me. "That's enough of a head start, I think. Go get her, buddy!"

I sat there, paralyzed.

"Get moving!" said Darren. "Your ten minutes has started. I'm not really into hurting little girls, but I'll sure do it."

I forced myself to stand up. "I'll kill you," I told him.

"Fine. But kill her first."

I glared at him, but that glare couldn't come close to showing the extent of the hatred I felt for him at that moment. Hatchet in my hand, I ran out the front door.

CHAPTER SEVENTEEN

Andrea was gone.

My first thought was that she'd ignored Darren's advice and had gone for the van, but I quickly ran around the vehicle and she wasn't there.

Shit! With all of these cacti, there were plenty of places to hide. I lowered the hatchet and listened carefully for the sound of footsteps.

There had to be a way out of this. Maybe draw Darren out of the cabin somehow, then surprise and subdue him.

I caught a glimpse of motion on the left side of the cabin, and took off running in that direction.

I didn't know what I was going to do, but it certainly wouldn't involve chopping off Andrea's head and bringing it back to Darren as a trophy.

Had there been a window in the little girl's room? I couldn't remember.

Stop being ridiculous, I told myself. Even if there was a window, no way was I going to be able to break it, crawl through, untie the girl, and take her to safety.

I hurried after Andrea, moving as fast as I could

without running into a cactus. I wanted to shout after her, to let her know that I wasn't going to hurt her, but I couldn't risk letting Darren hear that.

I didn't have a watch. Had a minute elapsed yet?

I heard a cry of pain up ahead.

I picked up my pace, letting out a cry of my own as several cactus needles slashed across my shoulder.

How could I get Darren to come outside?

I could pretend that I'd killed Andrea, but he wouldn't fall for that.

What if she pretended that she'd killed *me?*

What if Andrea screamed that *she* had won the game, and when Darren came out to investigate, I let him have it with the hatchet?

Holy shit, this could work!

I picked up my pace a little more. I just had to find her, catch her, and explain the plan.

I stopped running and listened.

No sign of her.

"Andrea!" I said in a loud whisper. "Andrea, listen to me!"

Nothing. I walked forward, keeping alert for any signs of movement.

"I can get us out of this. I just need your help. Andrea, can you hear me?"

She answered with a primal shriek as she came out of nowhere. She knocked me to the ground and I howled in pain as my arm smashed into a patch of cactus.

She showered me with punches. I used the hatchet to try to deflect them, but most of them struck my chest. I turned my head to the side as she tried to claw out my eyes.

I wrenched my cactus-pinned arm free and struck her in the jaw. The blow didn't even faze her. She kept punching, harder and harder.

I bashed the flat side of the hatchet into her skull.

She dropped to the ground, sobbing with pain. I pushed myself up with my shredded arm and tried to keep my voice as calm as possible.

"Andrea, please . . ."

She dove at me again, fighting with an unrestrained fury that was terrifying. She shrieked with each punch, and it took every bit of my strength just to defend myself.

She grabbed my uninjured wrist and dug her fingernails into it, hard enough to gouge through the flesh.

I cried out and dropped the hatchet.

She grabbed for it and missed.

I delivered another blow to the jaw. I heard something crack, but she didn't seem to feel this one any more than she'd felt the first. Her eyes were wild, crazed, almost feral. Even if we did get out of this, I wondered if she'd ever regain her sanity.

She grabbed for the hatchet again and got it.

I yelled "Shit!" as she swung it over her head, ready and willing to bring it down upon me. I frantically scrambled backward, colliding with another cactus.

The hatchet slammed into the ground in front of me.

I kicked at Andrea's face but missed.

She yanked it out of the dirt and took another swing. This one also hit the ground, but was delivered with enough force that if she *had* hit my leg, I had no doubt she would have split it in two.

I kicked her in the face.

I got to my feet, in my panic and confusion using a cactus to brace myself. The needles ripped through my palm, breaking off as they did so.

Andrea got to her feet as well.

"Please," I said, gasping for breath. "I can get us out of this."

She looked at me. How long had she been tied to the bed? What horrors had Darren shared with her?

"Please . . ." I repeated, only now realizing that I had tears flowing down my cheeks. The cactus needles stung so badly that if I'd had the hatchet, I might have chopped off my hand to ease the pain.

"You can't do shit," she told me.

"I can! I've got a plan!"

"Me, too. Bring him your goddamn head!"

She let out another shriek and rushed at me. I turned and ran. Thank God it was my arm and not my leg that had been stabbed by the needles.

Now what the hell was I supposed to do?

I outran her easily. Maybe if I knocked on the door and begged for my life, Darren would take pity on me and end the game.

No. He'd shoot me in the face in disgust.

There had to be a way to reason with Andrea, to let her know that we were in this together.

How much time did I have left?

I kept running. The fence was just ahead.

I narrowly dodged the armlike stem of a large saguaro cactus.

My ankle twisted and I lost my balance, staggering into yet another cactus. I screamed at the pain and fell to the ground, jamming the needles in my palm even farther into my hand.

Suddenly, death didn't sound so bad.

I heard Andrea approach. I did everything I could to force the absolute agony out of my mind and stood back up, as Andrea threw the hatchet at me.

It struck me in the face, handle first.

The pain literally blinded me. I could see nothing but blurry shapes and spots of light. I just wanted to lie down and go to sleep. Wake up in the morning. Or not at all. It didn't matter.

I couldn't see her clearly, but I could tell that Andrea was rushing toward me.

I threw a punch.

Technically, it was less of a punch than a slap. A slap with my needle-covered hand that got her right in the face. She stumbled backward, bellowing and digging at her eyes.

She struck something.

Screamed.

And fell to the ground.

As my vision cleared, I crawled toward her, gasping and sobbing and trying to remember to breathe. She lay there, facedown.

I rolled her over. Her eyes were closed, and a large piece of bloody cactus was embedded in her neck.

She didn't move.

And I knew what I had to do.

It took me a few moments to find the hatchet, but I picked it up and dragged it over to her body.

I tried to envision Darren's face on her head.

She whimpered.

Oh, Christ . . .

Andrea opened one eye. Her body trembled a bit. Blood trickled down the sides of her mouth.

"Don't hurt me . . ." she said in a soft, pleading voice.

Not too far away, the little girl screamed.

My ten minutes were up.

Andrea gave me a positively heartbreaking look. "I don't . . . I can't die . . . my kids need me . . . I can't die . . ."

"Mommy it hurts it hurts make him stop Mommy . . . !"

I yanked out the cactus that was lodged in her neck. Then I lifted the hatchet.

Please die before I do this, I mentally pleaded. *Please be dead when the blade hits.*

Andrea opened her other eye. I tried to avoid her stare as I lined up the blade with her neck.

The little girl screamed and screamed.

I slammed the hatchet down . . . but at the last second I lost my nerve. The blade struck her throat, nowhere near as hard as intended. It dug into the flesh enough to break the skin but not hard enough to kill her.

Andrea gargled blood.

"My hand!" the little girl shrieked. *"Please stop please please please it hurts so bad!"*

I gripped the handle of the hatchet tightly in both hands, as if suffering my own pain from the needles would lessen my guilt.

Andrea still stared at me.

I brought the hatchet down on her neck as hard as I could.

It went in deep.

I wrenched it out of her neck and blood splattered against my pants and shirt. Andrea's eyes were still open. She had to be dead, but she was still staring at me.

"*Stop it!*" I screamed at her, slamming the hatchet down a second time. It still wasn't enough to sever her head.

I slammed it down a third time. Then a fourth. Then a fifth.

The little girl cried and screamed and begged for Darren to make the pain stop.

I grabbed a handful of Andrea's hair and lifted her head. Part of it was still attached to her body, but with a few seconds of effort I ripped it free. Then as I shouted a flurry of words that made no sense to anybody, especially me, I ran back to the cabin.

Darren was sitting in a wooden chair just outside the front door. He had the little girl with him, but smiled and set down the straight razor as he saw me approach. Her arms and legs were covered with streaks of red.

"Let her go!" I screamed, lifting up Andrea's head. Blood from her neck ran down my already bloody arm.

"I can't just let her run around, not with all the cactus," Darren said. "But I'll lock her in the bedroom where she can't get hurt. We'll take her back to her parents tonight."

I stood there, gasping, vision shifting in and out of focus as I waited for Darren to return. He pushed the chair out of the way and walked toward me, slowly applauding. The gun protruded from his pocket.

"*Great* job, Alex. You did go into overtime, but it looks like she put up quite a fight." He gestured to

Andrea's head. "You can drop that if you want. Unless you like the way it feels in your hand."

I let her slick hair slide through my fingers. Her head fell to the ground.

"How did it feel?" Darren asked.

My entire body was shaking. "You've ruined my life."

"No I haven't. I've changed it. How did it feel? It felt good, didn't it?"

"The only way in the fucking world that it would have felt good is if that fucking hatchet had gone through your fucking neck."

"Ooooh, murder brings out your potty mouth, huh?"

"I did what you told me to. I won the game. Let me take the girl home."

"You just need some time . . ."

"I don't need any time! I need you to get the fuck out my life, you psychopathic motherfucker!"

Darren actually looked hurt. "It'll feel good once you get over the initial shock."

I shook my head. "I don't know what you think you're trying to accomplish here, but you're trying to convert the wrong guy."

"We could be partners."

"No way."

"We wouldn't take any shit from anybody."

"No."

"C'mon, Alex, think about it! We could do what we wanted! Nobody would mess with us!" He was sounding almost whiny. "You and me! We could catch them together, bring them back here, take turns! Think how creative we could be working as a team! Think how much fun we could have!"

"You can shoot me in the head if you want," I told him, surprised by how steady my voice was. "But let me make this absolutely clear: I will *never* kill for you again."

"Not *for* me, *with* me!"

"Not at all!"

For a moment I believed that Darren was actually going to burst into tears. "I thought . . . I thought I saw something in you, Alex. The same thing I have."

"You were wrong."

He nodded. "Yeah, I guess I was."

"So let me take the girl home."

Darren seemed to become suddenly aware that he had the gun on him. He slowly removed it from his pocket, looked at it as if unsure what it even was, and then pointed it at me and pulled the trigger.

I went down, screaming and clutching my upper leg.

He slowly walked into the cabin, defeated.

I just lay on the ground, eyes squeezed shut. When I opened them, I was staring at Andrea's upside-down head.

A minute later Darren came back out of the cabin. He crouched down next to me, waved a cell phone in front of my face, then stood up and hurled it into the air. The cell phone sailed far into the backyard.

"I'm really disappointed, Alex," he said, eyes glistening. "I can't make you into something you're not, I guess. You won't be seeing me again. Have a good life. Give Melanie my best."

He walked out of my line of sight. I heard him swing open the front gate, get in the van, and drive away.

Then I began to drag myself along the ground, struggling desperately to maintain consciousness.

PART THREE

ENEMIES

CHAPTER EIGHTEEN

"Tracy Anne, you stop that right now!"

My daughter turned to look at me, grinned her adorable grin, and then proceeded to fling another handful of sand at the little shit who'd knocked over her castle. He deserved it, of course, but as a responsible parent it was my duty to keep this feisty almost-four-year-old from hurting the boys. I went over to the sandbox, scooped her up, and perched her on my shoulders.

"Donkey ride! Donkey ride!" she shouted, squealing with laughter.

Neither Melanie nor I were completely sure where Tracy had gotten the phrase "donkey ride" from. The only thing certain was that Melanie thought it was a lot funnier than I did, mostly because Melanie never played the role of the donkey.

I walked through the park, thinking that it wouldn't be too much longer before Tracy became too old to ride on my shoulders without breaking noteworthy bones. But for now I would continue to be a good daddy and give her donkey rides whenever she wanted, low ceilings notwithstanding. After all, she was the greatest, most beautiful daughter who had ever been born in the entire history of the world.

And I had the greatest, most beautiful wife in the entire history of the world, too. I was quite a lucky guy. Everybody else had to be jealous.

There's a kind of love where you want to know everything about a person, where every smile, frown, or tear is a glorious mystery to be solved. Where every freckle is an object of fascination. Where you'd rather spend two hours sitting at a bus stop with this person than a week on a Caribbean cruise alone. It's an infatuation, and it can't help but fade with time.

Then there's the kind of love that's a true *bond*, where this person is your rock, where you can't imagine living apart, where you know that no matter how bad things get, no matter how long that dark night of the soul lasts, you can depend on this person to keep you sane.

Melanie was my rock.

The year after I killed Andrea was a bad one. Melanie and I hadn't been together long, and there was absolutely no reason she shouldn't move on to easier relationships. This was a time of parties, of new and varied boyfriends, of enjoying the last time in life before truly adult responsibilities take over. Not a time to be giving up all of that to help me through my trauma.

But she did. She stood by me during the police investigation. She consoled me when I woke up screaming in the middle of the night, babied me when I woke up crying. Melanie didn't judge me for what I'd been forced to do, not even when Andrea's parents (who hadn't seen their daughter in years) tried to slap a wrongful death lawsuit against me.

The little girl's father was a lawyer. He got me out of that mess. Her mother made me more chocolate chip cookies than one human being could ever eat.

Darren's van was found behind a grocery store. Darren himself was never found. I saw him quite often, even though I knew he wasn't really there.

After sitting out the spring semester, I went back to Shadle University in the fall, at Melanie's insistence. We got an apartment together, which her parents didn't think was particularly cool but which they allowed to happen, even giving us a nice housewarming basket of fruit.

Melanie maintained a straight-A average all through college, even during the semester where she helped sustain my mental health. I explained that this proved that she didn't really need to spend those countless hours studying. She agreed, and continued to spend those countless hours studying.

We had lots of really great sex.

I asked her to marry me three times before she graduated. She turned me down. I asked her to marry me again the day she graduated. She told me to ask her again tomorrow. I did, and she accepted.

My parents offered to pay for the wedding, which weirded me out so severely that I was unable to share the news with Melanie for a week. Her parents took this as a personal insult. I joked that we should get married twice to keep everybody happy. Her parents didn't think this was very funny. It was later easily resolved by having my parents pay for the honeymoon, which I think was standard operating procedure anyway.

We honeymooned in Jamaica. We saw so little of

Jamaica that we might as well have honeymooned in Peoria.

Melanie went on to get her master's degree, but not before getting pregnant. It was not a planned pregnancy, and I quickly discovered that my dear sweet wife was not quite so dear and sweet while with child. She used a great deal of language that she would have to stop using once the baby was born. She made more than one disturbing comment about my testicles. Then she started putting peanut butter on her Froot Loops, which was really uncalled for.

And when Tracy Anne Fletcher was born, she wept and said that she was the most precious little baby in the world.

However, now she wasn't quite so little. "Done with the donkey ride?" I asked.

"Noooooooooo!"

"You're going to snap Daddy's spinal column."

She giggled.

"Watch out!" I cried. "There's a low hanging branch on that tree up there! I hope no little girls get caught on it and hang there forever and ever!"

"Noooooooooo!"

"Oh my goodness! We're getting closer! What are we going to do? They're going to have to name it the Tracy Anne Tree because there'll always be a Tracy Anne dangling from it! We're almost there!"

I let out a theatrical scream and ducked down so that Tracy safely cleared the branch. "Hooray!" she shouted.

"That was a close one. I don't know what I would've done if you'd been stuck on that tree. I'd have to pay birds to fly up there and feed you. And you know what birds eat, right?"

"Worms!"

"Do you want to eat some worms to practice?"

"Noooooooooo!"

"They're good. Mommy and I eat them for breakfast sometimes. I like them with ranch dressing."

"You're weird."

"I'm not weird," I insisted.

"You're weird."

"How weird?"

"*All* the weird!"

"That's pretty weird! Is Mommy weird?"

"No."

"Just Daddy?"

"Yes."

"What about Kitty? Kitty's weird." Kitty was her favorite stuffed animal and not, technically, a feline.

"She is not!"

"She's the weirdest of them all! She's so weird that she gives weird lessons to people who want to be weird. If you keep sleeping with her she'll make you weird, too."

"No she won't!"

"No she won't. You know why?"

"Why?"

"Because you're *already* weird!" I smiled at the lady walking her dog. "Wanna buy a weird kid?"

"Sorry. I've got two of my own."

"Half price, today only."

"Daddy!"

"We accept coupons from all of our competitors."

Tracy began to drum her hands on top of my head.

"Remember what I said about giving Daddy a concussion, sweetie." I let her down and took her by the hand. "I think it's time to head home."

"Noooooooooo!"

"Yeeeeeessss!"

"Is Mommy there?"

"She will be when we get back."

"Hooray!"

"Hooray!"

Tracy was parked on the living room floor, sitting far too close to the television screen. Melanie pushed up her glasses and gave me a kiss.

"Have fun at the park?" she asked.

"Of course. Have fun at the gallery?"

"Of course." Though she was overwhelmingly busy going for her PhD, she also volunteered two hours a week at the local art gallery. She enjoyed doing it, and it gave Tracy and I some father/daughter alone time. "Tracy, you're too close to the TV."

"Okay," said Tracy, making no move to rectify the situation.

"Scoot back."

"Okay."

"Now."

Tracy scooted back a distance that might be visible with an electron microscope.

"You heard your mother," I said.

Tracy scooted back a foot.

"I'm sure she'll look just as good in glasses as you do," I told Melanie, giving her another kiss. She returned the kiss, but then frowned. "There was a message for you."

From the way she said it, I knew exactly who the message was from. "Aw, crap. Tomorrow?"

"Yeah."

"Damn it."

I loved my wife. I loved my daughter. I hated my job. I had not ended up in architecture, but rather the corporate world, doing meaningless financial garbage that paid well but chipped away at my soul one meeting at a time. When it had been eight to five, Monday through Friday, I could live with it, but now every other weekend I was being called in to work mandatory overtime.

"Can't you just say no?"

"Yeah, and then not hear the end of it all week. Better to just put in the few hours and be done with it. They say it's temporary."

"They've said it's temporary—"

"—for the past six months, I know. What can I say? I have a lousy job." I kissed her. "If I were too blessed, I'd float up into the heavens and it would be really inconvenient to try and get me down."

"We wouldn't want that."

"Nope."

Tracy giggled hysterically at the television show she was watching. It was a poorly animated, inane program about a family of dishes that went on magical adventures.

"Does she have to watch that?" I asked.

"It's her favorite."

"It's going to make her dumb."

"It's no worse than what we watched when we were kids."

"No, actually, it's much worse. We had *cool* shows when we were kids. This show is going to make her dumb, I swear." I noticed that Tracy had moved closer to the television again. "Tracy! Scoot back!"

"Okay."

"Do you want me to shut it off?"

Tracy scooted back about two inches.

"On the couch."

"I can't see it on the couch!"

"Yes, you can. Move back there or I'll turn it off."

Tracy stuck out her lower lip in a pout, but slid back along the carpet and leaned against the couch.

"*On* the couch."

"Mommy didn't say I had to!"

"Mommy's saying it now," Melanie told her.

Tracy looked at us with disdain, and then got up on the couch.

"We're such mean parents," Melanie said.

"The meanest. Tonight you should wear your witch hat."

"I think I will."

We kissed again, and then joined our daughter on the couch to share in the joy of unspeakably crappy television programs.

It was a long week at work, as all of them tended to be. Friday was particularly bad because I kept flashing back to a very special, very surprising move Melanie had made in the bedroom the night before. I wanted her to do it again. It sounded much more fun than working on the spreadsheet I had up on my computer screen.

Being horny at work really sucked.

Mr. Grove, my boss, walked up to my cubicle. He was short, bald, and quite overweight, though he carried it well. He drummed his fingers along the side of my wall.

"Gonna need you to put in a few hours tomorrow,"

he said. "We've got a video conference with Lavin at two."

"I can't do it. Taking care of my daughter."

"Can't your wife do that?"

I shook my head. "She volunteers at the art gallery."

"If it's volunteer work, she can get out of it, right?"

"I can't do Saturdays. I can come in on Sunday if you need me."

"How long is your wife there?"

"One to three."

"So you can work until then, right? And then put in a couple of hours after three?"

"Yeah."

Mr. Grove chuckled. "Good thing you're salaried or you'd blow the hell out of our department's budget. Nah, I'm just kidding, Alex. I appreciate all you do for us."

"Thanks."

"See you at seven."

"Yeah."

I went back to the fun-filled spreadsheet.

Melanie was not feeling up to doing the special move again that night, but we engaged in some traditional activities that were more than satisfying. I set the alarm for six, grumbling loudly about how unfair it was to lose a wonderful day of sleeping in.

"You don't get to sleep in anyway," Melanie said. "Tracy wakes us up with her cartoons."

"Yeah, but someday she'll be too old for cartoons and we'll miss it," I said. "On the other hand, my job will go on forever. A long, dark, empty forever."

"So when are you going to look for a new one?"

"I dunno. When Tracy's in college, I guess."

"Be serious."

"I just don't want to quit this job and find myself in something worse. At least the people I work with are tolerable. I could end up with one of those psycho bosses who throw furniture and breathe fire."

"Alex, you're not happy."

"I'm *very* happy."

"But you're not happy at work."

"It makes coming home all that much sweeter."

Melanie snuggled more closely against me. "Yeah, well, it would be sweeter to be woken up by cartoons tomorrow instead of the alarm."

"I'll just tell them I'm not doing any more overtime. I'll march right into Mr. Grove's office and say, 'Hey, you son of a bitch, you ask me to do any more overtime and I'll kick your ass from here to Scandinavia!'"

"Call me before you do it. I'll want to see that."

"Will do."

We kissed and went to sleep.

It really, really sucked when the alarm went off.

"Tracy Anne!" I shouted, as the bully kid ran off crying. She'd really gotten him good with that handful of sand. I was pretty sure he'd swallowed at least a few ounces. But, again, though he deserved it, I couldn't be responsible for raising a sand-flinger.

"You need to be nice to people," I told her, lifting her out of the sandbox.

"He was mean."

"Yes, he was. But if you're nice to people like that it drives them *crazy*."

"I want to swing."

"Then swing you shall."

I carried her over and gently placed her on one of the swings. "Do you want a great big push or a tiny little push?"

"I can do it myself."

"You don't want Daddy to help?"

"Nope. See?" She began to pump her legs. Very little happened. "Start me."

I gave her a push. She quickly got into the rhythm and began swinging herself. "See? I can do it!"

"Yep, you sure can!" Well, that was disappointing. I walked to one of the benches to watch the show. Only four years old (next week) and she no longer required my swinging assistance. Pretty soon she'd only need me for cosigning loans. Damn.

I watched her swing. She looked a lot like Melanie. The same blonde hair, deep blue eyes, and an almost identical smile. Not as much of a klutz, though, which made Melanie happy.

Something struck me in the back of the head.

I cursed and then automatically apologized for cursing. There was definitely going to be a lump there. I looked around and saw that I'd been hit with a baseball. A couple of kids, probably fifth or sixth graders, hurried over to collect it.

"Be more careful next time," I told them.

"Screw you."

I blinked. "I beg your pardon?"

"Screw you, old man."

Okay, I did *not* need elementary school kids saying "screw you" to me, and I most *certainly* didn't need to be called an old man at twenty-six years of age. "Excuse me, but you hit me with your baseball. You could really hurt somebody. There are little kids playing around here, so you need to be more careful."

"Gimme the ball back, bitch."

I couldn't believe it. I wasn't going to let this mouthy little punk talk to me like that. "Where are your parents?"

"Smoking crack with yours."

The kids laughed and high-fived each other for such a deliciously clever retort. I wanted to hit them in the back of the head with the baseball, but somehow I didn't think that would be mature behavior.

"You know what, get out of here," I told them.

"I said, give the ball back, bitch."

"It's mine now."

"Give it!"

"I'll tell you what. Get your parents to come ask me for it. We'll have a little chat."

The kid gave me the finger.

"Get out of here before I kick your butt."

"Ooooh, we should call the cops! He threatened us!"

"Here," I said, tossing the ball as far as I could manage. "Go get your ball, you little creeps."

"You throw like a bitch."

I glanced around to see if anybody else was hearing this. My God, if Tracy Anne ever started to behave like this, I was going to blister her little—

She was no longer on the swing set.

CHAPTER NINETEEN

"Tracy Anne!" I shouted. "Come back here, honey!"

It was okay. She had a short attention span and she'd gotten bored with the swings and wandered off, that was all. She was fine.

"Tracy Anne!"

I turned back to the kids. "Did you see where my daughter went? She was on the swings. She had a pink dress."

"Screw you."

"Come on, this is important, did you see where she went?"

The kid gave me the finger again. I hurried across the park, calling out for my daughter. She couldn't have gotten far. I'd only been distracted for a minute.

Sometimes a minute is all it takes . . .

No! I wasn't going to be one of those parents who had their children snatched away from right under their noses. She'd just wandered off, that's all.

I frantically ran around the park. No sign of her. "Tracy Anne!"

Oh, Christ. Where was she?

Five minutes later, I pulled out my cell phone. She could be in some stranger's car, miles away by now. How could I let those kids keep my attention away from her for so long? How could I ever tell Melanie what I'd—?

"Sir?"

A woman, the same woman who I saw walking her dog through the park on a regular basis, waved at me. She was holding Tracy by the hand.

"Oh, thank God!" I ran over to them, crouched down next to my daughter, and hugged her tightly. "Don't ever do that again, sweetheart! You had Daddy scared out of his wits!" I looked up at the woman. "Thank you so much!"

"She was behind the trees over there," said the woman, pointing.

"I owe you a million. I'll walk your dog anytime you want. Or I'll clean up after it when you walk it. Anything."

"I'll have a pooper-scooper specially made for you," the woman said. She ruffled Tracy's hair. "You stay by your daddy from now on, okay?"

Tracy nodded. The woman left.

"Promise me you'll never do that again," I said.

"I didn't mean to."

"I know you didn't mean to, but you have to always stay where I can see you. I can't see you when you're behind the trees."

"The man took me there."

The impact of her words was like a kick to the gut. "What man?"

Tracy sniffled. "The scary man."

"Did he hurt you? What did he do to you?" I realized that I was frightening her even more and forced myself to calm down. "Did the man do anything to you?"

She shook her head.

"Did he say anything to you?"

"He said happy birthday."

"Is that all?"

"And he gave me a present."

And then I realized that my daughter was holding an object with a small bow on it. A very familiar dark red pocketknife.

"Don't worry, Mr. and Mrs. Fletcher, we *will* get him," Officer Bradley Reitz assured me. "Your daughter's description should be a big help. She's a smart kid, that one."

"Yeah, she is," I said, tightly holding Melanie's hand.

The "scary man" had long black hair and wore sunglasses. Tracy had pointed to one of the other officers to indicate that he had a mustache and goatee.

"And he never brushes his teeth," Tracy said.

Officer Reitz had pulled up a picture of Darren on his computer screen and asked Tracy if that was the scary man. She said no. He did some astonishingly quick work with the mouse and keyboard, and then showed Tracy the same picture, doctored with sunglasses, longer hair, and a mustache and goatee.

She said it was him.

But of course I had no doubt. Nor was I supposed to. The pocketknife was more than enough to let me know that he was back, and now he was after my family.

We had police protection twenty-four hours a day.

Melanie cried a lot, and I comforted her and told her that everything was going to be fine. I believed it. If we were cautious and alert, he couldn't hurt us.

I truly believed that.

We sat at the dinner table. Tracy Anne took a way-too-big bite of her bread and wiped her buttery mouth off on her sleeve.

"Napkin," said Melanie.

Tracy used the napkin to wipe off her sleeve. "Mommy, where's my birthday present?"

"Your birthday isn't until tomorrow, sweetie."

"No, the one I already got."

"That wasn't a real birthday present, sweetie. You can't have that one."

Tracy Anne cried.

We put bars on the windows and upgraded our alarm system. The old alarm system had been top-of-the-line when it was installed, but now we needed more.

Tracy slept in our bed.

I personally walked her into the preschool class-room each day. I would've stayed in the classroom all day if I'd been able to (my finger painting skills could use some development, anyway). A cop kept watch over her day care.

I watched for Darren in every shadow, every corner, every face in the crowd. He couldn't hide from me, and he was *not* going to get my daughter.

But you can't live like that forever.

The police stopped their around-the-clock surveil-lance.

Tracy moved back to her own bed. Every time I

snapped awake, which was several times a night, I'd go check on her.

I had to let Tracy run and play with other kids, even if my heart gave a jolt every time I thought they were running a bit too far.

Weeks passed.

Melanie missed her period. Tracy overheard us talking, and bounced around the house shouting happily about the little brother or sister she was going to have. As it turned out, Melanie wasn't pregnant but stressed out to the point where it affected her body's internal rhythms. The doctor prescribed medication. Melanie refused to fill the prescription.

Tracy finally made the bully cry. Her sand castles remained intact after that.

I threw a huge surprise birthday party for Melanie. Everybody was required to show up as a historical figure without saying who it was, and during the party there was a contest to see who could correctly guess the most. We discovered that our friends had an extremely poor grasp of historical figures, but that Tracy made an adorable Joan of Arc. That night, I made love to Melanie while wearing my Napoleon hat.

Months passed.

We bought Tracy her first pet, a goldfish. Tracy decided that she wanted a great *big* goldfish and poured the entire canister of fish food into the bowl. Goldilocks perished. We told her that the fish had gotten so very big that it grew arms and legs and walked out of the aquarium and went off to live in the ocean.

My job continued to suck.

Melanie's parents' house in California was damaged

by an earthquake, and they came to live with us for three weeks. I realized that as much as I liked her parents, three weeks was way too fucking long.

Tracy lost her first baby tooth. Unfortunately, it was a direct result of trying to swing high enough to do a loop-de-loop.

I accidentally washed Melanie's favorite white shirt with the darks, which somehow progressed to the worst fight we'd had in our entire marriage, and which was resolved with absolutely exquisite make-up sex.

And I had a dream where Darren slept in Tracy's blood.

It was a year later when Melanie and I lay snuggled on the couch, watching television.

"Did you make the invitations?" she asked.

"All printed out and ready to go." I slid my hand over her clothed breast.

"Behave."

"It wasn't me."

She swatted my hand away. "Did you ask Mrs. Gonzalez if she could help?"

"I did."

"And?"

"She said of course. Some people get giddy at the thought of doing traffic control in a house filled with five-year-olds."

"Don't be sarcastic."

"I'm not being sarcastic. I think it's great that Tracy wanted to invite her entire class. I'm just wondering how a pair of outcasts like us created such a social butterfly."

"Maybe she'll marry well and bring us riches in our old age."

"Cool," I said. "Do you hear her?"

Melanie listened carefully. "Is she singing?"

"Yep."

"Maybe we should go check on her."

"Because she's singing?"

"She might be singing that she wants a glass of water."

"That sounds like her. Don't get up. I'll be back."

I extricated myself from the snuggle position and got off the couch. I carefully tiptoed down the hallway and listened at Tracy's door which, as always, was open a few inches to let in just enough light to keep the monsters out.

"Choppie choppie choppie," she sang quietly. *"And the head goes ploppie."*

I pushed open her door. Tracy sat up in bed, playing with a rag doll.

"Whatcha still doing up, sweetie?" I asked.

Tracy shrugged. "Dunno."

I sat down on the bed next to her. "It's pretty late. You've got school tomorrow."

She poked the birthmark on my chin. "Funny spot!"

I poked her chin back. "What song was that?"

Tracy raised her hand and pounded it three times against the doll's neck, like delivering a karate chop in rhythm with the song. *"Choppie choppie choppie, and the head goes ploppie."*

"Why are you singing that?"

"It keeps my dolls from coming alive."

"Don't you want your dolls to come alive? I think that would be pretty neat."

Tracy shook her head, very slowly and very seriously. "They'll get me."

"You have friendly dolls. What makes you think they'd get you?"

"The man told me."

This doesn't mean anything is wrong she could be talking about anybody it's just a song they could have taught it to her in kindergarten she's not in danger . . .

"Which man?"

"The nice man."

"Who's the nice man?"

"He said he'd protect me."

"Tracy, Mommy and I will protect you. We'll always protect you. Is the nice man somebody from your school?"

"No."

"Day care?"

She nodded. "Billy fell off the slide and he was crying and Mrs. Duza thought he had a 'cushun and the nice man came and talked to me."

"And he told you about your dolls?"

"He said the song would protect me from them." She chopped at her doll again. *"Choppie choppie choppie and the head goes ploppie."*

"Don't sing that anymore," I snapped, much louder than I'd intended. "You're supposed to always tell me when you meet a stranger. Always. You know that!"

"He protected me."

"Damn it, Tracy, he could have hurt you!"

Tracy looked at me as if I'd slapped her. Melanie hurried into the room. "What's wrong?"

"I think Darren is back again."

"Oh my God." Melanie scooped Tracy out of bed.

"Did you see him, honey? Did you see the scary man?"

Tracy shook her head.

"Do you remember what the scary man looked like?" I asked. "You saw him when you were almost four. Do you remember that?"

She shook her head again.

"It's him," I told Melanie. "It has to be." I wanted to scream and kick things and hold my daughter tight. "Did the man tell you anything else?"

Tracy nodded.

"What?"

"He said that some dolls came alive still."

"And what did he tell you to do?"

"Stab 'em with a pencil." Tracy bared her teeth and made a stabbing motion with her fist.

CHAPTER TWENTY

"We'll run," I said, pacing frantically but trying to speak softly and not wake up Tracy, who was in our bed. "We'll pack up, get the hell out of here, and move somewhere where he can never find us."

"Why won't he just go *away?*" asked Melanie, wiping her runny nose with a handkerchief.

"I don't know." The scariest part was that he was so patient. He'd waited eight years to show up again. Then another year between the pocketknife and the chopping song. Had he been spying on us all this time? Maybe he spent every day secretly watching Tracy at day care, just waiting for an opportunity like Billy falling off the slide. Or maybe this was exactly how he'd planned it.

Pocketknife before her fourth birthday.
Scary song before her fifth birthday.

Would he wait another year before he tried something else?

It didn't matter. We were moving. We'd move across the country, or go to Mexico, or go to fucking

Antarctica if we had to. Anything to get away from that maniac.

"I can't live like this," said Melanie. "I can't be scared all the time."

"We won't be."

"We *will* be! As long as he's out there, no matter where we go we'll always be scared. What kind of life will Tracy have?"

"The police will catch him."

"They haven't caught him in nine years! Why would they catch him now?"

"I don't know. I don't know what to do, Melanie! He's insane and he's fixated on me—!"

"On *Tracy*."

"—on Tracy, and I don't know how to handle the situation except to put a bullet through his brain. Which I'll do if I ever see the son of a bitch! But until then, we just need to get out of here. I'll quit my job, we'll pull Tracy out of kindergarten, we'll pack up, and we'll leave! We'll change our identity! We'll do whatever it takes!"

I could feel myself losing it. And this was probably exactly what Darren wanted. Why kidnap our daughter now, when he could make us fear for her safety for the next year? For the next ten years. For the rest of our lives.

The next day I quit my job. I'd wanted to do this since the day I started, but Darren had stolen the joy from this moment. Instead I felt sick to my stomach and depressed as I typed my e-mail of resignation. I'd fantasized about doing this hundreds of times, and even had a lengthy mental list of unflattering adjectives for Mr. Grove, but instead the e-mail was brief and regretful.

Melanie was absolutely heartsick over dropping out of school, but there was no choice. Most of her credits would transfer.

We had enough savings to sustain us for . . . well, not long at all, and that was if we cut into Tracy's college fund. That idea wounded Melanie more than anything else, but I swore that we'd replace it.

The plan was simple. We were going to get in our car and drive away. Darren couldn't find us if even we didn't know where we were going. We'd pack only what we could fit in the trunk of our car and drive off to a new future.

In a way, it was almost romantic.

It was also unnecessary, because as I sat in a booth at the local fast food burger joint, eating a flavorless lunch as I took a break from tying up the crucial loose ends of our life here, Darren joined me.

"Howdy," he said.

He looked horrible. He'd cut his hair short and the mustache and goatee that Tracy had reported were no longer there. But his face had a sunken look, as if he hadn't eaten in weeks, and his complexion was pale and sickly. He smiled at me, revealing rotted teeth.

"I've got cops following me everywhere I go," I told him. "You're fucked."

He shook his head. "No you don't. Your daughter does but you don't. Damn budget cuts." He chuckled. "By the way, I've got a gun. You cause me trouble and I'll start shooting people at random."

"Let me see the gun."

"Oooh, lost some of our trusting nature, huh?" He opened his leather jacket, revealing the handle of a pistol protruding from an inside pocket. He closed it up but kept his hand inside.

"You stay the fuck away from my daughter," I told him.

"No."

"If you touch her, I'll kill you."

"Maybe that's what I want. Can I have some fries?"

"Fuck you. They're mine."

"You get feistier every time we meet, Alex. I think Melanie is really good for you. I was pretty hurt that I didn't get invited to the wedding, though. Did you get the salad shooter I sent?"

I took a tasteless bite of my hamburger and didn't respond.

"You're actin' pretty brave there, buddy. Of course, you know that I'm not here to shoot you. If I wanted to do that, I've had hundreds of opportunities, and I'm speaking literally. Did Tracy sing you her song?"

Just lean over, you son of a bitch, I thought. If he got close enough for me to reach out and grab him, I'd slam the sick bastard against the table and bash him until his skull split open.

I might not even stop then.

"This is too public," said Darren. "Let's go for a drive."

"I'm not going anywhere with you."

He nodded at a booth behind me. "See that baby in the high seat? One shot and her head will look like the food they're trying to get her to eat. Then I'll shoot the mother, and then I'll shoot you. Then I'll slip out

that door right there"—he pointed behind me again—
"and flee the scene. I'll lay low for a year, maybe two,
and then I'll find your wife and daughter. Do you like
your daughter's fingers, Alex? They'd make a beautiful necklace, don't you think?"

"You rehearsed that, didn't you?"

"I don't get the feeling that you're taking me seriously," said Darren, pulling the gun out of his jacket.
"Let's rectify that."

"No!"

He quickly hid the gun under the table. "I hate
threatening babies," he said. "Don't make me do it
again."

"Where do you want to take me?" I asked.

"It's a surprise."

"I've seen your surprises."

"You sure have. How often do you think about that
hatchet going into her neck? I bet it made a great
sound, didn't it? Think she could see when you carried
her head around?" He shifted in his seat. "Get up from
the table slowly. Take the rest of the fries with you;
I'm starving."

I gathered up the fries and put them back in the
bag. Then, slowly as instructed, I slid out of the booth.

"Go out the back door."

I walked toward the back door, watching the baby
happily coo as its mother teased it with a slice of pickle.
I wondered if Darren really would have shot the baby
first.

Yeah, he would have.

I pushed open the door and walked outside the
restaurant. Darren stepped up right behind me and
shoved the barrel of the gun into my back. "Let's pick

up the pace," he said, as we moved across the parking lot.

I looked around for a cop, a security guard, anybody who could help me, but the only other occupants of the parking lot were a group of teenagers lost in their individual cell phone conversations. *Somebody* had to notice that he had a gun in my back, right?

"It's the blue one," Darren said, prodding me again. "It's unlocked. Get in the passenger side."

I opened the passenger door of the blue sedan and got inside. Keeping the gun pointed at me, Darren got in the driver's side. He switched gun hands, dug a set of keys out of his pocket, and started the car.

We pulled out of the parking lot, and then immediately into the parking lot of the grocery store next door. He drove around the back of it, next to a Dumpster, and then put the car into park.

"Get out," he said, waving the gun at me.

"You're letting me go?"

"Of course not. You're just switching seats. Get out."

I opened the door and got out. I considered making a run for it, but he could easily put a bullet into my back before I got anywhere close to safety. He reached down, pulled a lever, and the trunk popped open.

"I figured somebody at the restaurant would think it was suspicious if they saw you get in the trunk," he said, getting out of the car. "Gotta think of these things, you know. If anybody sees us, they're dead, so get in there quick."

I climbed into the trunk.

Darren slammed the lid shut.

* * *

I had a wristwatch that lit up when I pressed on the face. 1:37. 2:15. 3:19.

The car stopped at 3:44. I heard sounds that I was pretty sure were Darren refueling the vehicle. He didn't acknowledge my presence in the trunk with even a friendly tap on the lid.

We started off again. At 6:15 we stopped a second time, but I didn't hear any refueling. Probably a stretch and pee break. I wanted to pound on the lid, to scream for help, but I also didn't want to get anybody killed.

He refueled again at 7:42.

At 9:59, the car stopped. I heard something that sounded like an electric garage door opener, and then the car moved forward again and the engine shut off. I heard the garage door close, and a moment later Darren threw open the lid of the trunk. I blinked and shielded my eyes from the blinding light.

"Sorry about the ride," said Darren with no trace of sarcasm. "I couldn't risk anybody seeing you." He extended his hand. "C'mon, I'll help you out."

Though I would've liked to attempt some sort of amazing escape, my body was so cramped up after all those hours in the trunk that I simply took his hand and accepted his assistance. I promptly collapsed onto the cement floor.

The garage was tidy and nondescript, but I didn't like seeing the screwdrivers, pliers, hacksaws, and other tools mounted on the wall. I struggled to get back to my feet but my legs weren't working yet.

"Don't strain yourself," said Darren. "We're in no rush. We'll have ourselves a nice, relaxing evening, okay?"

"They'll be looking for me," I told him.

"C'mon, don't insult my intelligence. I know they're looking for you. It's not like you're some vagrant I yanked off the street. Melanie has gotta be heartsick right now. It kills me to do this to her, but you left me no choice."

"You have every choice in the world! You don't have to do any of this!" I used the rear bumper of the car to brace myself as I pulled myself to my feet. "You're the one who's always talking about controlling your own life."

"Okay, okay, I know what you're trying to do. 'A' for effort, buddy. Let's get inside. I'm sure you could use a drink."

Still unsteady, I walked with him inside the house. The living room was sparsely but tastefully decorated, with a pair of sofas, a recliner, and a small television. A large brown rug filled most of the center of the room. "Have a seat," Darren told me.

I plopped down on the recliner. My muscles were in absolute agony, but I tried to hide it as much as I could.

"I hate to seem untrusting, but there's a pair of handcuffs mounted to the side of that chair," Darren said. "Latch one bracelet around your wrist, please."

I did as I was told, snapping the bracelet shut over my left wrist.

"That's just temporary," Darren assured me. "I've got much better accommodations waiting for you. What do you think of the house?"

"Lovely."

"Two stories. Nice quiet neighborhood. And upstairs is my Gallery of Horrors. You'll get a kick out of it. Back in a second."

He disappeared into the kitchen. I tugged on the handcuffs, hoping that they might just pop free, but they held firm. Though I was scared shitless for myself, I at least knew that Melanie and Tracy Anne were safe for the time being.

Darren returned, balancing a tray with two tall glasses of iced tea, complete with lemon wedges. As he presented it to me, I grabbed the closest glass and gulped down the liquid fast as I could, letting it run down the sides of my mouth.

Then I threw the glass at him.

Though I'd desperately hoped for a direct hit to his face, Darren moved out of the way in time. The glass merely nicked his ear and shattered against the tile floor. He stared at me as if shocked by my poor behavior in his home, gently set the tray down on top of the television, and then punched me in the jaw so hard that it brought tears to my eyes.

"Don't *make* me get ugly!" he shouted, furious. "I will *fuck you up* if I have to! There are some really unpleasant times coming up in your life, so don't make them worse!"

I spat out some blood. "I figured you'd be more pissed if I didn't try to escape."

"No, see, this isn't about you anymore, Alex. That time is long gone. Right now this is about me. It's about me doing whatever I want to you. How about I show you?"

He stormed off into the kitchen. I yanked on the handcuffs, more frantically now, but he returned seconds later with a butcher knife.

"How about I give you a little slice on the cheek, huh, Alex? How does that sound? Sound good?"

"Okay, you've made your point."

"I don't think I have." He slashed the tip of the blade across my cheek. I winced and felt a warm trickle as he cut my other cheek even deeper. "You like that? Huh? C'mon, asshole, fight back! Try to kick me. See what I do."

"I said okay, you've made your point! Now get that knife out of my face!"

Darren stepped away. He looked a trifle embarrassed as he wiped the blade off on his pants leg and set it on the couch. "Just remember who's in control here," he said, softly.

"I won't forget."

"And don't patronize me." He sat down on the couch. "I don't even remember what I was saying. Oh, yeah, this isn't about you. It's about me. And pretty soon it'll be about Tracy Anne."

I stiffened.

"She's got what you had, you know. I can see it when I look at her. I could always sense it before, but I could never really *see* it before, y'know? It's beautiful. Just look into her eyes." He ran a hand through his hair. "You always fought it. I don't think she will."

"My daughter is not a killer."

"Not your choice. You can see it if you look. It's like a black fog. A beautiful black fog. You ever see it?"

"There's nothing to see."

He leaned back on the couch. "You're just not looking. Doesn't surprise me. Where do you think Melanie and Tracy Anne are right now?"

"Somewhere safe."

He nodded. "Yeah, I'm sure they are. But I can wait. That's where I screwed up with you. I was way too impatient. I thought that you'd see what you really were after you murdered whatever-her-name-was, but I messed that all up by rushing it. The fog wasn't completely there yet, not like it is with your daughter. I bet you it'll be even thicker the next time I see her. Hmmmm, I wonder when that will be?"

He got up off the couch and retrieved his own glass of iced tea. He took a long swig. "Ah, that hits the spot. You'll really wish you hadn't thrown that glass at me, because that means no refills, and you're going to get thirsty."

Darren set the glass back on the tray, and then bent down and grabbed a corner of the rug. He pulled it to the side of the room, exposing a small trapdoor. He winked at me and pulled it open. "I dug this all out myself," he said. "I've learned patience, but damn, it took forever. This ground is hard as a freakin' rock. Sorry there isn't much room, although it should be better than the trunk of my car.

"What'd I do with my gun?" he asked. A moment later he reached inside his jacket. "Oh yeah." He took out his set of keys, removed one from the ring, and tossed it to me. Then he pointed the gun at my face. "Unlock the cuffs."

I did so.

"This is the part where you really don't want to make any mistakes. Get in the pit."

"Listen to me, Darren. We can work something out."

"No, we can't."

"We can. I'm sure we can."

"You're getting dangerously close to making a mistake."

"If you shoot me, the neighbors will hear."

"There aren't any neighbors. That was a joke. And if there were, that'd be my problem, not yours."

"Darren, please . . ."

"Get in the pit!"

I stood up and walked over to the trapdoor. If the pit was bigger than the trunk of his car, it sure wasn't by much.

"Darren, you've got to listen to me. There's no reason for this. We can be friends again!"

"Treating me like I'm stupid is about as big of a mistake as you can make right now."

I was completely helpless. I couldn't let myself get locked down there, but I couldn't very well protect my wife and daughter lying dead with my brains splattered on the floor.

"I'll bring Tracy to you."

"What?"

"If you swear that you won't hurt her, I'll bring her to you."

"See, now, if I believed you, that would be a great little offer. Nice bluff, but sorry, no. Now please get moving."

I climbed down into the pit. It was just barely large enough for me to sit up, and didn't appear quite long enough for me to stretch out.

"You'll be in there for a while," Darren informed me. "It'll give you plenty of time to think. Think about your wife and daughter, and what I might be doing to them. See ya."

He closed the lid, casting me into complete darkness.

CHAPTER TWENTY-ONE

Being locked underground by a sociopath is highly overrated.

This is the kind of thought I used to keep myself sane. At first, I kept myself busy by screaming and pounding on the trapdoor until my hands were raw and bloody, not that I could see their condition. Then, for a change of pace, I curled myself up into the fetal position and cried.

Even so, I didn't realize just how bad things were for me until I'd gone three days without him checking on me. I'd managed the lack of restroom facilities as well as possible, trying to get it into the corner so that I wouldn't roll over into my own filth while I slept. The smell of shit and piss was sickening, but I could live through it. What I couldn't live through was a lack of water, and I was starting to wonder if I was ever going to get it.

Darren wouldn't just leave me to die down here, would he?

I did everything I could to stay sane down there. I played word games. I thought of happy times with

Melanie and Tracy. I sang. I tried to recite every single movie I'd ever seen in a theater. I made a game out of trying to guess what time it was before verifying it by pressing the face of my wristwatch.

On the fourth day, the watch light went out.

I felt something drip on me, probably imaginary, but I pictured Tracy lying on top of the trapdoor, Darren going at her with a hatchet, bleeding into my pit.

I stuck out my tongue, thinking how refreshing a drop of blood would be.

I giggled about that. Maybe I'd turned into a vampire. "I vant to drink your blood," I said. Or thought, since the words didn't seem to actually emerge from my lips.

Killer Fang the Rescue Dog. Too bad Darren chopped him all up, because otherwise he'd be digging me to safety right now.

I giggled myself to sleep.

When the trapdoor finally opened on the fifth day, I was so dehydrated and delirious that I thought it was Satan reaching down to grab me by the collar. I could see his red glowing eyes, feel the heat pouring from his skin, see his demonic tail swishing back and forth. Finally, he was taking me to hell.

Then I was floating. It was fun.

I became aware of my true surroundings as I woke up, lying on the living room floor. Darren was seated on the couch, watching me carefully.

"Tell me your name," he said.

"Alex."

"Good. You're not completely gone."

"Water . . ."

"Oh, yeah. I bet you'd kill for a drink of water, wouldn't you?"

I nodded.

"Too bad you're so weak. It'd be fun to test that out."

Either I lost consciousness for a moment or Darren teleported. He was hovering over me with a bottled water. "Here you go."

I took it from him and drank greedily, gasping for breath as I tried to gulp the entire bottle in one swallow.

"Whoa, whoa, take it easy, the water isn't going anywhere," Darren assured me. "This is your mental health day. I can't have you going completely bonkers. Today you get to stay outside of the pit. We've got food, water, books, DVDs; I even hooked up one of the old Nintendo systems. Bath first, though. You really need it."

I let the empty bottle drop out of my hands. My throat was still raw but I managed to ask: "What did you do to Melanie?"

"Nothing. Haven't seen her. I'm laying low, buddy. No rush. I've got all the time in the world."

He helped me into the bathroom, where a nice warm bubble bath had already been drawn. The water felt so good, so relaxing, that I wanted nothing more than to just slide under the surface and drown in it.

Put an end to my misery.

But then I'd never see my family again.

I stayed in the bath until the water had lost every bit of its heat. Darren fed me peanut butter crackers while I soaked, and nothing had ever tasted more delicious.

I spent the day eating, drinking, and watching immature comedies on DVD. I also spent it trying to figure out ways to overpower Darren, but I was always either handcuffed to the recliner or being held at gunpoint. Often both.

That evening, Darren hopped down into the pit with some paper towels and a baggie. I was warned of no fewer than six different consequences, all bad, if he heard so much as a scrape of the recliner across the floor. I watched the pit carefully, trying to figure out if I could drag the recliner over there and slam the trapdoor shut before he had a chance to make good on his threat, and decided that my chances for success were pretty decent if Darren happened to suffer a fatal heart attack and/or have all the bones in his legs snap for no particular reason.

And then I went back into the pit for three more days.

"Ready for another mental health day?" he asked, opening the lid. "Too bad. This is torture day."

He dragged me out of the pit.

Forced me up the stairs.

Showed me his collection of souvenirs.

Laughed as I screamed.

Strapped me to a metal table.

Took his time deciding what to use.

And went to work.

I don't think there was a regular schedule for the mental health and torture days, except that the two of them alternated and I thought it might have been one of each per week.

If my count was correct, there had been fifteen of each.

No, sixteen torture days. An ill-fated escape attempt earned me a bonus one of those. A long one.

Some days I wanted to die. Some days I vowed that I would *not* die until I'd seen my family again.

My hair grew down to my shoulders, although it also fell out in clumps. I often imagined that a nest of spiders was living in my beard. On my mental health days I begged Darren to let me shave, but he wouldn't allow me to have a razor, even an electric one.

I was emaciated, scarred, and so ghastly in appearance that if I ever did see Tracy again, she'd probably run screaming in terror from the monster who called itself her daddy.

At the end of what may have been the fifteenth mental health day, Darren disappeared into the bathroom for a long while. When he emerged, he had short blond hair, a dignified beard and mustache, wire-framed glasses, and looked like somebody who might teach Kafka and complain about the state of popular literature at a university.

"Like my disguise?" he asked, running his fingers through the false beard. "Not bad work, huh? Do I look trustworthy? Would I look trustworthy to your daughter?"

I jumped up, nearly wrenching my arm out of its socket.

"I've gotta scope things out, wait for the perfect moment, so I might be gone for a while. I'll put some food and water in the pit this time, just in case. And don't look so frowny, Alex. You've been waiting all this time to see them again, haven't you?"

The walls of the pit were closing in on me, making it impossible to breathe.

If he hurt either of them, I would kill him. I would pull on those handcuffs until I ripped my own arm off, and then I'd crush his throat with my remaining hand.

Or I'd strap him to his own torture table. Get my revenge, one minute for every minute he'd strapped me here. It would be a lot of minutes.

Or I'd just hug my wife and daughter close and never, ever let them go.

Though I don't know if this related to actual days, I slept four times before the trapdoor opened. Darren looked pleased as he extended his hand toward me.

"Success, baby! Oh, man, you would not *believe* how close this came to being a complete disaster. One teacher dead for sure, another one questionable, but I did it. I got 'em." He seemed practically giddy.

Through almost superhuman resolve I kept myself calm. This was it. This was when he might make a mistake. He couldn't watch three of us at once, and an escape opportunity might present itself.

But I was a little giddy myself. Though I would have given anything in the world, including my own life, for Melanie and Tracy not to be here with this madman, I couldn't help but feel happiness at the thought of finally getting to see them again.

I had countless questions to ask, but I remained silent.

After I got out of the pit, Darren cuffed my hands behind my back. He pressed his ubiquitous pistol into the back of my neck and shoved me forward.

"You've waited a long time for this, so don't mess up now," he told me.

We walked into the garage.

Three figures were kneeling on the cement floor, hands behind their backs, burlap sacks over their heads.

The smallest one was unquestionably Tracy Anne. Melanie was next to her, trembling and sobbing beneath the sack.

Darren moved past me. "Ta-da!" he said, dramatically yanking off the third person's sack and revealing a gagged and bruised Mr. Grove. "Bet you didn't miss this guy, huh?" He walked around Mr. Grove and kicked him in the back, toppling him over. "I'm sure you don't mind that I beat the shit out of him."

I kept myself calm. I had to bite the inside of my cheeks hard enough to draw blood, but I kept myself calm.

"And, of course, you know this lovely lady," he said, yanking off Melanie's hood. She was also gagged. Her face was also bruised. Her eyes were wild with fear, but they widened as she saw me.

"Sorry about the marks. Like I said, things didn't go as smoothly as I'd hoped. And our star of the evening, the lovely and talented Tracy Anne Fletcher!"

He pulled off my daughter's hood. If there'd been bruises on her face, I'm not sure I'd have been able to keep myself from rushing forward and trying to kill him, but the only marks on her face were tearstains.

"Nice little family reunion we've got here," said

Darren. "Wouldn't it be ironic if I just shot Melanie right now? I'm not going to, but wouldn't that just *suck?*"

I said nothing.

"Okay, I've got some setup to do, so you're going to have to go back into your pit," Darren told me, walking behind me. I felt the jab of a needle in my shoulder. "I hate using artificial means like this to keep you sleepy, but you're probably just a wee bit emotional right now and you might do something stupid."

I fell to the floor.

In my dream, Melanie accidentally walked into me with a duffel bag. I grabbed her, kissed her, and asked her to marry me, even while wondering why the bag was leaking blood.

The Gallery of Horrors consisted of two upstairs rooms. The bedroom was where Darren kept all of his souvenirs; mostly articles of clothing and body parts. Most of them were preserved in jars "because of the smell," although the teeth were in a glass display case.

I knew from one of the torture sessions that a small wooden box contained a shriveled scrap of flesh: one of Killer Fang's ears. He'd slept with it under his pillow the entire rest of the year at Branford Academy.

He'd murdered twelve people. "Not an impressive count for all those years, I guess," he'd admitted, "but I make them last."

The bedroom also contained dozens of drawings, both color and black-and-white, of his exploits. An art critic might say that what he lacked in technical skill he made up for in grisly passion.

And yes, this is where Darren slept each night.

The torture room featured, along with the metal table, shelves of tools. I'd become acquainted with many of them during my months here, including the acetylene torch, but nowhere close to all of them.

I was in this room, seated on the floor, when I woke up. My hands were cuffed together and chained through a metal loop in the wall that seemed to have been installed for that very purpose. Melanie was on the other side of the room, similarly chained. Unmoving. I stared at her, praying for something to indicate that she was alive, and relaxed when I saw her breathe.

Mr. Grove lay on the metal table, shirtless. Also unconscious. Apparently the legs of the metal table were retractable, because it had been lowered to just two feet off the ground.

A kiddie table . . .

"Melanie!" I said in a whisper. "Melanie!"

She didn't awaken.

"Melanie, please! Can you hear me?" I tugged on my handcuffs, but Darren hadn't waited this long only to botch the restraint process now.

A few minutes later, Mr. Grove began to stir. His light stirring suddenly turned into complete panic as he let out muffled screams through the duct tape over his mouth and jerked around as if being zapped with an invisible defibrillator. His terrified squeals were so high-pitched that in other circumstances they might even have been comical.

Melanie opened her eyes.

Focused on me.

And then she too burst into a panic, shrieking and

yanking at her restraints. I tried to soothe her, to reassure her, but how much reassurance could I give her when we were both chained to the wall in a house with a serial killer?

But her panic was short-lived. "Alex!" she cried. "Alex, oh my God, oh my God, I thought he killed you!"

I shook my head and spoke loudly enough to be heard over Mr. Grove's squeals. "No, no, I'm fine. I'm completely fine." The cuts, burns, and other assorted wounds gave away my lie, but my safety wasn't the important thing now.

"Tracy! What's he done with her?"

"Don't worry about her," said Darren, coming up the stairs and walking into the room. "How about we keep the noise level down to a dull roar, huh?" he asked, pointing the gun at each of us in turn.

"Where is she?" I demanded.

"Resting. And no, not in the pit, so don't look at me like that." He gestured to Mr. Grove. "Is he always this loud?" He set the pistol down on a stool next to the metal table, went over to the shelf, selected a large mallet, and showed it to Mr. Grove. "Don't make me use this."

Mr. Grove went silent.

Darren grinned and waved the mallet at me. "See, Alex, if you'd had one of these at work, your problems would have been over." He surveyed the room. "Looks like everything is all set. I'll go get Tracy Anne."

He left and headed back downstairs.

"What's he going to do?" Melanie asked, desperately.

"I don't know." I did know; I knew exactly what he

was going to do, but I couldn't say it out loud. Instead, I said: "I love you."

"I love you, Alex."

"We'll get out of this. I promise. We'll get out of here, and everything will be back to the way it was . . . no, it'll be even better, because we'll have a book deal and we'll never have to spend time apart ever again and we'll . . ." My voice cracked. "We'll be fine. We'll be happy."

I heard footsteps on the staircase. A moment later, Darren walked back into the room, holding Tracy by the hand. She was looking at the ground, shoulders shaking as she wept.

"Don't cry," Darren said, sounding a bit uncomfortable with the task of reassuring a child. "Nothing bad is going to happen to you."

"You leave her alone!" Melanie screamed.

"I knew I should've taped you up," Darren said, crossing over to the shelf. He retrieved a spool of duct tape and crouched down next to Melanie. She jerked her head around, trying to prevent him from getting the tape over her mouth, but after a few moments of struggle he managed the task.

Tracy stood there, frozen.

Darren turned his attention to me. "I need you to be part of this, and that'll be a lot more difficult if I have to tape you up, too. Think you can behave?"

I nodded.

"That's good, because if things go wrong, Melanie is going to be our cutting board." Darren stood up and returned to the shelf. He selected a scalpel.

Melanie looked at me, pleading with me to help our daughter, but of course there wasn't a thing I could do.

Darren knelt down in front of Tracy, getting down to her level. "Do you know who I am?" he asked.

Tracy didn't look up.

"Look at me, Tracy." He touched her chin, gently lifting her head. "Do you know who I am?"

She shook her head.

"I'm your daddy's friend. I've been his friend for a long time. I've known him since before you were even born. In fact, I've known him since before he even met your mommy. Isn't that neat?"

Tracy continued to cry.

Darren patted Mr. Grove's leg. "Do you know who this is?"

"No."

"Sure you do. You've seen him before, haven't you?"

"Uh-uh."

"You've just forgotten. That's okay. I'm sure you're a little scared, even though there's no reason to be. You know Mr. Grove, don't you? You've met him a couple of times."

Tracy nodded.

"And who's Mr. Grove?"

"Daddy's boss."

"That's right. See, you knew all along. Your daddy hates Mr. Grove. Mr. Grove keeps your daddy away from you. Did you know that?"

Tracy began to cry harder.

"Do you think that people who keep little girls away from their daddies are good people?"

"No."

"So Mr. Grove is a bad person, isn't he?"

Tracy Anne looked up at Darren. "You kept me away from Daddy worse."

"You're right, I did. But I did it because it was really important."

"Daddy's job is important."

Darren appeared momentarily flustered that he was losing an argument with a terrified five-year-old, but regained his composure. "Is Daddy's job more important than you?"

"No. Neither are you."

I didn't know whether to cheer or scream.

"You're very smart, Tracy. But how would you like to get back at Mr. Grove? Would you like to make him hurt for keeping your daddy away from you?"

"No."

"Yes you would. It'll be fun. We can make Mr. Grove pay for everything bad he's done. We can make him bleed."

"I don't want to."

"Sometimes we have to try things that we don't want to do. They're good for us. Watch this." Darren slid the scalpel along Mr. Grove's leg, cutting a line from his upper thigh to his knee. Mr. Grove thrashed and screamed through his gag.

"Your daddy has wanted to do something like that for a long time," Darren said. "He'd give anything to be holding this scalpel right now. Wouldn't you, Daddy?"

"Yeah, I would."

"And he'd like you to cut Mr. Grove. Wouldn't you, Daddy?"

"Tracy, sweetie, do whatever he tells you to."

"No, no, it's not what I tell you. It's what your daddy tells you. What do you think, Daddy? Should she cut Mr. Grove?"

"Yes."

"Tell her to do it."

"Tracy, I need you to cut Mr. Grove. It'll be okay, I promise." I had no idea how that statement could possibly be true, but maybe, just maybe, giving Darren what he wanted would make him release us. Guilt over Mr. Grove's unfair fate, Tracy's psychological trauma . . . we could work through these. There'd be nothing to work through if Darren became frustrated and decided to snap my daughter's neck.

"I don't want to," Tracy said, sniffling.

"Please do it," I told her. "Then we can all go home."

"He's right," Darren said. "If you kill Mr. Grove for me, I'll let you, your mommy, and your daddy all leave. Wouldn't that be great? I bet you've missed him a lot, haven't you?"

Darren placed the scalpel in her hand.

"Just cut his leg, to see how it feels."

Tracy violently shook her head. "No!"

Darren took her hand in his own, and pressed the scalpel blade against Mr. Grove's leg, the one that hadn't been cut yet. "All you have to do is push. Not even very hard. It's really sharp. Just slide it gently toward you."

Together they drew the blade across Mr. Grove's leg. Mr. Grove seemed resigned to his fate and didn't struggle nearly as much this time.

"And again," said Darren. This time, he released Tracy's hand halfway through and let her finish slicing the skin all the way down to his ankle.

Tracy studied the blood dripping from the blade almost quizzically, as if it were a particularly interesting species of butterfly.

"Did that feel good?" Darren asked.

"Kind of."

"Do you want to do it again?"

"Do I have to?"

"Only if you liked it. But you liked it, didn't you?"

"I don't know."

"You can say that you did, Tracy. It's okay."

Tracy's fingers tightened around the scalpel.

Oh my God what kind of monster has my daughter become?

And then she slammed the blade deep into Darren's thigh.

CHAPTER TWENTY-TWO

Darren let out a howl and instinctively smacked Tracy in the face. His feet slipped out from underneath him and he struck the floor, hard.

"The gun!" I screamed. *"Tracy, get the gun!"*

She spun around.

"The gun! Right there!" I jerked my head toward the pistol resting on the stool. "Get it!"

Darren grabbed for Tracy's leg but missed. Sobbing, she snatched up the pistol and pointed it at him. She was holding the handle with both hands. Darren got to his feet.

"Put your finger on the trigger!" I told Tracy, trying to convey the urgency without shouting and possibly scaring her into dropping the weapon.

Tracy did so. Darren hesitated, as if trying to calculate his chances of getting the gun away from a frightened five-year-old.

"Squeeze the trigger, honey! Do it now! Shoot him!"

Darren lunged at her.

She pulled the trigger. The gun fell out of her hands as it fired.

The bullet ripped through Darren's side, catching him low, just above the waist. He clenched his teeth together, clutched at his wound, and then screamed, *"Fuck!"*

He yanked the scalpel out of his leg.

"Get the gun!" I screamed.

Tracy grabbed the gun but Darren was already on her. He wrapped his arm around her neck and wrenched the weapon out of her hands. She screamed and flailed and thrashed and, though I don't know if it was intentional, slammed her fist into the bullet wound.

Darren cried out and stumbled backward into the metal table. It caught him behind the knee and he dropped to the floor again, landing right in front of me. The hand with the gun was out of reach, but I slammed my foot down on his other wrist as hard as I could, wishing that I weren't in bare feet. I didn't hear the crack of bones shattering that I hoped for, but Darren cried out once again.

I kicked him in the face.

He scooted out of the way, back against the metal table. He was completely enraged . . . and he still had the gun.

"Run!" I shouted at Tracy. "Go down the stairs! Run as far as you can!"

Tracy rushed out of the torture room.

Darren, limping but moving at a rapid pace, followed her.

I heard Tracy's footsteps hurrying down the stairs. Darren's were close behind.

And then a loud *thump*, followed by several more.

Somebody falling down the stairs.

An adult.

Silence.

I just sat there, listening. Had she gotten away? Had he fallen on top of her?

"Tracy . . . ?"

Crying. I was sure I heard crying. "I hear her!" I told Melanie. "Tracy, can you hear me?"

No response, but her crying was unmistakable.

Footsteps. Soft ones.

Tracy walked through the doorway, looking scared and pathetic and absolutely beautiful. I wanted to call her over, to tell her that everything was going to be wonderful, that we'd be the happiest family who ever lived. But there were practical matters to take care of first.

"I heard the man fall down the stairs," I said. "Is he moving?"

Tracy shook her head almost imperceptibly.

"I need you to keep being brave for Mommy and me. The man has a set of keys. They're in his pocket. Can you get them for us?"

"I can't . . . I'm scared . . ."

"I know you're scared, honey. But you won't ever have to be scared again. I need you to get his keys and to take his gun away."

And shoot him. Tell her to shoot him. To make his head explode, spraying her with blood and skull fragments and gray matter. Hey, she's already cut an innocent man, and stabbed and shot a not-so-innocent one, why would this be any worse?

Well, it could be a hell of a lot worse if she shot herself. She lucked out with the first shot. One twitch of her tiny hands and she could blow a hole in her foot. Let's see her get back upstairs with the keys then, huh?

"Tracy, there's a mallet over there, do you see it?"

She looked at me, uncomprehending.

"It's like a big hammer. On the floor. See it?"

Tracy looked where I was nodding and went over to retrieve the mallet that Darren had threatened Mr. Grove with.

"I want you to hit the man on the head with it, as hard as you can. Hit him a few times. Then get the keys and bring them up here as fast as you can. Can you do that for me?"

Tracy vigorously shook her head.

"Yes, you can, sweetie!"

"I'm scared of him."

"He won't be scary after you bash him! But you need to do it quickly, before he wakes up!"

Though if we were fortunate, Darren was lying dead at the bottom of the stairs with a broken neck.

"I'm *scared!*"

"You won't be! Once you get the keys Mommy and Daddy will protect you from everything! Please, sweetheart, you only need to be strong for one more minute."

I could almost see her physically summoning her courage. She left the torture room and hurried down the stairs.

"She'll be okay," I told Melanie. "It's almost over."

Melanie nodded, clearly trying to be strong, and I loved her for it.

From downstairs came a sound that was wonderfully similar to that of a mallet striking a skull. It was repeated three more times.

Silence.

"I can't find them!"

"Yes you can, sweetie! I saw him put them in his pocket!"

"I can't get them!"

Shit. Darren must've been lying facedown.

"Keep trying!"

"He's too *heavy!*"

"Just reach underneath him!"

Another silence.

"I found them! I found them!"

I listened with joy as Tracy scampered up the stairs and burst into the torture room. She was still crying, but she proudly held up the keys.

"Unlock Mommy!" I said.

It took several tries for Tracy to find the right key, and I kept looking back and forth between my family and the empty doorway.

The bracelet popped open.

I heard a noise from the staircase.

"Hurry! Get the cuffs off! Get them off!"

It was definitely footsteps.

Melanie pulled her hands free and immediately got to her feet. "Go free Daddy!" she told Tracy as she hurried over to the shelf.

Darren stepped into the doorway, holding the mallet.

Melanie grabbed a large hunting knife and threw it at him. It sailed harmlessly past his ear. Melanie grabbed for another weapon, a claw hammer, as Darren stepped all the way into the room. His hair was soaked with blood and his left arm was twisted at an unnatural angle.

Melanie ran at him with the claw hammer. He tried to deflect her attack with the mallet, but she got him in the shoulder and tackled him to the floor. Their landing was blocked from my view by the metal table.

"Mommy!" Tracy screamed, distracted before she could get the key into the handcuff lock.

I heard a loud *thwack* and a grunt from Melanie.

Darren got up. He let out a furious, animalistic roar, raised the mallet, and ran toward Tracy and me. She shrieked, dropped the keys, and ran to the other side of the room.

I tugged on the handcuffs and cried out in frustration.

Darren strode over to the shelf. I could only see part of Melanie behind the table, but I saw her take another swing at him with the hammer, one that didn't even come close.

Darren selected a hypodermic needle from the shelf and turned back to face Melanie. He kicked her, knelt down upon her, and slammed the needle into her.

As she took another swing at him, the hammer dropped out of her hand.

Tracy ran for the doorway, and Darren easily caught her by the arm. She bit down on his hand, hard enough to draw blood but not hard enough to keep him from slamming the needle into her shoulder.

He shoved her to the ground. She didn't get up.

"*Shit!*" Darren screamed, kicking the side of the metal table. "Shit! Shit! Shit!"

He picked up Melanie's claw hammer, turned it claw-side down, and began slamming it into Mr. Grove's body, screaming obscenities with each blow. He slammed it over and over and over, splattering my boss's face and chest. After nearly a minute he began to strike with a sideways motion, tearing off chunks of flesh with each swing.

Finally he flung the hammer as hard as he could against the shelf of tools, knocking several of them to the floor.

None within my reach.

"Why would she do that?" Darren wailed, digging a finger into the bullet wound in his side. "Why would she do that? Why couldn't she see?"

He grabbed Melanie and roughly dragged her out of the torture room and into the bedroom. He stormed back into the torture room, picked up Tracy, and carried her into the bedroom as well.

"Don't hurt them!" I begged. "Please! I'll do anything you want!"

I heard the bedroom door slam. Darren returned to the torture room and sat down on the corner of the metal table, facing me. "I thought we were friends."

"Darren . . ."

He jammed his finger into the wound again and bellowed with pain. "I should take everything away from you! I should!"

"Darren, please! Just give Melanie and Tracy back to me!"

"Why?"

"Because they're all I have!"

"That's a trite fucking answer! I should kill them!"

"No!"

"Give me a reason not to fuck them up."

"Because this is all my fault! Not theirs! I shouldn't have lied!"

"When?"

"When I said that cutting off the woman's head didn't feel good."

I had him. I knew I had him.

"It felt incredible, Darren, the way drugs probably feel. And it scared me. I should have listened to you, but I was scared. I'm sorry for being scared."

Darren stared at me, his expression now blank.

"But, please, don't hurt my family. We can hide all of this. That thing you saw in Tracy, that cloud . . . I saw it, too, and I was scared by it, but *you were right!*"

Darren lowered his head. "I think I was wrong."

"No, you weren't."

"I don't know. I don't know what I'm gonna do."

He stood up and slowly wandered over to the shelf, moving like a zombie.

"Darren, please, you can't hurt them! You can't hurt my family!"

Darren selected a small knife. "I don't know . . . shit, I just wanna go to sleep . . ."

He walked toward the doorway.

"No, don't leave!" I screamed, tugging on the handcuffs. "Talk to me! Let me make you understand!"

Darren walked into the bedroom and closed the door behind him.

I screamed after him, begged him, threatened him. Then I screamed at myself. At my parents. At my teachers. At God.

When I could scream no more, I just wept.

The bedroom door opened. Darren didn't even look at me. He just kept his head lowered and went down the stairs.

I heard a car drive away.

The keys that Tracy had dropped rested next to my leg. Picking them up with my toe was easy; stretching out on the floor and moving them up my leg with quick jerks of my body was not. It took all night to get them into my mouth.

I just kept telling myself the entire time that Melanie and Tracy were fine. No, not fine. Alive. Alive was all I needed.

After freeing myself from the handcuffs, I staggered out of the torture room, opened the bedroom door, and knew that I would never, ever stop screaming.

CHAPTER TWENTY-THREE

I remember very little of the next few weeks. The hospital stay, the funerals, Melanie's parents, my parents, the police . . . just a blur.

I do, however, very clearly remember the Christmas morning when I climbed into my bathtub and put a gun in my mouth.

PART FOUR

SOUL MATES

CHAPTER TWENTY-FOUR

The bag of bullets kept me going through those next one hundred and fourteen days. A bullet a day. A date scratched into the casing. One more day I hadn't killed myself.

I wondered if Darren would consider that the ultimate victory. I mean, how much more control could you possibly have over somebody than to drive them to take their own life?

Sometimes I feared that he was still watching me, ready to strike at any moment, ready to burst into my home wielding a scythe and just start lopping off body parts, cackling in malicious glee. Most of the time I didn't care.

I certainly didn't care as I lay there on the cold ground, colder than a spring evening in Arizona should ever be, shivering, unable to see anything beyond my breath misting in the air, trying to remember if there had ever been happier times.

Maybe there hadn't. Maybe I'd hallucinated it all.

No, there'd been wonderful times.

I closed my eyes and just lay there, right on the

sidewalk, thinking about my beautiful Melanie. My beautiful Tracy Anne. I could feel Melanie's touch on my chest. Her warm breath on my neck as she slept. Her slobbery tongue on my eyes.

I opened the eye that was not currently being licked by a slobbery tongue. The tongue belonged to a dog that bore minimal resemblance to my dead wife.

"Kassie, stop that!" said the dog's owner, tugging on the leash. Kassie, a miniature schnauzer, resisted these efforts and desperately struggled to continue with the licking, but was defeated in her goal.

I almost wished he hadn't pulled the animal away. Its warm tongue felt kind of nice in the cold air.

"Sir, are you okay? Do you need me to help you find a shelter?"

I shook my head.

"Are you sure? I'm not from around here, but I could probably . . ." He trailed off for a moment. "Is that you, Alex?"

I opened my eyes. Whoever this guy was, I didn't recognize him. Probably somebody who'd followed my story in the news. I'd nearly lost it near the beginning when some sick bastard asked for my autograph.

"It's Peter. We were roommates at Branford Academy."

I gaped at him. His face had gotten chubbier and his glasses had gotten thicker, but he did sort of look like . . .

As soon as he smiled, I recognized him immediately.

"Peter! Oh my God!"

He took my hand and helped me up. I started to brush off my clothes, more than a little embarrassed by my appearance. "Wow, this is . . . this is just completely bizarre. I wish you'd seen me looking better."

"I've seen worse. Not much worse, though. You've got blood around your eyes."

As I dabbed at my eyes with my fingers, Peter took a handkerchief out of his pocket. I reached for it, but he shook his head. "Let me do it. It's hard to see your own eyes."

I let him wipe the blood away, feeling like a helpless child. "What are you doing here? You don't live around here, do you?"

"No, I'm here for a dog show. Kassie here is going to win this year." He folded up the handkerchief and petted the schnauzer, which bounded happily around on its leash.

"So you're a professional dog trainer?"

He shook his head. "It's just a hobby. I thought about breeding them, but then you have to sell them, and I couldn't bear to give up any of my babies."

"So what else have you been doing?"

"You'll never guess."

"You've become a coal miner."

"Aw, you guessed." Peter frowned in mock disappointment. "No, I'm studying to become a minister."

"Seriously?"

"Seriously. And I'm only a couple of years away."

"Wow. So you're living a life of celibacy and all that?"

Peter laughed. "Not quite. I have a lovely wife named Debra, and God has seen fit to bless us with five children."

"Five? Wow, you *have* been keeping busy!"

"Yeah. Of course, Satan possesses at least two of

them on any given day, but he's kind enough to rotate so that Debra and I don't go completely bonkers. What about you?" he asked, noting my wedding band.

"Things . . . they haven't been good."

"I figured that when I found you lying on the ground."

I started to tell him what happened, but I couldn't say the words.

"Why don't we sit down?" said Peter, leading me to a bench. My side was covered with bird crap, but it wasn't like I was looking my most dapper this evening. Kassie sniffed an aluminum can with great interest.

"She died," I told him. "My daughter, too."

"Oh, Alex, I am so sorry to hear that. Did they go peacefully?"

"No. No, they didn't."

"What happened to them?"

"They were murdered. Butchered."

Peter closed his eyes. "I can't imagine what you must be going through. If this helps in any way, please know that they're in a better place now."

"That does help," I lied.

"I'll pray for them. And you."

"Darren killed them."

Peter's eyes flew open. "What?"

"Darren Rust. You remember him?"

"Of course I remember him! *He* killed them?"

"Yeah."

"That's . . . that's . . . my mind is reeling. Listen, my hotel is only a few blocks away. This sounds like it might be a long story, so why don't we hang out there and get some room service?"

"I don't want to burden you with my problems."

"Okay, you *do* remember that I said I was becoming a minister, right? Listening to people's problems is part of the job description."

"Yeah, but we're not in a church. I thought, y'know, it might be like asking for free medical advice from a doctor at a party. Doctors hate that."

"Don't be a dork."

"Is a minister allowed to call somebody a dork?" I asked, surprised that I was able to ask such a light-hearted question. Seeing my old friend again was a wonderful jolt to my system. I wasn't ready to dance or sing a merry tune, but I could get through this night without my bullets.

"I'm not a minister yet."

"Is an aspiring minister allowed to call somebody a dork?"

"No. I'm likely to burn in hell. Thanks a lot, dork."

Peter told me all about his post-Branford Academy life as we walked to his hotel. He'd met Debra in college when they fell asleep in the same economics class. They'd gotten married two months later, making both of their families incorrectly believe that Debra had to be pregnant. "But she got pregnant right after that," Peter said. "And again, and again, and again, and again. We could name each of our children after a failed form of birth control. But each of them is a blessing, even with the whole demonic possession thing they've got going."

At the hotel, we ordered a pastrami sandwich for me and a chicken Caesar salad for Peter. As we waited for the food to arrive, Peter brushed Kassie while I told him the whole macabre tale. He listened, fascinated and horrified, as I took him all the way up to this evening.

"I don't even know what to say," Peter admitted. "I don't pay much attention to the news, or you know I would've been there for the funeral. Funerals," he corrected himself. "I wish I could have helped you before you felt like you needed to give up."

I shrugged. "Not your fault."

"I know. I can't imagine that Jeremy knows about it, either. I'd think he would have called me about that if he'd heard."

"You talk to Jeremy?"

"Not often. He, uh, hasn't exactly followed God's path."

"Did he ever become a stand-up comic?"

"No. I think he tried amateur night once and it didn't work out. I wish he hadn't quit so easily. Two marriages, two divorces, no kids. Lots of anger, and I don't know why."

"Darren is a pretty good source of anger."

"Yes, but it goes beyond that. Jeremy is just . . . angry. I haven't spoken to him in a few months. We trade phone calls around the holidays and that's about it. I'll give you his number. He'd love to hear from you."

"Thanks."

"Why don't you fly back with me, Alex? You can meet my family and relax for a couple of days. Debra's a fantastic cook and she'll make you eat your own weight at any one given meal." He patted his belly. "She's given me this fashionable gut. Speaking of which, when is our food going to get here?"

"Can't you ask God to put a rush on that?"

"I could, but I never know how much to tip."

"Listen, I appreciate your offer, but I don't want to impose."

"You wouldn't be imposing. I've got five children. I won't even be able to see you through the blur."

"What if Darren follows me?"

"I don't let fear come between me and my friends."

"I do."

Peter considered that. "So you'll stay at a hotel. Under a fake name. He doesn't have a league of undercover agents, or satellites watching our every move from the heavens. He's just one man."

"One man who took everything from me."

"Not everything. You've got friends, and you've got your life. And pretty soon you'll have the biggest piece of cherry-rhubarb pie you've ever seen. I'm serious. She uses radioactive cherries or something. Anyway, you're meant to be there."

"Says who?"

"Says God."

"Ah."

"Don't worry, I'm not going to preach to you . . . too much. But I have faith. Jesus has never shown up on my doorstep, and the Voice of God didn't whisper in my ear that I should become a minster. I've seen the image of the Virgin Mary on a department store window and suggested that they buy better glass next time. I haven't witnessed any miracles that can't be otherwise explained, but I do believe that God has a hand in our lives, and that he gives us little gifts, to do with as we please. Like when I found you tonight."

"Coincidence."

"Probably. I was out walking my dog in a strange city, and I just happened to come upon my roommate from, what, fifteen years ago? It could be coincidence. Stranger things have happened. But I have faith, and I think that God may very well have wanted me to find you."

"So God made Kassie have to go potty?"

"He might have. And he might have given you that birthmark so that I'd recognize you. Or maybe God has no particular interest in my dog's bodily functions and tonight was just one of those weird things you can't explain. Why not embrace it either way? I'll embrace it as a gift from God, and you can embrace it as a wacky coincidence that resulted in you getting some awesome cherry-rhubarb pie."

"I don't think anybody has ever marketed a piece of cherry-rhubarb pie like you just have."

"You're flying over for dinner, right?"

"Sure."

The next day, I cheered on Peter and Kassie at the dog show. They came in second.

"Do you believe in doggie heaven?" I asked, as we waited for the plane to take off. I'd hoped that God would allow his ministers-to-be and their guests to fly first-class, but we were stuck back in coach.

"Of course. It's like human heaven except that you're encouraged to piddle in the streets whenever you want."

"And do you believe that it's blasphemy against the doggie gods that poodles be given such ridiculous haircuts?"

"You need a dog of your own," said Peter. "I'd donate one of mine, except that I've already planned to sneak a couple of my kids into your baggage when you leave." He suddenly looked distraught. "I'm sorry. That was a horrible thing to say. I shouldn't be making jokes about kids when you . . . I'm sorry."

"It's okay."

"No, it isn't. I can't believe I did that."

"Peter, it's okay. But I *will* be searching my baggage before I get on the plane."

"I'm an efficient packer. You'll never find them."

"We'll see." I tried to think of something much funnier to say, but my repartee skills had rusted with age, and instead I just settled back in my seat and enjoyed my friend's company.

"Welcome to the zoo," said Peter as we walked into his home.

He wasn't kidding. Though I thought that saying his children were possessed by Satan was a bit harsh, they certainly were possessed by the spirits of long-dead monkeys.

Debra was an absolute sweetheart. She gave me a huge hug and said how sorry she was for my loss.

Dinner was delicious and voluminous. It was the most I'd ever eaten in my life, and my futile attempts to explain that I was completely full were met with great amusement by Peter.

Right as Debra got up to retrieve a dessert that would certainly cause my body to explode if I so much as inhaled the aroma, the doorbell rang. The four children old enough to talk simultaneously screamed that they wanted to answer it.

He didn't look anything like his twelve-year-old self, but I immediately knew it was Jeremy.

* * *

"Am I allowed to smoke in here?" asked Jeremy, as he, Peter, and I relaxed in the living room.

"Sure, if you want to face Debra's wrath."

"How does that compare to God's wrath?"

"Smaller scale but much more frightening."

"I'll skip the nicotine. I'm supposed to be using those patches anyway." He looked at me. "So tell me how you ended up tangled up with that sick . . . Peter, are your kids listening?"

"Probably."

". . . with that sick rascal anyway?"

I told him the whole story. Jeremy's face turned redder and redder as he listened. By the time I finished, I thought he might start ripping chunks out of the couch.

"So it's simple. We kill him."

"Okay."

"I'm serious. You need closure on this. That rotten little psychopath has had power over you . . . over us . . . for more than half of our lives. It's time to take it back."

"I don't even know where he is. For all I know, he's dead."

"And for all you know, he's watching through the window right now. Sorry, Peter, but it's true. Alex, if you want to move on with your life, you need to end this. You're young, you've got more time ahead of you than behind you, and you can't waste it by always wondering when that son of a rascal is going to show up next."

"Well, if he'd be considerate enough to show up at my doorstep, I'd be more than happy to end this."

"So flush him out."

"How?"

"I don't know. Put out a big sign that says 'Free Beer for Lunatics.'"

"Ha ha," I said.

"Ho ho," Peter chimed in.

We looked at Jeremy expectantly.

"What?" he asked.

"It's your line," Peter said.

"I have no idea what you guys are talking about. But I'm serious; we've got to flush him out."

"Whoa, hold on," said Peter. "I don't want him flushed out around me."

"Of course not. You've got a lot to lose. I don't have squat except for three alimony payments."

"Three?"

"Three as of last month, yeah. I'd kind of hoped for an annulment of that last one, but it didn't work out."

"Sorry to hear that."

"Yeah, well, shit happens. I mean poop happens. Anyway, we can get this guy. He wants you to be his partner in homicide, right? Why not go on a killing spree of your own?"

"Oh, sure, that'll ease my mental torment."

"Not a real one. Fake him out."

"Sure. I'll just walk down the sidewalk, pretend to kill a few people, and wait for him to show up."

"You know, you're very sarcastic for a suicidal. Didn't you use to do magic?"

"Yeah. I gave it up when I spent those months locked in the pit. Too hard to see the cards."

"Well then, smart-ass, it's possible that you're

familiar with the concept of illusion. You see, an illusion is something that appears to be there, but really isn't. For example, in the fabled floating woman trick, audience members will see a floating woman up onstage. And yet the magician possesses no supernatural powers with which to float this woman. Most magicians give up by this point, but others, the really clever ones, they think to themselves, 'I know, instead of trying to call upon paranormal forces to float this woman, I'll just do an *illusion* that makes it *look* like the woman is floating, and then I can still get my paycheck.' Yes, the concept of illusions has been very popular with magicians across the world, which is why it's so surprising to me that you've never heard of it."

"So you're saying that I should fake a murder?"

"No, I'm saying that you should float a woman." He looked at Peter. "Was he this slow when we were roommates?"

"Actually, I think you were the slow one."

"That's what I thought."

"I'm sorry," I said. "I'm not trying to be sarcastic, but this idea sounds a little preposterous."

"Why?"

"Because . . . I don't know why, actually." Maybe it wasn't that preposterous. "We'd have to find somebody good with special effects."

"That shouldn't be too hard."

"Let's think about this. I could go on a fake killing spree, it could get captured on tape, and Darren would see it on the news and think that his whacko plan worked. And we'd be ready for him."

"Sure!" said Jeremy. "We'd hire some actors, put some blood packs on them, have you walk into a restaurant or something with a gun, open fire, and have somebody tape it. All the media would cover it."

"You're right, they would," I said, starting to get excited.

Peter rolled his eyes. "Scale it back, you guys."

"Why?"

"Because you'd have to find actors who could die in a believable enough manner that when experts reviewed the tape for the umpteenth time they wouldn't say, 'Hey, look at the shoddy performance of victim number three.' Also, where are all of these people going to hide out while you wait for Darren to show up? You'd have to find actors willing to vanish for a while and let their families believe that they were dead. And I'm pretty sure authorities will be able to tell a squib hit from a real bullet hit."

Jeremy frowned. "I thought priests were supposed to inspire."

"I'm not a priest. I'm studying to be a minister."

"But he's right," I said. "We just need to scale it back. One victim. Somebody willing to disappear for a while."

Jeremy raised his hand. "I'm willing."

"Really?"

"Put me in a hotel room with cable and I'm yours."

"So we'd only have to do one convincing death. Do either of you know any special effects people?"

"Not me," Jeremy admitted.

"I don't," said Peter, "but again, keep scaling it down. Unless the effect is absolutely seamless, you'll get caught. If the video is exposed as a fraud, Darren will know you're up to something, and you've blown this kind of opportunity forever."

"So maybe the victim doesn't die," I said.

"Exactly."

"I just threaten to kill him."

"Exactly."

"And if I'm making the video myself, there's nobody else involved."

"Exactly."

"This is gonna be awesome," Jeremy said. "I haven't been this excited about something in ten years!"

"What about your wedding days?" Peter asked.

"They still make the top five. Jeez. Two of 'em do, anyway."

"So when do we do this?" I asked.

"We don't," said Peter. "I mean I don't. I've got a wife and five kids. God doesn't want me to live in fear, but God also doesn't want me to be dumb enough to attract a serial killer with a snuff video."

"Absolutely understood," I said.

"But I won't say anything. Maybe I'll make myself unavailable. Debra and I have been wanting to take the kids on a family cruise."

"How do you afford a cruise for seven people on an aspiring priest's salary?" Jeremy asked.

"Aspiring minister. We do all right."

"I can see that, but how?"

"Debra writes."

"Really? She's published?"

Peter nodded, a bit uncomfortable.

"What does she write?" I asked.

"Romances."

"Wow."

"Erotic romances."

Jeremy and I exchanged an unbelievably amused look.

"Debra writes smut?" Jeremy asked.

"It's not smut. It celebrates romance and the human body."

"So you read smut?" I asked.

"No. Just hers. I look for continuity errors."

"Like, what? There were seven people in the bed in the previous chapter and now there are only six?"

"There's a market for this! *You* have five kids and see how resistant you are to those royalty checks! I don't have to discuss this with you!"

"Can I find these in my local bookstore?"

"Yes, but she writes under a pen name. And I'm not going to tell you what it is, because the two of you are just immature enough to mail me highlighted pages."

"I would never *dream* of doing that," said Jeremy, the picture of innocence. "How much of it comes from real life, you hot stud muffin?"

Peter laughed. "I've already said too much. Now who's up for more pie?"

CHAPTER TWENTY-FIVE

Two days later, Jeremy and I were in my home. Though Peter owned a video camera, and though we happily tormented Peter with graphic speculation about the bedroom antics that had been recorded by that very video camera, borrowing it didn't seem like a good idea. We wanted as few ties to Peter as possible. So I rented one from a local shop.

We'd decided that the subtle approach was not necessarily the best one, and so the tape was to be a direct message to Darren. I would hold the camera myself, and show Jeremy in my bathtub, bound with duct tape. Then I would speak to the camera, letting Darren know that I would be ending Jeremy's life "where the rope burned your skin."

The problem was that the video wasn't working. Jeremy didn't look scared enough. I didn't sound convincing at all, and I kept flubbing my lines.

After the ninth or tenth failed attempt, I slammed the video camera down on the bathroom sink and ripped off the duct tape that covered Jeremy's mouth. "Let's just call it off."

"We can't."

"They won't even air this. The people in the news-room will laugh themselves silly. We'll end up on some bloopers show."

"No, we can do this," Jeremy insisted. "We just have to really sell it."

"I don't know how."

We were silent for a long moment.

"What if you didn't just threaten me with that knife?" asked Jeremy.

"You mean, actually cut you?"

"Not deep, but a real cut. Don't even tell me where you're going to do it. Just slash me a couple of times when you film me in the tub."

"I can't do that."

"Sure you can. You cut me, and then you cut yourself. Two good slices across your chest. When they blow that up, look at it pixel by pixel, they'll see that it's real."

"I can cut myself easier than I can cut you."

"You can do both. Make me scared of you." He chuckled nervously. "But I'm trusting you not to slash my eyeball. No face cuts."

"Jeremy, this is going *way* beyond any friendship obligations you might have."

"It's not about friendship. I'd lose an arm to see that piece of shit get what he deserves. Don't cut off my arm, though, please."

"I won't."

"I trust you. Now do you trust me?"

"Of course."

"We'll find out. Take off your shirt and go get a picture of Melanie and Tracy."

I unbuttoned my shirt and tossed it aside. Then I

picked up my favorite photograph. Melanie was at my side, looking positively radiant, almost glowing as she held two-year-old Tracy Anne in her arms. It was a lousy picture of me, of course, but I didn't look at myself.

"Let me see it," said Jeremy.

I showed him the photograph.

"She's beautiful. Both of them are."

"I know."

"I bet they were more beautiful with blood running down their faces."

I lowered the picture. "Okay, I already don't like where this is going."

"Do you think they woke up while he was cutting them? Maybe they were awake the whole time, able to feel every last bit of agony."

"I know what you're trying to do. It's not going to work."

"I bet he laughed when he did it."

"Seriously, Jeremy, this is just going to piss me off."

"They're gone forever, you know."

"Knock it off."

"Peter told me that they're probably burning in hell."

"Okay, *knock it off!*"

"Your wife and your daughter are burning in hell and you're all alone and Darren is out there laughing his ass off. You said he kept souvenirs, right? Did they find all of Melanie? Did they find all of Tracy?"

I didn't respond. I hadn't even thought of that awful possibility. I just stood there, letting the hate and sorrow flow through me.

"You think maybe he brought Melanie's nipple with him? What do you think he brought from Tracy? How much do you think it *hurt* while he was cutting them up? How much do you think Melanie hated you as she lay there? How much do you think Tracy hated her daddy, who promised to protect her but let somebody cut her up? Do you think she was thinking good thoughts about you when he sliced off her fingers? She died hating you. She's burning in hell hating you."

Tears were pouring down my face.

"Pick up the camera," Jeremy said.

I picked up the camera, pressed record, and then spun it around to tape myself. "I'm Alex Fletcher, and this message is for Darren Rust. You were right. Goddamn you, you were right!"

I grabbed the straight razor from the edge of the tub and·slashed it across Jeremy's arm. He cried out in pain. Then I slashed his cheek from the corner of his chin to just past his left eye.

Oh, shit, I'd cut deep. Way too deep.

Don't lose this.

I rubbed my hand on his bleeding arm and held my palm up to the camera. "Yeah, this feels good. You made it feel good, you son of a bitch!" I placed the camera on the sink and stood in front of it. "You made it feel really"—I slashed my chest with the razor— "fucking"—another slash—"good!"

I pointed to the camera. "You did this to me, Darren. You took away everything I had, and the only way I can fucking cope is to take it away from other people!"

I grabbed the camera from the sink, nearly dropping it. "Remember Jeremy?" I asked, pointing the camera at my bleeding friend. "It's *his* fault this happened! He started it all!" I spun the camera around to record my face. "You wanna share him? Huh? This is what I've become, so I fucking well better embrace it! I'm gonna rip his fucking guts out where the rope burned your neck. You wanted to turn me into a killer?" I held my bloody palm up to the camera again. "Mission accomplished."

I pressed stop and set the camera back down on the coffee table.

"You cut my face," Jeremy said.

"Jeremy, I'm so sorry."

"I'm pretty damn sure I asked you not to cut my face. Band-Aids would be nice. You need some, too."

My chest was covered with blood. I hadn't even felt the cuts. I opened the medicine cabinet and grabbed some bandages, cotton balls, gauze, and antiseptic.

"You cut my face," Jeremy repeated.

"I know. I'm sorry."

"I hope you at least didn't tape me pissing my pants. I'd like *some* dignity when this is over."

I glanced at his soaked crotch. "I didn't even no-tice." I opened the antiseptic and poured some onto a cotton ball. "This is going to burn."

"Well, no shit."

We were silent as I cleaned and dressed his wounds and then my own.

"I'm sorry for what I said," Jeremy told me as we sat on the couch.

"It's okay. It worked."

"Peter never said that they were burning in hell."

"I know."

"And they didn't hate you."

I didn't respond.

"Should we take a look at our masterpiece?" Jeremy asked.

We popped the tape into the VCR and watched it. I didn't even recognize myself. That wasn't me. It was a stranger who'd completely lost his grip on sanity.

It was terrifying to watch myself like that, knowing that my words were just lines but that my emotions were completely real.

God, what if Darren had been right about me all along?

We could've been traveling the countryside, hacking up innocent people for sport, laughing at their misery and having a grand ol' time.

It sure would've been a better life than what I had now.

The tape ended.

"Now *that*," said Jeremy with a satisfied grin, "is one convincing video."

It was not a flawless plan by any stretch of the imagination. Television stations might not air it. Darren might not see it even if they did. They might omit the crucial "where the rope burned your skin" line. Darren might see through the whole thing and laugh at our pathetic attempt to trick him.

Or Darren might be dead.

I could handle him being dead. But I couldn't handle never knowing. Jeremy was right. I needed resolution.

We decided that Jeremy would indeed hang out in a hotel room for the duration of the plan. Optimally, he would have camped out with me in the woods outside of Branford Academy, but I didn't see how that could work. I could hang out there as long as necessary, but to sustain a faux captor/victim relationship twenty-four hours a day just didn't seem feasible.

This way, Jeremy would be all nice and comfy in his hotel room, and he could keep tabs on the situation through newspapers and television. If he had anything crucial to share, he could give me a call on my cell phone.

Jeremy wore a ridiculous disguise and paid for the hotel room in cash. He wished me luck, gave me a hug, bitched at me one last time about cutting his face, and left.

I dropped ten packages with copies of the tape, addressed to various local news outlets, into a mailbox and then drove down to Branford Academy. Feeling no nostalgia whatsoever, I left my car in the parking lot of a twenty-four-hour supermarket and walked the eight miles to the woods.

I didn't know the exact tree we'd used to hang Darren, but I found a clearing that looked like it might be the right place. I sat down, leaned against the tree, and prepared myself for a long wait. I had a backpack with food, water, a couple of really thick paperbacks, a flashlight, toilet paper, caffeine tablets, and other assorted necessities. The gun I kept on my lap.

It was not, truth be told, a very pleasant camping trip, especially when I discovered that my heavy sweater wasn't doing much against the cold. But at the same time, when you've spent months living in a dark pit, hanging out in the woods really doesn't sound all that bad.

I wondered if anybody had watched the tape yet.

I wondered what my parents would think. It would certainly justify their excessive reaction to the stolen condoms.

Maybe I'd win an Emmy for Best Performance in a Fraudulent Video.

As night fell, I started to get really anxious about what was happening, but I told myself to be patient. Be patient, stay alert, and think about how wonderful it was going to be when Darren finally showed his deranged face.

When it was completely dark, I allowed myself to fall asleep. If Darren came looking for me in the darkness, his flashlight would wake me up. I still woke up several times, flinching awake and then sitting there, listening carefully for any signs of noise, but there was nothing.

The entire next day passed without event. I tried to dig into the first novel but it was astoundingly boring, so I moved on to the second one, which was even worse. I wondered briefly if it would be safe to make a bookstore run, but decided against that idea.

I sat there quietly, wondering if I was the biggest idiot who ever lived. Nah. Top twenty at the max. Lots of people had done things more stupid than setting themselves up as a psycho killer and waiting out in the woods hoping for a real killer to decipher an obscure clue.

It wasn't *too* obscure, was it?

No. Unless Darren had completely lost all rational thought (which was a very legitimate possibility) he'd be able to figure it out. As long as he saw that portion of the tape. But even if the television stations didn't air the uncut version (and they'd at least bleep out my frequent use of the F-word), the complete video would certainly make its way onto the Internet. Darren would see it for sure.

Maybe he'd even watched us making it.

Now that would suck.

I slept even more poorly the second night, cursing Jeremy and his warm, snuggly bed and his cable TV and his hot shower and his *USA Today* delivered every morning. That bastard. I hoped his shower ran out of hot water just as he'd finished shampooing his hair.

Had Melanie really hated me as she died?

Had Tracy?

No. They weren't even conscious at the time.

As far as I knew.

Had Melanie hated me as she sat there, trapped, watching Darren try to turn our daughter into a murderer?

It wasn't my fault.

Although it was my fault for becoming friends with somebody like Darren. For letting him into my life.

Okay, you've been over this shit a million times, so let's think of something more productive, all right? How about sending a little more hate Jeremy's way? I bet he's got a nice fluffy pillow. Two of 'em. Maybe even three.

I slept against the tree, which was not particularly fluffy.

By the next afternoon, I was thoroughly convinced that I was the biggest idiot society had ever produced. The biggest dipshit, numbfuck, dumb-ass ignoramus who had ever been allowed to reach adulthood. I should've been discarded at birth to keep my genes from lowering the world's collective IQ by a good three points. God, was I dumb.

I needed to just gather my things, walk back to town,

admit that it was all a hoax, face the lawsuits, and get some rest. Living a life of fear was starting to sound like a halfway decent idea.

How many kids had been afraid to go to sleep last night because of my video? How many of them worried that the crazy man with the straight razor might be hiding in their closet? How many nightmares was I creating just to end my own?

Christ, this was out of hand. Time to pull the plug.

But if I gave up now, that was it. Darren would know that I was trying to set him up. I might never get a chance to face him on my terms, not his.

I could wait another few hours.

Just as it started to get dark, I heard footsteps. I picked up the gun and listened carefully.

It was only one person. I stared in the direction from where they were coming, aimed my revolver, and waited.

C'mon, you warped freak. Show yourself. Take a nice little bullet through the head.

"Alex . . . ?"

It wasn't Darren's voice. Or Jeremy's. It was an old man's voice.

"Who's there?" I called out.

"It's a friend, Alex," said the voice. I still couldn't see who it belonged to.

"Tell me who you are."

Now I could see the figure, mostly hidden through the branches. "Promise me you won't shoot me."

"I won't shoot you." I lowered the gun. "Jeremy isn't here. If you hurt me you'll never find him."

The figure stepped into view and I recognized him immediately. He had to be in his late seventies or early eighties by now. Previously there had been nothing frail about him, but no longer.

"Mr. Sevin?"

CHAPTER TWENTY-SIX

"Please don't shoot me," he said, raising a hand in defense. "I'm an old man, but I'd like to stay around a while longer."

"What are you doing here?"

"I saw you on TV." He tapped the side of his head. "I may not remember all of my students, but I do remember the ones who caused me trouble. And not many caused me as much trouble as you did." He chuckled softly, but then turned serious. "Why don't you give yourself up?"

"Are you here alone?"

"Yes. I'm slower than I used to be, but I can still get to where I need to go. Mr. Fletcher, I know you went through some hard times, but this isn't the way to resolve it."

He couldn't possibly be here alone. Even if he figured out the clue, he wouldn't just walk out here to confront me by himself, would he? He had to have told the police. And if I didn't end this right now, I was likely to get myself shot.

I dropped the gun and held my hands in the air. "You've got me!" I called out. "I'm unarmed!"

Mr. Sevin let out a visible sigh of relief.

"Where are the cops?" I asked, looking around for people lurking in the shadows.

"There aren't any cops. I told you, I came alone."

"I don't believe you."

"Well, it certainly wasn't my choice. But it was the instructions the caller gave me."

And then another figure pushed through the branches. It wasn't a cop.

"Didn't they ever tell you in Sociopath School that you never drop your weapon?" asked Darren, stepping into the clearing. He was wearing explosives. A lot of them.

He had a gun in one hand and a small black object in the other. "I certainly hope that if there *are* any cops watching, that they note my attire," he called out. "If I drop this detonator, you can kiss these woods and everybody crawling around in them good-bye!" He grinned at me. "So, Alex, how've you been?"

Darren looked good. As if he'd been working out, eating right, and maintaining inner peace through meditation. He was an almost exact duplicate of his college self.

"I've been better," I admitted.

"Yeah, looks like it. Mr. Sevin, hey, it's been a long time. You should really work on your phone manners."

Mr. Sevin was clearly scared, but he stood up to his full height. "There's nothing to be accomplished from this. Give yourselves up, both of you."

"Sorry. We're not your students anymore. But when we were, I know damn well that there were times when Alex here wanted to put a bullet through your brain. Weren't there, Alex?"

"We don't have time for him," I said.

"Oh, believe me, we've got plenty of time."

"I mean it; give yourselves up," Mr. Sevin insisted.

"You just worry about yourself for now," Darren told him. "Alex, get your gun."

I reached down and picked up the revolver. I could see where this was heading and I can't honestly say that I was pleased with that particular direction. Even when I set a trap for him, Darren managed to get the upper hand!

Maybe the explosives were fake. Maybe I could put a bullet right between his eyes (or through his nose; I wasn't picky) and end this right now. Hell, even if we *did* all blow up, I would sure get credit for taking control of the situation.

But I wasn't quite in the mood to die right now.

Darren grinned. "So, Alex, I understand you've got yourself a hankering to commit some cold-blooded murder. Why not start with the guy who ruined your life?"

"That would be you."

"Don't be that way. If Mr. Sevin hadn't fallen for the doctored journal, none of this would have happened. Go on, shoot him."

I pointed my gun at Mr. Sevin.

"Not so tough now, are you, old man?" asked Darren. "Kind of hard to discipline your students when they've got implements of death, huh?"

I slowly walked toward Mr. Sevin, keeping my gun pointed at his forehead. The poor man was clearly terrified, but continued to stand tall.

"You helped me discover really messed-up things about myself," I told Darren. "I don't know whether to thank you or kill you."

"Let's go with thank me."

I pressed the barrel of the revolver against Mr. Sevin's forehead. "But you got one important thing wrong, Darren."

"What's that?"

"You assumed that I'm interested in a decrepit, pathetic, shriveled old fuck like Sevin." I shoved Mr. Sevin to the ground and turned my attention to Darren before he even hit. I heard him land with an "*ooomph*" but I didn't hear a cry of pain. "I don't give a shit about him. I'm way past that."

"Point taken," said Darren.

"Nice suit. Are those explosives real?"

"They sure are."

"So what do we do now?"

Darren pointed his gun at me. "You're coming with me. I've got some real fun planned. If you're not going to kill Mr. Sevin, I vote we get a move on, just in case he did call the police."

"Fine with me."

We hurried silently through the woods. This was absolutely maddening. I had a gun and I had Darren in my sight and there was nothing I could do about it.

Yet.

Before too long we reached the edge of the woods, where a beat-up gray truck was parked.

"Sorry we aren't traveling in style," said Darren. "Get in."

I got in the passenger side without arguing. Darren hurried around to the driver's side and climbed into the truck as well. We slammed our doors shut and he put the key in the ignition. "It's gonna be a bitch doing this with one hand," he said, referring to the detonator in his left hand.

"I could hold it for you."

"I don't think we've hit that level of trust yet." He started the engine, slammed on the gas pedal, and we sped off.

"Where are we going?" I asked.

"Not far," said Darren. "By the way, nice video."

"Thanks."

"Were you fuckin' with me?"

"No."

"You sure?"

I lifted my shirt, revealing the bandages on my chest. I tore those off and Darren whistled as he looked at the wounds.

"Ouch," he said.

"I went a little nuts."

"They look infected."

"They probably are."

We were cruising down the street, far exceeding the speed limit. It was light traffic but I still worried that we'd bash into somebody and he'd drop the detonator.

"So where's Jeremy?"

"Somewhere safe."

"Did you already kill him?"

"Not yet."

"Look, I was wrong about you. I was wrong about your daughter, too. We're not alike, you and me. What I saw in that video wasn't you. I came out here to stop you from hurting Jeremy."

Say the fuck what?

"I've had a lot of time to think," Darren continued. "What I did to Melanie and Tracy, that snapped everything into sharp focus. I didn't hurt them, by the way. I want you to know that."

I was so filled with revulsion at his statement that it was all I could do not to reach over and throttle him, detonator or not. "I saw what you did to them."

"But I didn't *hurt* them. They were unconscious. They didn't feel a thing."

"You hurt them plenty before you killed them."

"I'm trying to ease your mental load here, Alex."

"You're doing a crappy job."

"Okay, okay, I deserve that. Believe me, if I could take back what I did, I'd do it in a second. I'd take back everything. I'd run right upstairs and tell Peter that his dog got hit by a car and I'd watch him cry and none of this ever would have happened." He smiled ruefully. "But it's a little late for that, I guess."

"Yeah."

"But it's not too late for you."

We pulled through the front entrance to Branford Academy. Darren floored the gas pedal as we bounced up onto the main lawn and sped across the campus toward a very familiar building.

"It's not called Dorm B anymore," Darren informed me. "It's now the Wolfe Building. They named it for Mr. Wolfe after he died a few years ago of a stroke. I never liked him, but I thought that was kind of sweet."

The truck gave a jolt as we hit some sort of bump and for a heart-stopping moment I thought the detonator was going to bounce out of his hand. It didn't, and we pulled up right in front of the building.

"Let's go," said Darren, throwing open the door. "Let's make some haste."

I got out of the truck as well, and together we hurried into the building. Darren immediately pointed his gun at the security guard. "You! You grab some kid, and you tell him to go door-to-door telling everybody to stay in their rooms! I don't want to hear a single goddamn sound but that one kid warning his buddies. And I don't expect to see a single cop in this building. If I see a cop inside, I'm blowing this place apart. Only two people die tonight if you don't screw up. You got it?"

The security guard just stood there, frozen in terror.

"So, what, you're gonna let a building full of kids die because you're too stupid to move? *Go!*"

The security guard hurried down the hallway. Darren gestured for me to follow him. "Upstairs," he said. We ran up two flights of stairs to the third floor. The hallway was unrecognizable with the new brown carpet and cheerfully decorated walls, but I knew where we were headed.

Darren let out an incredulous laugh as we reached room 308 and he tugged the red Summons off the doorknob. "They've got a bloody door," he announced. "Some things never change, huh?"

He threw open the door and waved his gun at the four young boys inside. "Get out! Now!" The frightened boys wasted no time in running for the door. "You make sure your buddies don't leave their rooms!

As long as we're not disturbed, nothing bad happens!" Darren shouted as they fled down the hallway.

Darren gestured grandly inside the room. "After you," he told me.

I walked into the room, which was decorated with posters of rock bands I'd never heard of, scantily clad women, and a large map of the United States. Darren followed, shutting and locking the door behind us.

"So," he said with a big sigh, "we're finally home again."

"What are we doing here?"

Darren ignored my question as he tapped the cleavage of one of the posters. "We never would've been allowed to put this up," he said. "They've really let this place slip since Sevin retired."

"What are we doing here?" I repeated. "There's no escape route."

"You noticed that, huh?"

"Do you really have enough explosives to bring the building down?"

Darren tapped some of the explosives on his chest, making me flinch. "I think so. Didn't test it out, obviously. Too bad we wouldn't get to see the building collapse. We could cheer and dance in the rubble. But, really, that's not what this is about. It's not about these kids. It's about *these* kids," he said, pointing the gun at himself, and then at me.

"We're way past being kids."

"Oh, I don't know. I still feel immature."

"So once more, why are we here?"

"I don't know. You called me. It was your video, right?"

"No. The video was to get you out to the woods. I

thought we were going to be partners, not trap ourselves in our old room."

"Partners," Darren said, thoughtfully. "See, I'm still having trouble believing that. Just call me cynical. You know what I think?"

"What?"

"I think that when you succumbed to those quote unquote messed-up feelings, you just couldn't handle it, and you decided that you needed a guide. Somebody who knew how to sort this all out. You probably aren't acquainted with all that many serial killers."

"You're right, I'm not."

"Do you see flashing lights?" Darren stepped over to the window to get a better look, then closed the curtain and returned to his spot. "Yep, the cops are on the way. That was damn quick. More news coverage for you."

"So, are you here to . . . guide me?"

"No. This isn't you. I told you, I was wrong. You're no killer. I saw it when you brought back that lady's head but I didn't want to admit it to myself. I'm here to clear your conscience."

"How?"

"Give me your gun."

"I'd rather not."

"You know that if you don't give me your gun, I'm just going to warn you that I'll blow this building up, and then you'll decide that you don't want me to blow this building up and will go ahead and give me the gun that I asked for in the first place. So let's skip that step, okay?"

I handed him the gun.

"Thank you." He flipped a switch on the detonator

and a small green light turned red. He undid a couple of straps on his shoulders. Keeping my gun pointed at me, he removed the vest of explosives and carefully set it down on the floor. "Feels good to get that heavy-ass thing off. It was hot."

"It looked it."

Darren walked over to me and pressed the barrel of my gun against my forehead. "Take my gun," he said.

I took the gun out of his hand.

"Open your mouth."

"I don't want to die."

"Yes, you do."

"Not anymore."

"You need peace, buddy. And I'm giving it to you. We'll die together. You'll get to end the life of the guy who murdered your family, and I'll get to end your life before you do something truly horrible. Open your mouth."

Some sweat trickled down into my eye and I blinked it away. What should I do? Confess that it had all been a setup?

"Don't make me tell you again, Alex."

I slowly opened my mouth. He slid the barrel of my gun past my lips.

"Now you put your gun in my mouth. On the count of three, we'll pull the triggers. We'll die to-gether like soul mates."

He slid the barrel deeper into my mouth and I felt like I was going to gag. "Do it."

I pointed the gun at his face. He opened his mouth, not taking his eyes off mine.

I placed the barrel of the gun on his tongue.

"One . . ." he said, as well as he could with a gun barrel on his tongue.

Just blow his head off!

"Two . . ."

I pulled the trigger.

Click.

Darren pulled back his head, sliding the barrel of the gun out of his mouth. "You were early," he said. "I guess my lack of trust was justified, huh? Drop the gun and get down on your fucking knees, Alex."

I did as I was told. He kept the gun in my mouth.

He looked really, really pissed.

CHAPTER TWENTY-SEVEN

"So what the hell was that?" Darren asked, jostling the gun in my mouth so that it smacked against my teeth. It wasn't all that long ago that I'd had a gun in my mouth, wishing desperately for the courage to pull the trigger, but those times were no longer. I didn't want to die. And I was *not* going to die like this, at Darren's hands.

"Were you just gonna splatter my brains against the wall and then dance on out of here?"

He thrust forward with the gun so that it hit the back of my throat. My gag reflexes went berserk and I grabbed his hand to try to pull it free, but he kept the gun in place.

"Puke on it," he said.

And as he jammed it forward even farther, I did just that.

He removed the gun and I doubled over, coughing and gagging. "You didn't answer my question," he said. "Were you going to splatter my brains and dance on out of here?"

I spat on the floor and then wiped my mouth off on my sleeve. "Why was the gun empty?"

"Because it was a test."

"So you were going to kill me and leave?"

"No. When you pulled the trigger at three we were going to have ourselves a nice little laugh, and then I was going to load the gun."

"Bullshit!"

"Bullshit yourself. I don't know how much you've read up on suicide pacts, but they only work with people you can trust. Thread your fingers together and put them behind your head, execution style."

I spat up some more vomit, just missing his shoe. "Screw you."

"Do it."

"No."

"That's not an option."

"I'm making my own options."

Darren stared down at me. I stared up at him right back.

Blink first, you motherfucker.

We held the stare.

Darren blinked first.

"All right," he said. "Maybe you passed the second test."

"I slept in their blood," I told him.

He furrowed his brow. "Whose blood?"

"My wife and daughter's. After you killed them. I slept in their blood."

"Did you now?"

"Yeah."

"Well, that was an odd thing to do."

"And I finished the job you did. You missed some parts."

"Is that so?"

"It's the truth." *I'll kill you for making me say these things.*

"Gee, somehow I have this crazy feeling that you're screwing with me again, Alex."

"I kept pieces of them. You were right, I'm a sick person. We both are."

"So, gee, tell me, what piece of Melanie did you keep?"

"Her nipple."

"Oh, dude, you *are* a sick person, just for making that shit up! Even I don't slice off nipples. Not my arena."

"I keep it with me."

"What'd you do, make a ring out of it?"

"I keep it in my pocket."

"Eeww, so it's all linty and stuff, huh? I sure hope you've never run it through the washer accidentally."

"It's in a box."

"Nipple in a box, huh? Do you ever stick it on and wear it? Now *that* would be some messed-up, kinky shit."

"I've never worn it. I just look at it."

"Wasted opportunity."

"And touch it."

"Freaky."

"And taste it."

"Okay, you've almost got me believing you now, you wacky pervert!"

"Do you want to see it?"

"Oh, sure, let me see the souvenir nipple. That'd be swell."

I slowly lowered my arms and stood up. Darren stepped back a bit but didn't try to stop me.

"Do you want to take it out?" I asked.

"No, no, actually, I think I'll just trust you on the whole nipple thing."

"It's in my pocket right now."

"I believe you."

"Do you know what else I did to them?" I asked.

Lose focus for one second just one second . . .

"What's that?"

"I rearranged their bodies, and I soaked up some of their blood, and then I—"

I smashed my palm into his hand, bashing it and the gun he held into his face. The blow took him completely by surprise and got him in the upper cheek, sadly missing his eyeball by a couple of inches.

Before he could recover, I tried to wrench the gun out of his grip. I gave up on that after a few seconds and smashed the gun into his face a second time, getting him in the mouth. Shards of broken teeth sprayed from his lips as he stumbled but kept his balance.

I dove at him, tackling him to the floor. The impact took our combined breath away, but I had so much adrenaline rushing through my body that I barely even felt it.

As he tried to point the gun at me, I smashed my fist against his lower arm as hard as I could, hoping to snap it in two. I didn't break any of his bones, but the gun did fall to the floor.

He jerked his head up and bit my arm. His broken,

jagged teeth pierced my flesh, and though the act of biting with those exposed nerves had to be one of the most painful experiences imaginable, he refused to let go. I tore myself free, leaving a chunk of skin in his mouth.

Darren spat it out and threw a punch that struck my solar plexus hard enough that the adrenaline was not sufficient to block the pain. A second punch got me in the jaw. I might have had the upper hand with the element of surprise, but Darren was still by far the physically stronger one, and almost before I realized it our positions had switched, with him on top.

I cried out as Darren grabbed me by the ears, crushing them, and slammed my head against the floor. The thin carpet did little to soften the impact. When he repeated this, a lot of my fighting spirit drained out of me.

Darren seemed to realize this. He spat some blood and tooth fragments into my face. "Is this how you wanted to die? Huh? I gave you the chance to go out with some dignity!"

"You gave me the chance to die next to a lunatic!"

He bashed my head against the floor a third time.

"We were friends, Alex. Best friends. I've already admitted that I was wrong . . . you weren't like me at all. But I stayed true to our friendship right up to this very day and I even wanted to die with you!"

"Do you know why you wanted to die with me?" I asked. "Do you really want to know?"

"Why?"

"Because you're fucking insane!"

My punch got him directly in the mouth, knuckles scraping against his already-ruined teeth, and I was somehow able to shove his body off mine. He fell onto his side, making noises as if he were choking on his own blood.

He grabbed the gun.

I kicked him in the stomach with both feet.

The gun went off, shattering something glass that I couldn't see.

I kicked him again and heard the *snap* of one or more ribs breaking. Darren screamed, but it was a scream that sounded like it was driven more by rage than pain.

I saw a flash of metal as he whipped the gun toward me and pulled the trigger again. The gun fired, I felt a hot pain tear across my cheek, and then the only thing I could hear was my ears ringing.

I pounced on him, slamming my hand against his chest, hoping that I struck the broken rib and jabbed it into a vital organ. Or even a nonvital organ, as long as it ripped up *something*. I heard Darren's shriek over the ringing in my ears, so at least I wasn't deaf.

He punched me in the face. It blurred my vision for a moment but I'm pretty sure I didn't feel anything.

I wrenched the gun out of his hand. He punched me again, and that blow I *did* feel, along with the one that followed it. Darren grabbed the barrel of the gun and pulled it out of my grasp, then threw the weapon across the room.

With a burst of strength that somebody that badly hurt really shouldn't have been able to achieve, Darren pushed me off him. I struck the wall, hard.

We both very slowly got back to our feet.

Darren wiped away some of the blood that was trickling down the corners of his mouth. He said something to me that I think was "Truce?" but I couldn't hear him.

I tried to lunge for him, but all of a sudden the impact of all of the punches I'd received hit me in the form of a nasty dizzy spell. I fell back against the wall and tried to remain upright.

Darren staggered over to the closest desk. He grabbed a handful of pencils out of a pencil holder and held them like a knife.

I pushed myself away from the wall like a swimmer pushing away from the side of the pool and hurtled toward him. Darren swung at me, ripping the sharpened pencil tips across my arm, not cutting deep but tearing a path from my wrist to my elbow. I tackled him and we smashed into the desk, toppled over a chair, and fell back onto the floor.

He jabbed the pencils at my throat but missed. Missed my throat, anyway . . . they got me across the same cheek that had been grazed by the bullet.

I decided that this would be a perfectly fine time for the police to burst into the room.

Darren slammed the pencils into my chest. For a horrifying instant I thought he'd actually plunged them deep into my flesh, but then I saw that they hadn't penetrated farther than the lead.

I yanked most of them out and returned the favor.

Once again he managed to shove me off him. I smacked into the chair, feeling as if the impact might have broken my back. I quickly grabbed the edge of the desk and pulled myself up, kicking Darren away before he could stab me with the pencils again.

He hurried across the room, going for the gun.

I grabbed a hardcover textbook off the desk.

Another dizzy spell hit me.

When I got an instant of focus, I saw that Darren already had the gun.

I threw the book. It struck him in the face, corner first, and then dropped to the floor.

Darren pointed the gun at me.

It was only a split second of awareness that I was going to die, but my mind went through a million thoughts. I wanted to pretend that I didn't care. When that bullet tore through my forehead, I'd be in a better place. I'd be with Melanie and Tracy. I'd be at peace.

But I wasn't at peace. Not yet.

And I didn't want to die.

Please don't let me die.

The gun fell out of his hand.

And then Darren fell to the floor. He just lay there, groaning in pain, face covered with blood. Helpless.

Dying?

I staggered over to the gun and picked it up. No, he wasn't dying. He was hurt bad, but unless one of those broken ribs was jabbed up into his heart, it wasn't fatal.

I'd been waiting for this moment forever. I couldn't even conceive of how beautiful it was going to look when his forehead blew apart. What kind of artwork would it leave on the floor?

I pressed the gun between his eyes.

Darren gave me a bloody grin. "I lied," he said, though I could barely hear him.

"About what?"

"Tracy Anne. The needle was almost empty when I jabbed her. She woke up."

My finger tightened on the trigger.

"She was awake for probably six or seven minutes."

"Shut up."

"I hurt her."

"*Shut up!*"

"Just thought you should know."

A rage more powerful than anything I'd ever felt tore through me. I hated him more than when he mutilated Killer Fang. More than when he forced me to murder Andrea. More than when he kept me in the pit. More than when he killed Melanie and Tracy.

I hoped that Darren could see the black cloud in my eyes.

I hoped that it scared him to his very soul.

And if it didn't . . . well, he'd learn true fear, because I wasn't going to give him a quick, merciful death by a bullet to the head. He was going to *suffer*.

Darren Rust was going to learn that he wasn't the only one who could enjoy the fine art of torture.

I went over to the other desk and found a pair of scissors.

"How many fingers do you think I can cut off before the cops break in?" I asked. "If the guard told them about the explosives, it'll probably be a while. I bet I can do all ten. What do you think?"

Darren didn't respond.

I knelt down next to him. The fight was completely drained from him, but I sure as hell hoped that the screams weren't. "What's the matter, asshole?" I asked. "Nothing to say?"

Darren was silent as I opened the scissors and slid them over his middle finger. He was less silent as I squeezed them shut.

I laughed as he bellowed in pain. I'd hoped that his

finger would slice right off, but though there was blood, the scissors didn't seem to be doing their job. I squeezed tighter and tighter, yet they weren't going through the bone.

I didn't give up.

Darren begged for mercy. I loved hearing it.

Blood trickled down the back of his hand, but still the scissors wouldn't cut through the finger. Darren's face was contorted into a wonderful mask of agony.

"Hurts, huh?" I asked.

I squeezed for a few more moments until it was clear that the scissors weren't going to work right. I pulled them away from his finger, closed them, and then raised the tip just a few inches above the same finger.

Then I slammed it down as hard as I could.

That got a *great* scream out of Darren.

It still didn't sever the digit, so I stabbed the tip of the scissors into it over and over. It was sort of like an extremely poorly played version of that game where you spread your fingers out and try to slam a knife in between them.

Darren howled in pain.

Now I was making progress. The finger was almost detached.

With a flick of the scissors, it popped off.

Nine to go.

Nineteen if I decided to move on to toes later.

I pressed the tip of the scissors against his ring finger of the same hand, and then . . .

. . . realized what I was doing.

Dear God.

I tossed the bloody scissors aside. Melanie might have wanted me to avenge her death, but she sure as hell would never have wanted to see me like this. This was subhuman. This was exactly what Darren would have wanted, assuming that he weren't the recipient.

I could just shoot him. Kill the fucker and make it all go away.

Take control of my life.

Darren's screams had faded to a pitiful whimpering.

And as I looked at him, my rage vanished. Simply vanished. Instead, I felt strangely at peace.

Completely serene.

Maybe I'd died. Maybe he'd killed me during our scuffle. Maybe I was floating toward that white light at this very moment, and just couldn't see it.

No. I hurt too much to be dead.

Instead, I laughed.

"Let me talk to you about control," I told him, amazed at my calm, steady voice. "Control is when you decide not to kill a worthless piece of shit like yourself, because you don't need to. It won't bring Melanie back. It won't bring Tracy back. It will just mean that I caved in to the feelings you tried to give me all this time. And I can't think of one good reason why I should let you win.

"I don't need to kill you. I don't need to complicate things when the police finally burst in here. Do you know what control is? Control is realizing that shooting somebody in cold blood, even you, will cause enough nightmares to far outweigh that brief moment of euphoria."

"Coward . . ." Darren whispered. I couldn't hear him but I could read his lips.

I shook my head. "No. I have options, Darren. You didn't take away my life; you took away my family. But with you gone, I can move forward. I can find a new job and I can root for Peter's dog to win prizes and I can learn new juggling tricks and I can encourage Jeremy to perform some more crappy stand-up comedy and . . . all kinds of stuff. I can be happy again."

Darren turned his head and spat out a huge amount of blood. "You're just scared to do it."

"I've never been less scared in my life. You always talked about power, Darren. Well, how about this? I wish you nothing but the worst. And if I'm really concerned about revenge, why on earth would I let you off so easily as to kill you? Your ass is going to prison. You don't like people telling you what to do? You're gonna be dealing with that twenty-four hours a day, seven days a week, buddy. You might even get to be somebody's bitch. Whether it's prison or an insane asylum, every bit of your freedom is gone, Darren. It's over. What do you think about that?"

"Don't do that to me . . ." Darren begged. He looked small and sad and frightened.

"Oh, I can't *wait* to do that to you."

"Shoot me, Alex. I deserve it."

"No. You don't deserve it. That's the whole point."

"*Kill me.*" He tried to scream the words, but was too weak.

"No. It's my choice. And I choose that your sadistic, pathetic, murdering ass gets dragged off to prison."

Darren began to weep.

I picked up the vest of explosives and tossed it onto one of the top bunks. "Anyway, I'm going to send a kid out to tell the police to come on in. Hopefully I won't accidentally get shot. That would sure screw up this start of a whole new life, huh?"

EPILOGUE

I knelt by the twin graves, feeling a little self-conscious and uncomfortable. There was so much I wanted to say, but I was having trouble finding the words.

"Melanie? Can you hear me?" I asked.

I waited for a long moment, as if expecting a response. It was hard for me to find the words, but I didn't need to say them out loud. Melanie and Tracy would know.

So much to tell about these past two months. I had, in fact, been shot by one of the cops while trying to surrender, which put a bit of a damper on my victory party. However, the superficial leg wound gave me a lot of bargaining power, and it was pretty easy to convince authorities that I was not the bad guy. Mr. Sevin was not so easy to convince, and would no doubt go to his grave believing that I was quite the hooligan.

On the basis of his superb performance in the video, Jeremy was quickly offered a small role in a major motion picture. He got an agent who managed to screw him over in record time. But he'd loved his two days on the movie set, was dating an aspiring actress (who, he confided, would always remain aspiring), and was currently waiting tables and going to auditions. He'd considered cutting himself at each audition as a gimmick, but I talked him out of it.

Darren remained under twenty-four-hour suicide watch. As the prosecuting attorney said, he couldn't so much as "scratch his balls without asking permission." I never spoke to him. There was no need. He wasn't going anywhere.

I didn't have permanent hearing loss, which was nice.

Some nights I woke up crying, and some nights I woke up screaming, but most nights I slept through until morning. I had plenty of nightmares about what I'd done with the scissors, and I thought about it a lot while I was awake. Ultimately, though, it was something I could live with. Darren was responsible for the twin graves in front of me. I could have done much worse than chop off his finger.

I met somebody. Christine. The timing was bad and I wasn't even close to being ready to fall in love again, but I liked being with her and she liked being with me.

"All I can offer you is friendship," I'd told her.

"I'll take it," she'd said.

I missed Melanie and Tracy terribly, and I'd always miss them, but my life would continue. I stared at their graves and said the only words I could manage.

"I'm happy," I said. "I hope you are, too."

I set down the flowers, wiped the tears out of my eyes, and walked toward the cemetery gates. Killer Fang II, a gift from Peter and his family, would be anxiously waiting for me at home, and that puppy and I had a lot of playtime to get in before the day was through.

ROBERT DUNBAR

Author of *The Pines*

As a winter storm tightens its grip on the small shore town of Edgeharbor, the residents are frightened of much more than pounding waves and bitter winds. A series of horrible murders has the town cowering in fear. Mangled victims bear the marks of savage claws, and strange, bloody footprints mar the beach. A young policewoman and a mysterious stranger are all that stand between this isolated community and an ancient, monstrous evil.

"*The Shore* is every bit as much of a classic as *The Pines*." —Hellnotes

THE SHORE

**"Among the classics of modern horror."
—*Weird New Jersey* on *The Pines***

ISBN 13: 978-0-8439-6166-9

NATE KENYON

**Finalist for the Bram Stoker Award
and author of *The Reach***

The biggest news in the small northern town of
Jackson was the reopening of the local hydropow-
er plant. Until the deaths. First a farmer was found
horribly mutilated in his field. Then a little girl disappeared from her home. Deep in the woods a
deputy came upon a chamber of horrors straight
from a nightmare. And through it all, one child is
haunted by visions of the mysterious "blue man,"
a madman who brings with him blood and pain
and terror, a terror spawned by forces no one can
understand.

THE BONE FACTORY

ISBN 13: 978-0-8439-6287-1

JOHN EVERSON

They're coming. They are a race of sadistic spirits known as the Curburide, and they are about to arrive in our world, bringing with them horrors beyond imagination. The secret to summoning—and controlling—them has fallen into the hands of a beautiful, sexy and dangerously insane woman.

Ariana has dedicated her life to unleashing the demons in our realm through a series of human sacrifices, erotic rituals of seduction and slaughter. As she crosses the country, getting ever closer to completing her blood-drenched mission, only three figures stand in her way: an unwilling hero who has seen the horrors of the Curburide before, a burgeoning witch…and a spiteful demon with plans of his own.

SACRIFICE

ISBN 13: 978-0-8439-6019-8

☐ **YES!**

Sign me up for the Leisure Horror Book Club and send my FREE BOOKS! If I choose to stay in the club, I will pay only $8.50* each month, a savings of $7.48!

NAME: _____

ADDRESS: _____

TELEPHONE: _____

EMAIL: _____

☐ I want to pay by credit card.

☐  ☐ MasterCard. ☐ DISCOVER

ACCOUNT #: _____

EXPIRATION DATE: _____

SIGNATURE: _____

Mail this page along with $2.00 shipping and handling to:
Leisure Horror Book Club
PO Box 6640
Wayne, PA 19087
Or fax (must include credit card information) to:
610-995-9274
You can also sign up online at **www.dorchesterpub.com**.
*Plus $2.00 for shipping. Offer open to residents of the U.S. and Canada only.
Canadian residents please call 1-800-481-9191 for pricing information.
If under 18, a parent or guardian must sign. Terms, prices and conditions subject to
change. Subscription subject to acceptance. Dorchester Publishing reserves the right
to reject any order or cancel any subscription.